One Handful of Earth

By Ellie Gunn

warm regards,

Ellie Gunn

ISBN 978-0-557-08849-2

A novel for Clan Gunn everywhere.

"But when the sky darkens and the prospect is war
Who's given a gun and then pushed to the fore
And expected to die for the land of our birth
When we've never owned one handful of earth."
Ed Pickford

Clans in the Strath of Kildonan, 1813

Clan MacDonan
Alexander (Alec) and Isabella Rose (Bella)
Robbie, Rose and Tommy
Motto: Love, the Source of Courage
Pipe Music: The Wild Glen

Clan MacLennan
Hugh and Mary, Les
Motto: This is the Valour of My Ancestors
Pipe Music: MacLennans' Lament

Clan Sinclair
Neil and Catherine
Margaret, m. Ian MacDonald
Motto: Commit Thy Work to God
Pipe Music: The Sinclairs' March

Clan MacKay
Janet
Walter and Annie
Jamie, Sarah
Motto: With Strong Hands
Pipe Music: MacKays' March

Clan Gunn
John and Helen
Motto: Either Peace or War
Pipe Music: The Gunns' Salute

Clan MacLeod
Robert and Lorna
Motto: Hold Fast
Pipe Music: MacLeod's praise

Glossary

An t-Earrach – Gaelic toast to spring

Aye (eye) – yes, always, continuously

Bairn – baby or little child

Bannocks – oat or barley sweet bread

Bog – permanent standing water

Bracken – type of fern and generic streamside plants

Brae – hillside

Breagha an-diugh – Gaelic lovely day greeting

Broch – ancient circular stone fortress

Byre – shed for animals, sometimes part of a cottage or attached to the side

Ceilidh (kaylee or keelie) – Gaelic party

Cnoc – a small hill

Cottar – tenant farmer without permanent land

Cruisie – metal flame holder, usually brass, can burn grease, peat or slivers of pine needles

Failte – Gaelic welcome

Firth – river estuary and bay

Glen – valley between hills or mountains

Griddle – flat iron pan for baking, really known as girdle

Hearth – fireplace on floor or enclosed, center of family activity

Kirk – the Presbyterian Church of Scotland

Lad – boy or young man

Lass – girl or young woman

Loch – lake

Madainn mhath – Gaelic morning greeting

Mo nair'ort – Gaelic for stop, cease

Moor – broad land without tree cover or running water

Peat – lowest layer of decomposing bog heather, cut in blocks in early summer to dry

Pewter – tin alloy with other metals

Reel – fast tune with repetitions for line dancing

Shieling – mountain grazing land for cattle

Slainte mhath – Gaelic toast to good health

Strath – broad river valley

Strathspey – easy going tune for slow dancing

Tartan – plaid woven cloth, made with local plants in pattern specific to a
clan

Thatch – roof covering made of straw, reeds and other long, narrow plant
fiber tied together in bundles

Tinkers – landless traveling merchants

Weans – small children free from their mother's milk

Wee – little, small

Wee dram – shot of whiskey

One Handful of Earth

Chapter One

Love, the source of courage. Clan MacDonan

Saturday, 20 March, 1813. Morning, Kildonan

A PROLONGED DELUGE pushed the river to the verge of its banks, threatening to flood the pastoral valley, the Strath of Kildonan. Familiar rocks disappeared. The deepest pool moved in a circle. Three lads played on the slippery edge, challenging each other to toss the biggest stone.

Up on the hillside, Bella MacDonan brushed her auburn hair away from her face, made a loose braid and twisted it at the nape of her neck. She pulled her new linen cap over her hair and hummed a lively reel as she prepared her home for the spring *ceilidh* that evening. Storytelling, feasting, and dancing would be a welcome treat after the loneliness of a dark winter. The morning chores went well, and all three of her nearly grown children were off on their assigned tasks.

The baking project was under way, so there was no putting off the cleaning. A pile of debris by the door needed moving before her son Tommy ran in and scattered it. She swept out the dirt and paused at the door to greet Tommy, who was returning from his daily mission to find the chickens' newest laying place. His black curly hair fell forward as he ran down the lane toward her. He was barefoot as usual, and it looked like he'd crushed a fresh egg in his shirt pocket. His sixteenth birthday was quickly approaching, yet at times he seemed twelve again.

"I found three eggs, Ma." He handed her the basket. Bella tried to push the hair out of his eyes, but he jumped back, quicker than her reach. She smiled at his pleasure in dodging and now being taller than her.

Tommy turned and ran back up the hill to continue the search.

She carried the basket inside, lined up the eggs on the table and took the basket out to the ledge by the door, hoping he would come back for it. The hairbrush in her apron pocket bumped against her leg. She grabbed the handle and cleaned out the loose strands to throw for the birds to make their new nests. For the first time she noticed several gray hairs among the reddish-brown strands. She remembered her mother combing her own long hair, saying, 'when the hair turns gray, the children move away'.

Her own three children were close to the age of marriage, but she doubted any of them would go far from home. Robbie, the oldest, would inherit their land and build his own cottage nearby. Rose had her hopes on Les MacLennan, the lad who lived down the hill. And Tommy, well, she kept him close by her side.

A stream of sunlight called her around the corner for a look at the outside world. A creek-side path wove through banks of heather, roses, and stands of bracken fern just coming to life after the long winter. Buds were breaking on the hazelnut trees, a hopeful sign of spring.

Peat smoke curled from every thatched roof. The MacLennans were straight below the MacDonans and their community stretched along the river to the MacKays in the downstream distance.

Her eyes fixed on a group of children throwing rocks too close to the surging water. Her breath caught in her chest as her five-year-old nephew Jamie MacKay picked up a huge chunk of an ancient crumbled wall. He staggered to the brink with the heavy load and pitched his rock. She stared in horror as he lost his balance and plunged head first into the rushing current.

"Jamie!" Bella dropped her brush, picked up her long skirts, and ran down the path.

"Robbie. Tommy. Help!" She hoped her sons would hear her. Dashing past the MacLennan cottage, still far away from the bottom of the hill, she yelled for her friend, "Mary! Jamie's in the river." No one appeared to help her.

She caught a glimpse of Jamie's head as he paddled along the surface and tried to climb up the sliding mud. There was nothing to grab, and he fell back in the water, going under again. The other lads tried to hold out their hands, but the distance was too great. One of them searched the ground for a stick while the other ran home for help.

Bella threw off her shawl and ran faster. When she got to the side of the river, he was gone. She scanned the water, looking for a sight of him. His dark hair and two small fluttering hands emerged downstream. He was floating on his back at the edge of a whirlpool just above the falls. Bella sprinted along the river path yelling "Help!" whenever she had the breath.

A few people, who lived near the MacKays, heard the commotion and stepped outside to investigate. When Bella pointed to Jamie in the water, John Gunn grabbed a length of rope from his barn, and Martha Fraser carried a blanket as they both headed for the river's edge.

Annie MacKay heard Bella's cry when she stepped outside to look for Jamie. Their cottage was close to the river; Jamie knew enough to stay back. She saw Bella gesture to something in the water. It was Jamie! She pulled off her boots to go after him.

A great splashing broke the river's flow as a stranger on horseback galloped into the river and rode straight for the whirlpool. Churning water was up to the animal's belly. The rider led his mount to the edge of the swirling pool, leaned over, and scooped Jamie up with one arm. He wrestled the limp body across the saddle in front of him and carefully turned back the way they had come, where a rocky path gave the horse a foothold.

The red-haired young man made his way to a small crowd of people. "Jamie, Jamie lad," Annie called as she ran to her son.

Bella arrived a moment later as the rider dismounted and lifted the limp body down. Jamie's skin was gray, his lips were blue, and he wasn't moving. His mother reached for him and tried to cradle him in her arms, but Bella pulled him away, laid him on his stomach in the grass and pushed the river from his lungs. She pushed on his back again and again as more water poured out.

She turned him over, put her mouth to his, and blew air into his chest. Nothing.

Bella had once revived a newborn with water in his lungs. She was sure the same procedure would work for Jamie, but sensed she had only moments to get him breathing again. Martha Fraser was holding onto a shaking, sobbing Annie; John Gunn and the young man knelt next to Jamie.

"Help me turn him," Bella said to John. They quickly flipped Jamie onto his front again, and Bella pushed on his back. More water came out. She pulled Jamie toward her, put her mouth on his, blew, paused, and breathed into Jamie. He coughed.

Bella turned him on his side as he choked, gasped, and turned pink again. Annie dropped to his side and tried to pick up her squirming, crying child. His wool sweater was sodden and his dripping trousers were twisted around his waist. Martha tried to drape the blanket around them.

"Annie, take him inside quickly and get his wet clothes off." Bella directed as Annie struggled to stand up with Jamie in her arms.

"Here, I can carry him easily," the rescuer said, as he stretched out his long arms to take Jamie. Annie handed him over gratefully and led the way to her cottage. Bella followed trying to catch her own breath. Martha ran ahead to open the door, and John tied the horse to a nearby tree.

A small crowd of neighbors gathered as the news spread from cottage to cottage along the Strath. Tommy arrived in time to see a tall, red-bearded man carry a small bundle into the MacKay cottage. When Bella spotted Tommy coming down the path, she waved at him to hurry.

"Ma, what's happened?"

"A stranger rescued Jamie from drowning. Can you greet the man and see to his needs while I help Annie?"

"Aye. Shall I take him home?"

Bella nodded and hurried inside.

Annie was peeling off Jamie's drenched clothes, and their hero was building up the fire on the floor. Jamie's granny struggled to sit up in a bed to the side. Janet MacKay had severe stiffness in her joints this time of year and could not walk unaided.

"Bring him here, Annie. I shall warm him up fast," she said. Jamie, naked and shivering, crawled under the blankets next to his granny.

"We are grateful to you." Bella turned her attention to their guest. Annie nodded, too overcome to offer hospitality.

"My son is outside," Bella said. "He will take you home and make a pot of tea." Standing close to him, she realized he was younger than she had thought. He looked a bit familiar; maybe she had seen him when he was a child.

"That would be lovely. I hope the child will recover soon." He saluted Jamie, who gave a weak smile in return, waved at the women and made his way to the door.

Tommy was outside, busy practicing his formal greeting in Gaelic. English would not do for someone who rescued wee Jamie from drowning. Suddenly the stranger was in front of him.

"*Failte! Madainn mhath.*" Welcome! Good morning. That didn't seem grateful enough for such a deed. He added in English, "You will always be remembered," as he looked up at the young man. He was probably his brother Robbie's age, twenty, and quite a bit taller than any of the MacDonans or MacKays.

"How do you do? My name is Nathaniel Reed." He put his hand out for a shake.

"Tommy MacDonan," he replied as Nathaniel gripped his hand. "Come up to our cottage and dry off or change clothes if you like. Your trousers are a bit wet."

"Soaked, I believe. If I stand by a fire for a few minutes they should dry. Can you spare a bit of hay?" They walked to the tree where John had left his horse.

"Sure, sure, come along to the byre. We have rough oats for the animals. Did you go right into the river on your horse? I'm afraid I missed it."

"Yes, Scout doesn't care much for moving water, but he did exactly what I told him anyway." Nathaniel stroked Scout's head as he untied the rope. "Honestly, all I did was carry him to land. It was your mother who revived him."

THE FOLKS GATHERED outside the MacKays' cottage turned their attention to Tommy and the visitor. Those who had seen the rescue from a distance were pointing to the whirlpool and mimicking the rider scooping Jamie from the water. A few people were praying for Jamie's soul when Bella miraculously saved him. It would be a grand story for the *ceilidh* tonight.

Scout got settled in the byre with the MacDonan mare and milk cow, and all the animals were tossed a handful of hay. Tommy led the way to the lower cottage door, which opened into a room they called the barn. The animals lived there until the larger byre was built several years before. Now the barn was a gathering place, a food storage area, and in summer, a sleeping place for Robbie and Tommy. Nathaniel dropped his saddlebags by the door. The fuel for their fire was stored in the corner, so Tommy grabbed a few blocks of peat on his way inside and added them to the floor hearth in the center of the room. He moved the kettle closer to the fire and made sure there was enough water for a pot of tea.

While Tommy was busy, Nathaniel discreetly looked around the cottage. It was long and quite narrow with beds stacked on top of each other against the walls. Wooden doors closed on the widest bed, while patchwork curtains covered the others. A small table under the only window was covered with some kind of dough, as if a baking project had been started and interrupted by the near disaster in the river, he guessed.

A tantalizing aroma of herbs, rosemary or thyme, he thought, and potatoes wafted from a large cooking pot on the fire's edge. The dry biscuits in his saddlebag were no longer appealing.

"Pull up a chair to the fire." Tommy motioned to wooden straight back chairs lined up along the wall. Nathaniel picked up a chair, thinking it was certainly short for his legs. But when he sat by the fire his trousers dried quickly, and the smoke from the fire stayed above his head. Tommy handed him a mug of hot tea, and he nodded his thanks.

"I hope the boy is feeling well by now. His name is Jamie?"

"Aye, James MacKay. My father's sister Annie is his mother, and he's also a fourth cousin on my mother's side."

"I have a distant cousin here in the Highlands myself," Nathaniel said as Bella walked in. He believed he witnessed a miracle when the dead boy breathed again from her touch. Her hair had come undone and her clothes were wet. He was noticing the outline of her lean body when Tommy jumped up to grab her hand and ended his thought.

"Is Jamie well?"

"Aye, thanks to our friend here." She flashed a radiant smile at Nathaniel.

He stood up and introduced himself. "Nathaniel Reed. I am glad to have been of service."

"We are grateful you rode up when you did, Mr. Reed, and were willing to risk your own life to save a foolish young lad." Bella motioned for him to sit again.

"I'm afraid I didn't think of my own life until we were at the whirlpool's edge and it was a bit late to change my mind." Nathaniel drank more tea and tried hard not to stare at the soup pot as his empty stomach grumbled.

"How did he end up in the river?" Tommy shook his head, as if he himself had never been close to falling in the river.

"He tried to throw a stone that threw him instead," Bella said as she poured herself a cup of tea. She pulled a chair close to the fire next to

Tommy. "The soup needs to cook a bit more, Nathaniel, but I hope you can stay to have a taste. Or were you on your way through the Strath?"

"I am not sure how much further I have to go. I have a map in my saddlebag, if you could point the way."

"Of course, get your map, and we will try to help." Bella hung the soup pot from the ceiling hook and lowered it close to the fire. Nathaniel finished his tea and went to the barn to get the map from his saddlebag.

Tommy stood up and began pacing. He ran his hand through his hair. His dark eyes were wide with concern and something new, the responsibility he had been given to greet the stranger.

"Ma, what do we do now? Uncle Walter has to thank him." Tommy leaned closer to whisper. "Da would want to shake his hand, too. When are they coming back?"

"Walter is fishing up the glen and should be back very soon. Your Da and Ian are late coming back from the coast. We'll have to do the best we can." She looked toward the barn doorway. "Is his horse fed?"

"Aye, I put him in the pasture with our animals." His eyes widened. "That is the biggest horse I have ever seen."

"He made a daring rescue." Bella had kept her focus on Jamie and had no idea who else was nearby. "You didn't see it?"

"No. I was looking for more eggs in the bracken." He poked at the fire in frustration.

"Did you find any?"

"Aye, but I put them down somewhere. Oh, here he comes!" Tommy hopped up as their guest appeared at the open doorway. "Come in, come in."

Nathaniel took his spot by the fire.

"Have you come far this morning?" Bella asked.

"I arrived at Dunrobin Castle a few days ago and have ridden this morning from Helmsdale. I left at first light, hoping I could make the trip back before dark, with enough time to look at the pasture my father wants to lease."

Bella frowned. "You must have taken a wrong turn. There is no pasture for lease here."

Chapter Two

Do and hope. Clan Matheson

BELLA GRABBED HER wooden spoon and gave the soup a thorough stir. The pasture along the river was all being used by the village. He must have come too far north.

"Damn! I thought I'd followed the landmarks correctly." Nathaniel unrolled the map. Tommy was shocked with his quick use of the word "Damn," which he would have been sent to stack peat for saying in the home. He glanced at his mother, but she was searching for bowls in the cupboard.

Nathaniel was looking around for a place to spread out the map, since the table was full of flour. Tommy picked up a boat-shaped metal container, their cruise lamp, stuffed it with slivers of peat, lit it from the fire, and motioned him to the floor by the wall hearth. The second fire, for baking or extra heat, added light and was near the window.

Once the map was spread out, Tommy pointed to Dunrobin Castle's spot on the North Sea. They both finger-traced the marked route north along the coast until it turned west at Helmsdale, and followed the river to its widest spot, right to Kildonan, their village. Tommy sat back stunned, Nathaniel perplexed.

"You followed the map correctly," Tommy explained, "but this land belongs to Clan MacDonan." He turned to look up at his mother's face. She was standing above them watching as Nathaniel tried to find some other valley nearby.

Nathaniel replayed his memory of the conversation he overheard between his parents. He was sure his father said he wanted to lease pasture in Sutherland County, west of Helmsdale, in a valley called the Strath of Kildonan. He planned to surprise his father with the news that he had already seen the land. What would he say now?

"Leave your map," Bella said to a bewildered Nathaniel, "the soup is ready. Tommy will show you where to wash up."

When the two lads headed out to the privy and washroom, Bella examined the map. There was no doubt that someone had traced a route to their door. There had been rumors that the Countess of Sutherland's English husband had a plan to increase his wealth. No one knew the exact details, except that it involved a crossbred sheep, the Cheviot.

Bella filled two bowls with potato-leek soup and put them on a shelf by the baking hearth. She wondered how much Nathaniel knew about the plans being made at Dunrobin. "Time to find out," she said to herself, as they were at the doorway. Bella took off her apron, poured herself another cup of tea, and pulled her rocking chair near the hearth fire.

She motioned Nathaniel to sit in a chair, while Tommy dropped to the floor on the braided tartan rug. Nathaniel's hands were clean and relatively smooth, she noted, with just a few scrapes and scars. He was used to hard work, but did not do it all day, she decided. He had perfect manners and a sensitive disposition, to his mother's credit, no doubt. Yet here he was riding alone in the stormy Highlands looking at land for his father.

Once they had both devoured most of their soup, Bella began her gentle interrogation.

"You have arrived to visit Kildonan at a fortunate time. We are celebrating the first day of spring with a *ceilidh*. I hope you can stay."

"Thank you, I would enjoy a *ceilidh*, but plan to be back in Helmsdale by dark."

"Do you speak the Gaelic at all?" Bella asked.

"I understand some of the Gaelic but do not speak it well. My father is from the border region, on the English side. My mother is a MacLeod. Her father was from Skye, so she speaks both languages. She says we have cousins in the far north, but has yet to meet them, as she grew up in Edinburgh."

Tommy pounced on an opening in the conversation. "I hear Edinburgh is grand."

"It is a huge old city with people everywhere. Men play fiddles and pipes in every public house and games happen in any open field. I am at University there. Well, I was, but I left school to come North."

Tommy eyes sparkled with pleasure to be talking with a person close to his age who had been to such a famous city. Studying the maps his father brought home from Inverness made him so curious about life outside their glen. Someday he would explore the world, or at least the rest of Scotland.

"So you have been at Dunrobin," Bella said. "Did you see the Countess Elizabeth?"

"No. They say she is in London for another month at least, until the weather in Scotland improves."

"That could be three months," Bella said. She tried to keep her voice calm, although her teeth were clenched and she longed to rip the map to shreds. "Who gave you the map with the route to Kildonan marked so clearly?"

"The Earl's Factor, Patrick Sellar, who has been corresponding with my father. He has stationed himself in a wing of the castle with men all around him. I could not get an interview myself, but one of his aides gave me the map."

Bella poured them another cup of tea. Her hands were shaking. The lads talked about games in the big city, while Bella tried to calm her racing heart.

She could plainly tell Nathaniel that the land was not available and send him quickly back to Dunrobin. That might make Sellar angry. Although the MacDonan Clan had leased this glen for 300 years, they did not actually own it. Every succeeding Earl and Countess at Dunrobin held the written deed for the vast land of Sutherland. She wished Alec would come home soon to see the map.

After drinking the rest of her tea, Bella stood up and moved to the baking table. "I must continue with my baking while the fire's hot, but perhaps you would like to stretch your legs a bit before riding again," she said to Nathaniel. She looked at Tommy with raised eyebrows and a sideways nod. He knew that look. It meant you'd best do whatever she kindly suggested.

"I could take Nathaniel up to the falls." Tommy volunteered quickly for his favorite walk.

"Ah, good idea," Bella said.

"Thank you, ma'am, for everything. I'd be keen to have a stretch." He and Tommy brought their bowls to the counter. Nathaniel put on his coat and started out the door. Tommy grabbed his coat, threw back a smile at his mother, and pulled the door shut behind them.

Bella took several deep breaths and tried to figure out what to do. It was tempting to tell the English lad to go home, but he had saved her nephew's life. Highland hospitality required great kindness for a life saved. He seemed like a decent young man, but now that he knew people lived on this "pasture," what would he tell his father? And where was Alec? He should have been home yesterday.

Her husband Alec's trip south with their neighbor Ian MacDonald included a search along the coast for small stones polished and smoothed by rough surf. Alec created belt buckles and brooches with the agates and pewter. After working on the land all his life, he was pleased to have his sons take over the daily chores. During the months of long light he traveled to Golspie and spread his creations on a blanket by the Inn or at the gate to Dunrobin Castle. Folks with a bit of money in their pockets stopped to look at his work and paid for his efforts. The coins were used to buy food they could not grow, books to read, the tools Alec needed, and a glass window for Bella, an extravagance for their village.

Bella looked out her window for a glimpse of Tommy, but they were already around the corner. She needed a plan of action. "Most important," she said to herself, "send someone to look for Alec." Bella moved the soup pot to a cooler spot and made sure both fires would keep going for the baking, whenever she got to it. She wrapped her shawl around her shoulders and strode out the door.

Bella turned down the lane, heading to the MacLennans' cottage, where she had sent Robbie after breakfast to collect chairs and benches for the gathering. She reached the door in a few minutes and after a quick "Hal-loo," went inside. Mary, her dearest friend, was weaving by the fire. Her dark hair was tied back in a scarf, and her broad freckled face broke into a smile as Bella arrived. Mary's son Les and her Robbie were eating biscuits and drinking tea. Les's pipes were at his feet and Robbie had his fiddle next to him on the bench. Everyone looked up to greet her.

"Ma, what's the matter?" Robbie asked, noticing her agitation. He was quieter than Rose and Tommy but had the most sensitive disposition.

"Go look for your father, please."

"Right now? Is someone hurt?" He stood up and put his coat on. Les and Mary gathered around her, waiting for the news.

"No one is hurt, but Jamie's had a near drowning. An English lad rescued him. Tommy is taking the lad to the falls, but Alec is late and I would like him home quickly."

"What! We missed a rescue? Did you see it?" Robbie asked his mother.

"I saw it. I yelled out on my way to the river, but you must have been playing the pipes and did not hear me," Bella said.

"Ach, we were practicing for the dance tonight." Robbie shook his head in disappointment to miss a change in their routine.

Mary took her hand. "Will Jamie live?"

"Aye, but Annie will need help. The close neighbors are there, but she would be comforted by a visit from you."

"Shall I go with Robbie?" Les asked. He had his coat on and reached for his cap.

"Can you gather chairs and benches and take them to the barn instead?" Bella had thought that was what Robbie was doing.

"Right away," Les said.

Robbie was out the door ahead of her. Mary put her arm around Bella. "Your usual calm has been disturbed, my dear, and your clothes are wet. Were you in the river too?"

"I would have been soon enough if the English lad had not come along, but I was holding Jamie until he could breathe again. My clothes will dry soon enough." She wiggled out of Mary's embrace before she was kept longer and given a cup of tea.

Bella ran to catch up with Robbie's long strides. His wavy brown hair hung past his ears and bounced behind him, as he had resisted her offers to trim his hair or beard lately. They hurried along the lane to the byre, while Bella explained the situation.

"I want your father to see the map and talk to the lad before he leaves. Ride the mare out, so he can get back quickly, and you bring the pony and cart."

Robbie nodded and ran toward the mare grazing in the lower pasture. When Bella returned to the cottage door, she looked for Tommy and Nathaniel. She spotted them walking up the brae. She took a deep breath and went inside, satisfied that her plan would work.

As she stood by the fire to dry her dress, the scene by the river replayed in her mind. Tears came without any way to stop them. There had been no time to realize how truly frightened she had been that Jamie would die. Her bed looked so inviting, she could crawl under the covers and cry, but this was no time to fall to pieces. She looked at the familiar objects nearby to steady her. The braided rug made from her Da's old shirts was comforting, and the rocking chair with the heart carved in the center reminded her that Jamie still lived. Alec would be home soon and it was the first day of spring. She brushed aside the tears. It was time to get ready for the *ceilidh*.

***

ONCE THE FLATBREAD dough from the table was warming on the stone griddle, Bella started the bannocks to keep her hands busy. Tommy said he'd left the eggs outside, so she stepped out to look in his usual spots. The gathering of neighbors in her home that evening would be a relief from the worries of the morning. She quickly found four eggs along the mossy ledge and returned to her project.

Her hands flew to the task as she stirred in fine oat flour, chopped hazels and with a flick of her wrist tossed in the last handful of raisins Alec brought north at Christmas time. Her mood lifted as she daydreamed about warmer days ahead, when the soil would turn easily and she could scoop up handfuls of earth to plant seeds again.

She spread the bannock dough in big wet spoonfuls onto another griddle and flattened the tops with the wet paddle. Each bannock cake spread into a round shape large enough to cut into a dozen pieces. The bannocks would be a great surprise for the *ceilidh*, as it had been a lean winter. Each household rationed staples to survive until spring. Everyone was thin this time of year, but no one was starving. She had hidden a package of flour, a sack of nuts, and the raisins for this very day. By the time several trays of bannocks had baked, she heard the outer barn door open and Alec's deep voice call out for her.

Alec walked in the cottage and into her arms. He was a hand taller than Bella and broad enough across the shoulders to wrap her in his arms securely. She put her arms around his narrow waist and he kissed the top of her head. She looked up into Alec's brown eyes hoping for comfort. The usual easy smile was gone. His forehead was wrinkled and his lips turned down.

"What's wrong?" Bella asked.

"It was good you sent Robbie out to look for me. I was trying to get home fast. There is worse news than a stray English lad."

"What is it?"

Alec moved out of her embrace to slip off his cap and coat. "Ian and

I slept at the Inn in Golspie during the rainstorm. We met several men from the Rogart village whose families had been tenants of Clan Ross for generations."

"Had been tenants?" A chill swept up her arms.

He poured himself a cup of tea. "The Earl of Sutherland hired a pair of lawyers to run his estate while he and the Countess are in London. The Factor, a man named Sellar, told Ross to put his tenants off the land."

Bella faced him. "Sellar gave the map to the English lad. Tommy took him to the falls so you could see his map."

"Let's see it then."

She unrolled the map near the window and they both studied it.

"Aye," Alec said. "It is to our door." He rolled the map back up and laid it across the floor fire. The paper caught and burned bright orange as they gazed at the flame until it turned to ash.

"What will we say when the lad returns for his map?" Bella asked. "Burning it does not change anything."

Alec ran his hand over his face to try to clear his mind. "The map got him here. He no longer needs it. Sellar is our problem, not the lad and his map." He sat in the rocker, pushed back to steady it, and drank down half his tea. Bella sat in the chair by the fire, her blue eyes focused on his face.

"Sellar told Edward Ross that the Earl purchased thousands of sheep that can survive the Highland winter, so his people would have to leave to make room for them. They evicted all the Rogart tenants and torched their homes."

"Burned them out? Oh, no. Where did they go?" She moved closer to hold his hand.

"Everyone's scattered, Bella. The men we met were young and single, looking for any work to trade for food."

"How could anyone do such a thing?" She withdrew her hand and covered her eyes to try to block the image of burning cottages and frantic people.

"When the tenants were gone, he went back and evicted Edward himself."

"Even Ross, the old Chief's grandson! Then no one is safe. Are they coming here next?" Bella hurried to look out the window, but only their neighbors were outside.

Alec joined her. He put his arms around her and she rested her head on his shoulder.

"Bella, I am afraid for us, and for everyone in the glen."

She looked up at Alec. He had never admitted fear before. His tear-filled eyes were searching hers for reassurance.

"Alec, I cannot believe the Countess would evict us. Can you?"

"She may have left it to her husband to decide." He looked around at the pans of bannocks. "Is it the *ceilidh* already?"

"In a few hours."

"Have you heard if MacLeod is coming?"

"No one has said one way or the other."

Alec started putting his coat back on. "I want to make sure he is here for a council we need to have first. I'll go upriver a bit and send a message along to the other clans too."

"You just got home. Aren't you hungry?" She stood in front of him, hoping to talk him out of leaving again. "You need to meet the English lad. Did Robbie tell you Nathaniel rescued Jamie from the river?"

"Aye. I want to thank him, and I will be back soon. Try to get him to stay the night. He may know something that will help us. Does he seem like a decent lad?" Alec asked.

"He is polite and sincere. I think Tommy has taken quite a liking to him." Bella handed him a bannock.

"Thanks, dear. We'll have the council first and then those wanting to tell stories and dance can still celebrate." He was out the door.

Bella followed him outside and after a brief kiss, Alec was gone again. He walked down the lane toward their daughter Rose, who was helping Les carry a long bench up the path. From behind Bella might have mistaken her husband for Robbie, except for the weariness of bad news on his shoulders. Alec spoke to them for a few moments, then continued down to the river path as they hurried up to the barn.

Bella ran ahead of them to open the door. "Put the bench against the wall," Bella said to Rose and Les, as she tried to calm herself.

"Mother, what is going on? Da told us he's off to announce a council in the barn this afternoon. I thought we were having a *ceilidh*." Rose pouted and dropped her end of the bench, as Les scrambled to put his down in unison.

"Come sit by the fire and I'll tell you what he told me. And let's have some soup now as we may not have time later." They followed her into the cottage and Bella gave the soup a stir. "Bring some bowls, Rose. You and Les can sit on the floor by the hearth." She pulled her rocker close to the fire.

When they were gathered with steaming bowls of soup in their hands, Bella stirred hers around and around as she tried to formulate a gentle way to talk about the danger they faced. She looked at Rose, just barely seventeen, her body that of a woman now, with Alec's wavy hair, but her own auburn shine. She had Bella's family's deep blue eyes and expressive brows and was both quick to judge and to forgive. She was becoming the best young weaver in the glen, and her talent playing the small harp impressed everyone. Bella thought of herself at that age, brimming with untested self-confidence.

And Les was practically her child too; he spent so much time in their home. He folded his long legs under his slender torso, and hand combed his thick brown hair neatly across his wide freckled brow. Bella knew he preferred life to be the same every day and resisted any kind of change. *And why does it have to change? Maybe they won't come here.* She stopped stirring and let out a breath when she realized they were waiting for a blessing.

"Dear Lord. We give thanks for our food. We pray for your continued blessing on our home and family. Amen."

Rose looked at her mother thoughtfully. Something had changed since the breakfast blessing.

"Have some warm bannock, too." Bella stood up and walked to the table, picked up her sharpest knife and cut a bannock cake in half, again and again until there were twelve pieces. She looked at the knife in her hand in a new light, wondering if she could stab someone who wanted to burn her house down or hurt her children. 'Yes, it would be possible,' a voice inside her warned. She put the knife down carefully, put four slices on a wooden board next to Rose, and returned to her spot by the hearth.

"There's been some trouble down south that could come here," Bella said. "That's what the council will be about. It's the Earl and Countess who may want to use our land to run sheep."

"There is not enough pasture for more sheep," Les said.

"I am afraid they may want us to leave, with our animals," Bella said.

Les heard the word "leave" and stopped eating.

"How could we leave? This valley is our home." Rose put down her bowl. Bella tried to blink away the tears she felt gathering.

"There is no easy way to tell you. The Earl's soldiers forced everyone in a glen to the south to leave. The cottages were all burned down. The land will be rented to sheep farmers from the Lowlands, who will use the pasture."

"They cannot do this to us, they have no right!" Rose was up pacing, her face red, fists clenched and body stiff. "The MacDonans have lived in this valley for generations. We are responsible for caring for the land, not some renter from England."

"I know it seems impossible, dear. I can hardly believe it myself. Your father has only heard this news two days ago. The lad who rescued Jamie has a map to pasture for lease in Kildonan. That is why the council has been called, to talk about what to do."

Rose stopped pacing and knelt by her mother. "Ma, what if they burn us out? What about Margaret and the other women who will give birth soon?" Bella put an arm around her daughter. "They cannot live on the hillside in the open air," Rose said and began to cry. "How can anyone be so cruel?"

Chapter Three

Endure bravely. Clan Lindsay

WHILE BELLA, ROSE, and Les consoled each other around the fire, Tommy and Nathaniel walked up to the waterfall, oblivious to the anguish below.

When they approached a large pile of boulders, Tommy, in the lead, turned to the left, but Nathaniel veered to the right. Stepping back, Tommy grabbed his new friends coat sleeve to pull him left.

"Nathaniel, around it sunwise, you don't want bad luck, do you?" Tommy asked.

"Bad luck? The way you walk around a heap of rocks?"

"Oh, aye. Don't you know? It's always important to pay attention to where your feet are stepping. Left foot forward across a threshold, sunwise around any circle of stones and especially around a peat bog, which if you try to walk straight across, could be the death of you."

"A peat bog, surely not." Nathaniel looked to see if he was joking, but he kept a straight face.

"In between the heather are patches of quicksand, and many a foolish Englishman has been lost to one," Tommy said, a frown creasing his brow. They climbed on a flat boulder for a view of the river below.

"You can't be serious."

"I am. Uncle Neil told me about an English fellow who was heard yelling for help in an especially nasty bog, over Cnoc Coire behind us." Nathaniel glanced over his shoulder at the rounded hilltop. "Some lads on their way to a shepherd's hut brought rope and threw him a line. They pulled and pulled, but his legs wouldn't come out. They were cursing the man's weight when he cried, 'Boys, can you not pull my horse out too, or shall I let go of the stirrups?' The lads were so disgusted they were ready to drop the ropes and walk away." Tommy coughed to hide his smile.

"What a foolish man." Nathaniel shook his head and then looked down at the marshy ground around the boulder they were standing on.

"That's the English for you," Tommy said, then added, "no offense to you, Nathaniel."

"None taken. What happened then?"

"Weel," Tommy said in Uncle Neil's style, "the smartest lad in the bunch said, 'Let go of your horse for now, we'll get him later.' So the Englishman let go and was dragged safely to dry land."

"And the horse?"

"Still waiting for the lads to return, all these hundred years."

They both burst out laughing and tried to push each other off the rock into the nearest bog.

"I guess you had me going there for awhile." Nathaniel admitted with a grin.

Tommy hopped off the boulder and they continued up the hill. They hiked to another outlook and stopped for a minute. This time the view was to the east. A series of rounded hills flowed as far as they could see. Trees dotted the landscape where streams provided year-round water. Wisps of smoke from cottages below them swirled with the light breeze.

"Ah, this highland air does me good, and your company, Master MacDonan," Nathaniel bowed with a flourish, "is the liveliest I've had in quite awhile."

"What? Is everyone in England serious then?"

"People make jests, but it is all very controlled and a bit stiff, quite acceptable to be amused, but not proper to laugh 'til your belly aches."

Tommy shook his head and gestured the way to a path further up the hill.

"You best not meet Uncle Neil then. He is the best storyteller in the Strath, maybe even the whole glen. He'll be telling jokes at the *ceilidh* tonight. There's a perfect time to listen to him—after he's had a couple of drams of his own whiskey, but before he's sampled someone else's stronger brew."

"It is a bit of struggle for me to understand everything you say, just a word or two mind you, but I doubt if I would understand jests with a slurred speech too."

Tommy stopped to stare at him. "What did you miss?"

"I don't know, in the middle of a sentence your words roll together a bit fast."

"And you speak so slowly, my friend Nathaniel, that I want to light a fire under you to speed things up a bit."

"I'm afraid I've turned into a proper Englishman, slow and precise. My father would finally be proud."

"A few days in the glen should have a good effect on you then. That is if you can stay a few days. Ma and Da would be happy to have you." Although there were several cottages with extra rooms where visitors could be lodged, Tommy had no intention of letting this interesting visitor stray very far. A door had been opened to the outside world with Nathaniel's arrival, and Tommy was eager to step through it.

Nathaniel frowned and rubbed his forehead. "I should probably just go back to the castle and return the map. Why did they give me a map here, where people live? It must have been a mistake. My father can get his own map when he comes north. I won't even tell him I've been here."

The sound of the waterfall reached their ears as soon as they rounded the bend. A grin broke Tommy's serious expression. "Race you to the falls!"

Nathaniel prided himself on his sprinting ability, but being on unfamiliar ground on a rough path with Tommy jumping from boulder to boulder like a goat was more of a challenge than he could match. He tried to keep up until they reached a flat spot where a deep green pool was rippled by falling water.

Tommy stretched out on his belly on a large rock at the edge of the water and hung his head over, scooping water by the handfuls over his head, face and neck. Nathaniel shrugged, sprawled on the edge and did the same.

"It is strange that the water is so clear, yet it tastes of the earth," Nathaniel said after drinking his fill.

"The water comes down a stream from the peat bogs. 'Tis the taste of that horse, buried for one hundred years."

With that, Nathaniel splashed a handful of water at Tommy, who returned it full force, so that in just a few minutes they were both soaked. Tommy raised his hands in peace.

"Ach, we'd best get back soon, but let's go just a wee bit higher, from the top of this rise we'll see the whole Strath below us."

So they climbed higher, following the water for a ways, and then Tommy took a smaller path to the west and they scrambled hand over hand. When they rounded a corner, the Auld Broch came into view. It was built of massive stones, chiseled or broken to fit, one upon the other, in a large circle. As the lads circled it, sunwise, with Nathaniel counting his long strides, they reached, "forty-eight, forty-nine, fifty! Tommy, this is huge. Who lived here?"

"No one knows really, it's just always been here. Some say the ghosts of Viking warriors killed in a raid haunt it. Others say it was built before the Vikings, by the painted men."

"The painted men! That sounds like one of your Uncle Neil's stories."

"Well, he probably has a tale if you ask him, but my Da says they were real, so I believe they were."

"It's quite deserted and in a desolate place as well. Is it used for anything?"

"No one really uses it, it doesn't belong to any clan, see? And there's no roof so it doesn't work as a shelter. But I've heard my brother Robbie whisper to lasses to meet him at the Broch."

Nathaniel whistled in surprise. "Do you think they did?"

"No lass in this village would dare go so far away by herself to meet any lad, even Robbie, who is surely the favorite of many."

"And what about yourself? Are you anyone's favorite, Tommy?"

"Only me Ma's." They both laughed. There were very few lasses that Tommy cared to think about in the glen. If they weren't closely related to him, they giggled too much.

"I was someone's favorite once," Nathaniel said, "but her family chose an important man for her husband, and that was it for me."

"You seem important to me," Tommy said.

"Thanks, but compared to her husband, I am not much at all."

"So it's already done then, the wedding?"

He nodded, looking away. "I suppose I left Edinburgh to get away from it all. An excuse to not put on a brave face, if no one I knew saw me. And looking around, not seeing another soul but you, I guess I've succeeded in running away."

"But did she say she really wanted you?"

"I'm afraid she was impressed by the other chap's money."

Tommy couldn't think of much to say after that, so they wound their way back down the path, the sound of the waterfall thick in their ears. Nathaniel was in the lead this time, and Tommy tried to squeeze past when the path widened a bit.

"I am used to shops everywhere. How to you buy what you need?"

"We grow all our own food in the Strath. For example, Ma's got a way with chickens, so we usually have the first eggs in spring, which we share or trade. My brother Robbie mends stone walls for fresh fish and my sister Rose weaves blankets and shawls."

"I didn't know you had a sister," Nathaniel said over his shoulder.

"Aye, she's older than me and tries to be the boss. I would stay away from her."

"Advice well taken."

"Do you think you will stay for the *ceilidh*?" Tommy asked.

Nathaniel was saved from deciding by their arrival back in the village.

Smoke was pouring from all the chimneys, giving the air a pungent sweet smell of oats and peat. Although they had gotten warm running up the hill, now Nathaniel felt a bit of a chill and looked forward to another cup of tea.

When they reached the cottage door, Tommy opened it for Nathaniel and motioned him inside. Bella looked up as they entered.

"Ah, you are back. How did you enjoy yourself, Nathaniel?" she asked, approaching him with her hand outstretched.

"Very much, thank you," he replied, taking her hand. Bella led him to the hearth where Rose and Les were sitting. Rose's eyes were red from crying about the evictions, and her cheeks flushed as the handsome young stranger approached with her mother. She and Les stood as Bella made introductions. Rose curtsied and looked down as was proper, while Les shook the hand Nathaniel offered.

Tommy announced that Nathaniel was thinking of staying for the *ceilidh*, which prompted Nathaniel to ask if that would be too much of a bother.

"You are very welcome to stay," Bella replied. "My husband Alec has gone out for a few minutes but is hoping to meet you."

"So Da is back from the coast. Where has he gone now?" Tommy asked.

Bella hesitated, wondering how much to say in front of Nathaniel.

Rose answered for her. "He's gone to announce a council, so we can decide how to stop lowlander sheep farmers from stealing our land." Gone was the blushing maiden. Rose had her arms folded across her chest and was glaring at Nathaniel.

"Rose!" Bella gasped in surprise.

Tommy stepped in front of his sister. "*Mo nair'ort!* Stop it! Do not insult our guest."

"I will insult anyone whose motives for coming here are deception and thievery." Rose raised her voice at Tommy.

Bella interrupted Tommy's next retort by moving between them, one arm around each of their shoulders. "There is much we do not know, but I believe it is fair to ask Nathaniel what his intentions are, before we find him guilty."

Tommy added, "I invited him to be a guest. You don't even know him, so just be quiet for once."

"Please forgive my intrusion," Nathaniel said. "I am leaving, but please believe I had no idea anyone lived in Kildonan."

Bella saw her plan for Alec to question Nathaniel disappearing. "You are still welcome to stay."

"Thank you for the delicious soup," he nodded to Bella. "And for the great stories," he said to Tommy, and then added, "I don't want to be left with my feet in the stirrups." He turned and walked out the door.

Chapter Four

Truth prevails. Clan Napier

"DAMN!" TOMMY KICKED a block of peat that fell into the fire and sent sparks onto the clay floor. There was silence in the cottage until Rose turned away from everyone and began crying again. Les touched her shoulder, but she pushed his hand away. Trying to comfort a crying lass was beyond him, so he headed home.

"Come and sit by the fire with me," Bella said. "Do not speak to each other yet, there is something I want to say." Tommy sat on the floor and poked the fire with a stick. Rose took the chair and turned it away from her brother.

"We have never had someone feel so uncomfortable in our home that he had to leave, until now." She put her hand up to Tommy before he could blame Rose. "It is something I hope to never see again. I do not completely blame you, Rose. We have been threatened and you meant to protect us, but Nathaniel himself is not the threat. I sense our lives are about to change, but in what way I do not know. What I want you to remember is that love and courage keep us together and when you are in doubt about what to do, I want you to act with love. Do you agree?" They both nodded. "Then I will promise to try my best to do the same."

She added, "Just sit quietly now and do not speak while you ponder what has happened."

NATHANIEL HAD SCOUT'S halter in his hand, ready to walk out of the pasture, when he saw someone walking toward him.

Alec met him at the gate. "Ah, must be the English lad," he said, one hand on the latch to keep it closed. "Alec MacDonan here," he put his other hand out for a shake. "I hope you aren't leaving so soon. My wife thinks highly of you, and I'd like you to stay longer."

"Hello, Sir. It's good to hear someone thinks highly of me, as I am afraid I did not make a good impression on your daughter."

"Ach, it pains me to hear that. Rose is often hasty in first impressions, it takes her awhile to warm up to strangers. There aren't many people who ride into the glen as you have done." Alec stroked Scout's forehead. "We are grateful for your swift action to save Jamie." He smiled at Nathaniel. "Well, it is up to you of course, to go or stay, but you are very welcome, despite whatever Rose said."

Nathaniel glanced back up at the cottage and saw Tommy waving him back.

"Perhaps I will see to my horse, give him a brushing and a walk around, while I sort things out."

"Good enough. I will speak to Rose," Alec said, gesturing with a nod of his head to the cottage. "I'll come back in a few minutes to see how you are doing. Ah, and keep your eye out for my oldest son Robbie, he'll be coming along with a pony and cart soon enough."

"All right, thank you." Nathaniel got a brush from his saddlebag and stroked Scout's mane.

As soon as Alec got back inside, Rose and Tommy began talking to him. "Wait, wait, one at a time, and let me sit down. I've been walking for three days." Alec grabbed the rocker as they gathered around him.

Tommy spoke quickly, "Da, we cannot let him just leave, he does not mean any harm, I swear it. He told me why he came here, and I promise, he did not know anyone lived here."

"He has agreed to wait and see to his horse while we talk things over," Alec assured him, "but," he said as Tommy started for the door, "I want you to stay here now so we can hear each other out." Tommy scowled a bit, but then sat on the floor next to Alec's chair. "Now Rose, have you been rude to a guest?"

"Yes, Da, I lost my temper after hearing about Rogart."

"What about Rogart?" Tommy asked.

"Can you be patient a bit longer, Son?" Tommy reluctantly nodded. Bella was standing behind Alec, her hands on his shoulders. "Bella dear," he leaned back in the chair to look up at her, "what shall we do now?"

"Rose and Tommy can apologize for shouting at each other, while you and I step outside for a minute."

Alec rocked himself out of the chair as Bella offered her hand and they both looked back at their children waiting for apologies to begin.

"You have never shouted at me before," Rose began as Bella and Alec went to the ledge outside the upper door.

"Alec," Bella said quietly when they were away from the door, "I am trying to be courageous as I have asked them to be," she nodded toward the house, "but what if we are evicted and separated from Tommy."

"We need to tell him now."

"My knees are weak with fear, Alec."

He looked at the sky and noticed how quickly the light was changing, "It is time, dear. The council will begin soon."

"Stay by my side, will you?" Bella wanted to make sure he didn't plan to leave again.

"Of course, love." He held her face in his hands and kissed her lips.

When they went back inside, Rose and Tommy were still talking by the hearth. Tommy had told her enough of Nathaniel's personal story that she agreed he was not the enemy.

"Rose dear," Bella said, "your Da and I want to talk with Tommy alone for a few minutes. There are still chores to be done before the *ceilidh* and your apology to be given to Nathaniel, if you are truly sorry."

"I am sorry and will tell him so." Rose gave Tommy's hand a squeeze and went outside through the barn.

***

"TOMMY," ALEC SAID, "let's the three of us walk up to the long flat rock."

"Am I in trouble for cursing? I am sorry. I lost my temper."

Neither of his parents answered, so Tommy started for the door, and as Bella wrapped her shawl around her shoulder, Alec squeezed her hand. Tommy waited just above the cottage and they made their way along the wide path above their home to a large level rock, big enough for four or five people to sit side-by-side, and high enough to dangle their legs over the edge. The rock faced the sun and provided a good view of the whole village and river below.

For a few minutes they all took in the view. The sunlight on the river turned the water a deep blue, a breeze played with the catkins on the hazel trees and birds called to each other from the copse of trees along the stream. They could see Rose and Nathaniel below, standing together at his horse's head, Rose offering a bit of hay to the horse and Nathaniel moving the brush down its mane. People lived in such close proximity, it was considered rude to stare at people going about their work, so they all returned their eyes to the sky, where white puffy clouds moved high above them toward the hills and Bella began to speak.

"Tommy, when Rose was just a wee bairn, not even walking yet, two soldiers from Dunrobin Castle rode to Kildonan. They asked for me at the MacKays's and then came straight away to our cottage. One was a MacKay cousin, who was a guard at the castle. He said the Countess Elizabeth had sent for me, and asked if I would come to Dunrobin at once to assist her. You know I was raised along the coast to the south, and my mother was a midwife who assisted women in the countryside and at the castle." Tommy nodded, twisting his hands and glancing around, while he waited for her to get on with the point so he could see about Nathaniel.

"So I knew 'assist' meant an important woman was having problems in childbirth to send so far away for a country midwife like myself."

"Well Ma, you are the best, everyone says so," Tommy said, hoping a compliment could end the story.

Bella paused instead, trying to calm her racing heart. "I gathered my birthing supplies, left Rose and Robbie with your father and Mary, and left on a third horse they brought for me. We rode hard to Helmsdale, were given fresh horses, and reached the castle after dark."

"What time of year was it?" Tommy was more curious about the story now, imagining his mother riding off in the dark on a mission with officers of the Countess.

"This time of year, exactly," Bella said."When we reached Dunrobin, I was taken to a small bedroom on the third floor overlooking the sea that was kept for personal servants. The Countess herself was in childbirth, but the infant had not arrived after two days of pain and she was worried. Being her fifth delivery she thought it would be easy, but it wasn't."

"I would think the Countess would have the finest doctor attending her," Tommy remarked. Bella glanced at Alec, who nodded at her to continue.

"Ordinarily she would have the best physician available. Except her pregnancy was a secret. Her husband, the Earl, had been indisposed for the past year, and could not have fathered the child."

Tommy started to panic. The story his mother was telling was beyond anything he wanted to hear. He looked around for a way to escape the ending. In desperation he jumped off the rock and tried to walk away, but Alec went after him and said, "Hold on, Son, it's almost done."

Bella was wringing her hands and looked poised to run also. "I helped her find a position that would ease the delivery. When I could see the bairn's head and told her it was almost over, she said, 'If this baby is born alive, will you take it to raise as your own?'"

Bella stilled her body and looked straight at Tommy. "I said 'Yes', Tommy dearest, and then you were born."

Chapter Five

Courage. Clan Cumming

TOMMY ROCKED BACK on his heels and might have fallen over had Alec not been holding onto him. He seemed to be lost inside himself and did not speak for several minutes, while Bella held her breath and clutched the edge of the rock.

Finally he came back and lowering his head said, "So I am a bastard. Does everyone know but me?"

Bella exhaled.

Alec had tears in his eyes but managed to answer. "Only Mary MacLennan, your mother, and I know the truth about your birth."

"So Rose is not my sister? Nor Robbie my brother! Why have you told me this now?" Tommy finished the angry outburst and tried to run away without looking at Bella, but Alec would not let him go and kept a firm hold around his chest. Tommy struggled to get free and then, giving up, began weeping. "And you," he finally looked at Bella, "who are you if not my mother?" Alec relaxed his grip on Tommy.

"I am the person who loves you most in this world." Bella's eyes filled with tears.

Tommy rushed to her and dropped to his knees and clung to her legs as he did as a small child. She stroked his head while they both wept. Alec stood close to them, not touching, just waiting for whatever was next.

When he could stand and speak again Tommy said, "I have so many questions and do not know where to begin." He took a breath, "Who is my father, if not my Da?" he glanced at Alec's mouth, but did not meet his eyes.

Bella managed to stop crying. "My third cousin, Henry Gunn. He was born at Dunrobin. His father was the Earl's Falconer. The Countess was learning to hunt with hawks, and Henry was helping teach her."

"Where is he now?" Tommy looked at the sky while she told him about his father.

"The Countess told me she sent him in the army as soon as she discovered her condition," Bella said. "I do not know where he is now."

"I am sorry that we have to tell you at all, Son," Alec said. He tried to put his arm around Tommy but was shrugged off. "There was an eviction in Rogart last week. If it comes to that here, and we are separated, well, we wanted you to know about your true heritage."

"I don't have much of a heritage, being a secret bastard, do I? I cannot think what to call you now or how to think of myself even." Tommy kicked the ground, hands in his pockets and his face averted.

"We will just be here with you, you can talk to us or not," Alec said.

Finally Tommy stirred. "I need to walk up to the Broch and think about all this." He looked up the brae he and Nathaniel had climbed that morning when he was young, naïve Tommy MacDonan, a different person than he was now. He wondered what Nathaniel would think. It was too much to consider all at once.

"Will you be alright?" Alec asked. He folded his arms on his chest to keep himself from hugging Tommy.

"Send Robbie to the Broch when he gets home, would you?"

"Of course," Alec replied. He offered his hand, but Tommy just waved it away.

He left without another glance at Bella, his usual sprint subdued to a rapid, head down stride up the path to the Broch.

Alec and Bella walked slowly back to the cottage, arms around each other, not speaking until the doorway when Alec said, "You did the best anyone could have done to break it to him gently. I hope he realizes soon how lucky he is to have you for his mother." Bella hugged him quickly and then pushed open the cottage door. Alec continued down the path when he saw Robbie had arrived.

Bella walked inside and noticed all the unfinished food preparation for the *ceilidh*, which no longer seemed important. She went to the privy and then washed her hands and face with cold water, which helped bring her back to the present, at least enough to know she felt raw and weary. Telling Tommy about his birth was the hardest thing she had ever done, harder even than the childbirth she had endured with Robbie and Rose. At least childbirth is an act the body can surrender to, while telling Tommy felt like she was pulling up every word from a deep well.

The fires were both dwindling. She didn't care anymore about fixing food, but she added more peat, at least to have some light for company. "I am certainly feeling sorry for myself," she said, kneeling to the flame. It only flickered in return, but somehow that was enough to give her a little energy back. She poked the fire until the color changed and the deep red coals were glowing with a life of their own. A sudden memory of her grandmother "reading" the peat coals came to the front of her mind. "Ah, lass," her grandmother said, "I see a handsome laddie sweeping you off your feet," and in darker times, "'Tis a scarcity coming, hide away meal for the next season."

Ruby and gold vibrations moved around the fire. Deep love, certainly, but blood and power too. The coals were clustered in small groups, the families in the glen perhaps. As she tried to make out how many groups there were, a large chunk fell from the edge and scattered the scene. "Danger." Her grandmother's voice was final.

Robbie stood at the open doorway alone. He looked so much like his father, outlined with the light behind him, that she thought the wavy hair and broad shoulders belonged to Alec. Robbie took the chair to her side and looked into the coals himself, as if he had a question.

"Da told me about Tommy," he said. Bella started, not sure how he would respond, but Robbie touched her hand. "Ma, I was surprised, no doubt about it, but I have this memory of you going away when I was a wee lad. You came back with a bairn, I never saw your body get big, like the other women. I was puzzled but never knew what to ask."

They sat shoulder to shoulder, both still gazing at the firelight. "I think it was very brave of you to go to the castle and care for the Countess and then be a mother to Tommy, never knowing if she might come to take him back. He has been a good brother to me." He stood up. "I'll be off to find him now."

"That is the most words you have ever said at once."

"Perhaps I was waiting for something important to say."

Bella stood as Robbie walked toward the door. "Tell him I will be waiting to see him," she called after him.

There was something stirring inside her. It was a tight band around her heart that had begun to loosen with the long held secret out of her body. Tommy would have a lot of questions and his future was still uncertain, as was her own it seemed, but at least she could now be totally honest with him.

She wondered if Alec was telling Rose and felt that she wanted to be part of whatever happened next. She splashed her face again, wiped up with her apron, had a long drink of water then wrapped her woven cloak around her shoulders and tied the belt at her waist before going outside.

THE WEATHER WAS improving and by noon all the clouds had moved on. Bella paused for a moment to notice the smell of warmer air and let the sun soak through her layers of clothes. Satisfied with the calm, warm feeling, she walked down the path and across the lane where she could see Alec, Rose, and the MacLennans gathered outside sunning themselves along the garden wall.

Mary was in the center, knitting as usual. Her linen cap was neatly pinned over the thick braid that circled her head. Bella reached her hand to her own head, wondering if she still had her cap, or if she had lost it, again. It was there, although most of the pins were gone and it was flopping behind her. She pulled up the edges, tucked her loose hair underneath as best she could to look like the sensible matron she was supposed to be.

Hugh was leaning against the wall, ready to remember a chore that needed doing if he got stiff and wanted to move around. Les had his pipes out and was polishing the wooden chanter with a soft cloth.

Alec put his arm out as she approached, so she slid under his shoulder, stretching her left arm around his waist. Rose had moved over to make room for her and was busy tapping her heels against the wall.

"Da says you want to tell us something important. That is why we are resting, even though the *ceilidh* starts soon," Rose said. She leaned back and looked at her mother.

"I need to tell you all something about Tommy before the *ceilidh*." It was time they heard the truth. Tommy would need their comfort if he would not accept hers.

When she got to the part about the Countess having a lover, Les slid off the ledge and walked a short distance. He could still hear her voice, but could leave quickly if necessary. Hugh lifted his whiskered chin as if to test the wind, in case a storm was approaching.

No one moved while Bella described her ride to the castle and the birthing. "I brought Tommy home and we have pretended all these years that he is our natural son."

Rose's eyes widened and she sucked in her breath, finally grasping what her mother was saying. "Tommy," she whispered, "is related to the Countess?" She leaned closer to her mother, who nodded her confirmation. "But, well, I've heard some women pretend, that is…," Rose was hanging onto her braids, twisting them around while she tried to figure out what to say. She was hoping Les would just walk away. "Couldn't she just say the Earl, you know…was the father."

"Her pregnancy was kept a secret from the Earl, who was in London most of the year. If I had not arrived before the birth, the maid would have been ordered to smother him." Bella paused. She had not told anyone that before. "Being distantly related to her lover, and hidden in a far away glen, made me a person she trusted to take her bairn away."

"Oh, Ma. You just told Tommy right now, when you went to the flat rock?"

"Aye. He has gone up to the Broch and asked for Robbie's company." Bella wished he had wanted her company. She would have to wait patiently and trust that time would come again.

"Shall I go too? What will we do when we see him?" Rose looked up at the hillside.

Alec looked too, although the Broch was not visible from the village.

Mary put her arm around Rose, who leaned against her shoulder for comfort. "We will treat him as we always have, no better and no worse. And we will all do whatever he needs to feel like himself again."

"Aye," Hugh added. "Himself will need to look for eggs, and run up the hill, and have a cuppa tea, maybe even a wee dram of my finest barley whiskey to celebrate, now that he is almost sixteen."

In a way it seemed like yesterday to Bella. The intensity of the birth, the surprise of suddenly having another child and then the person Tommy became all rushed together. He was as much her son as Robbie was, and she wanted to make sure he knew that.

Chapter Six

With generosity. Clan MacNicol

ALEC MACDONAN'S CALL for a council spread to the very top of the glen, reaching members of twenty clans. The original MacDonan settlers had arrived in 1536. Over the decades MacKays, Sinclairs, and Gunns from Caithness territory to the north joined them. Murrays and Frasers from the Dornoch Firth migrated from the southern peninsula.

The river valley stretched 25 miles from its source in the hills above the Borrobal Forest eastward to the North Sea. Small villages dotted the wide flat strath along the Kildonan River. Other folks lived in crofts, the smaller farms, on the gently rolling hills or alongside the streams that flowed into the river.

As fathers divided land for their sons for twelve generations, the valley became a patchwork of adjoining oat fields and cattle pasture. The grass barely met the needs of the animals in good times. In bad weather, snow covered the ground for months or flooding made the fields inaccessible. Despite the hard times, the people in the glen were deeply attached to their land and continued to hope and pray for a good harvest each season.

The intensive vegetable gardens in the heavily mulched raised bed system, the run-rig, supplied year-round greens, but the people were dependent on milk, fish, and meat for winter nourishment. After poor harvests young people would leave the glen for jobs in the south and send money back to their parents.

The second British war against the American colonies was raging in the swamps of Louisiana in 1813. For several years the Countess of

Sutherland had urged local lads to join the army, promising three acres of land upon their return. The newest pastor of the Kildonan Kirk was chosen by the Countess, breaking the tradition of being elected by the people of the parish. The Reverend made the rounds to the strongest lads in the glen, encouraging them to do their duty to the King and country.

Robbie was slightly interested, but doubted he could kill anyone so declined. Thinking it would be a grand opportunity to see the world, Tommy volunteered but his mother told him he was too young at 15 to even consider it. And now, with the evictions to the south and the council about to begin, making promises for the future seemed an underhanded way to clear the glen of young men who could defend their homes.

Alec expected the twenty Clans in the glen could at least send a spokesman with the short notice. The MacDonans returned home as the MacLennans gathered their bagpipes to bring to the council and hopefully for a dance afterward.

Bella glanced at the path to the Broch hoping for a glimpse of her sons returning. She and Rose waved in their direction, but did not see them.

"Ma, can we talk more later? I want to go for a walk."

Bella nodded, relieved to put it aside for a bit. Rose started down the path to the river.

Alec stepped inside the barn and came back outside with a basket of shot glasses and a bottle of Hugh's best whiskey, which had been saved for the first *ceilidh* of spring.

Bella leaned against the ledge at the end of the barn and tried not to worry about the future.

"May I pour you a wee dram?" Alec said with a dramatic bow to Bella.

"That would be lovely," she replied with a smile. "I believe my stomach would be warmed and my brain would benefit from some distraction."

"Here's to your everlasting beauty and charm, my love." They drank the dram at once and he refilled their glasses.

"Here's to your strength and kindness." Bella raised her glass to Alec. As they emptied their glasses, Hugh came around the corner of the barn with his pipes under one arm and another bottle in the other hand.

"Getting a start on me then, are you? Well, after the events of the day, and what is ahead of us, I would say we all need a good dram or two."

Alec poured a glass for Hugh. "I best have one more, I cannot let Hugh drink alone." Alec filled his and eyed Bella's glass in her hand.

"I would wait for Mary, but I do not see her." Bella raised her glass toward Alec. The three friends stood for a moment waiting for just the perfect sentiment for this round.

"To Bella," Hugh said, "the most courageous woman I know."

"To love," Bella said, "the source of all courage."

"*Slainte mhath*! To our health," Alec said, as they tipped their glasses together and drank.

"This might be your best batch." Alec nodded at the bottle in Hugh's hand.

"Well, do not forget the '94," Hugh said with a chuckle. "It was the year Les was born, and we had that dry weather in September. I will never forget the huge heads on the barley."

The barley story was cut short as Mary and Les walked up, arms loaded with baskets of food and their own bowls and mugs. Les had his pipes under his left arm just as his father carried his. The MacLennans had been pipers to a northern clan chief for generations. Now that the chiefs had abandoned the Highlands for lowland profits, the MacLennans tended their animals and crops like everyone else and led the people to dance, instead of to war.

"Not as much glory, but a lot more pleasure, and safer too," Hugh was fond of saying.

As they headed into the barn, people from nearby crofts arrived and then a group of people from Suisigil, the next village upriver, was seen rounding the bend. They were followed by a small wagon full of children, pulled by a pony. Alec and Bella greeted everyone as they entered the barn, Alec and Hugh offering a dram to the men, while Bella sought out women who were feeding bairns to settle them by a fire in the cottage. The small children, the weans, broke away from their parents and were already immersed in a game of shrieking and running. The noisy and chaotic scene was welcome after the winter's isolation and everyone was quite at home at the MacDonans.

Rose showed her latest weaving project to the lasses her age. The colors stretched on her loom were the MacDonan pine green and deep blue. She planned to sew a shirt for Tommy's birthday with the fabric, but looking at it now she wondered if he would still want the family plaid. The other girls were laughing at a riddle one of them told. She missed their company during the winter storms and they whispered around the loom about the changes in their lives and families. When any lads walked by, they turned to smile at them, in hopes of finding a dancing partner. As soon as it was polite to excuse herself, Rose went to look for Nathaniel.

The women wore colorful full-skirted dresses for dancing and tied a shawl over their shoulders to stay warm. The more prosperous had shoes, but many went barefoot. Anyone with a piece of family jewelry or bits of finery wore it proudly. Bella had pinned the round brooch Alec made for her to her shawl and adjusted her cap in a small mirror at the last minute.

Homespun peat-dyed trousers were the men's choice, as the kilt had been outlawed after the Culloden massacre in 1745. Their shirts were woven wool with bits of colored yarn, dyed by the women who collected lichen for a soft green and heather for red.

Alec thought most people had arrived and were settled on the chairs and benches arranged in rows of semi-circles, so he nodded to Hugh MacLennan, who stood in the center of the barn with his pipes tucked under his arm and the chanter in his mouth. Hugh began with "The Swallow's Tail," a cheerful tune that dipped and swirled. John Gunn joined in on his fiddle and several men pulled whistles out of their pocket.

When the song ended to cheers, Alec shouted above the commotion, "Hugh will play a few more tunes before the council begins, as I see more folks are arriving. Get friendly with your neighbors so we all fit in the barn. If you are in want of food, Mary MacLennan has biscuits and fresh cheese in her basket, or carry your mug to Neil Sinclair, who is pouring his fine brew by the door."

This caused a stir among some of those already settled and several people made their way to Mary, bringing back a handful of biscuits for their families. Quite a few men took Neil up on his offer and returned to their bench to share the drink.

John took the lead this time, and the fiddle set off slowly, while Hugh held a long bass note. It was a song they all knew well, a sad song of lost love and lonesome lochs that reminded them of stories told around a fire. The song ended with an uplift and John played a lively tune of happier times, of summer, of a good harvest, and a pretty lass.

Alec slipped into the cottage to look for Bella. She was standing close to Margaret MacDonald and had her hand on Margaret's very pregnant belly. He squeezed closer to Bella in the crowded room full of women and babies. One young mother with a bairn at her breast noticed him and bent her head down, pulling her shawl over the baby. Bella looked up to see Alec moving toward her. He got close enough to ask, "Tommy?" She shook her head no.

He stepped out the hillside door and looked up the brae. No sign of either of his sons. He walked around the outside of the cottage to the barn door. Les was leaning against the wall, pipes still under his arm. "Are you not going to join your father?" Alec asked with a hand on Les's shoulder.

"Maybe later." He was looking across to the pasture fence, where now Rose and Nathaniel were brushing the horses, their backs turned to the barn.

"Come inside, lad, the council is about to begin and we need every man's view." Les nodded, glanced at Rose and followed Alec inside.

***

ROSE AND NATHANIEL reached their arms toward the mare and Scout at the same time, Rose withdrawing hers quickly lest she touch Nathaniel accidentally. Rose was trying to think of what she could say that did not lead to Tommy, yet it was all she could think about. Nathaniel was feeling more comfortable around the MacDonans, but at the same time he felt unbearably English and out of place, especially with the possibility that his own father's interest in the pasture might lead to the eviction of the very people he was beginning to care about deeply.

"Rose, what do you think I should do? Should I go to the *ceilidh*, or go back to Helmsdale? I don't really belong here. I sound awfully English, and I will not know enough of the Gaelic to reply if someone speaks to me."

"Well, you rescued the MacKays' son. Everyone will want to thank you and toast you. I don't suppose you can sound less English, but maybe if you had different clothes you would be less conspicuous."

"I only have the clothes on my back." Nathaniel looked down at his riding trousers and matching vest, the fancy cuffs on his shirt, and the soft leather jacket. "I started out with more clothes but they are all filthy after a few weeks traveling."

"If you just had a homespun shirt and threw a plaid over your shoulder you would look more at home, even if everyone knows you are English. I do not expect Robbie would mind if you borrowed his other shirt. I know it is clean as I washed it recently."

"Are you sure he would not mind?"

"If you left your fancy shirt in its place, he would not mind a bit, I promise."

"How will we do it? The cottage could be full of women."

"Come around to the hillside door. I will go in and get his shirt, then you step around the corner to change."

Rose went inside where only a few women were left sitting by the fire as their small children played on the floor. In times past councils had been to plan battles and the women were left out. Now with the challenge to their homes in their glen, everyone was invited.

Robbie's shirt was just where Rose had left it on the hook by his bed. She removed the shirt, hoping Robbie would not mind after all, picked up a tartan blanket her Da wore on cold nights and carried her bundle to Nathaniel, who was waiting just outside the door. They returned each other's smiles as he took the package and stepped around the corner.

In a few minutes he reappeared, Robbie's shirt over his vest and the MacDonan plaid over his shoulder. "Weel lass," he joked, "would ye think I have been in this Strath all me life now?"

Rose tilted her head, looking him up and down. "If you were just barefoot...," she said.

"Never mind then, I will not trade Robbie my boots for his leather straps." They laughed together at the image.

"Let's go to the barn. I will find a place for you on a bench out of the way." She led the way through the cottage and dropped off the fancy shirt on Robbie's clothes hook. She found Nathaniel a spot in the barn at the very back, where he squeezed on a bench with the MacKays. Rose went to the front to sit by her mother.

Walter MacKay had found him earlier to shake his hand and thank him for saving Jamie and now put his arm on Nathaniel's shoulder in a gesture of friendship. Nathaniel settled in for his first highland *ceilidh*.

Chapter Seven

Brave and trusty. Clan MacLachlan

WHEN THE MUSICIANS finished a reel to a round of applause and hurrahs, Alec stood in the front row to formally welcome everyone. "*Failte*! Welcome! 'Tis a lovely day in the glen with the sun returning, the land coming to life again, and all of us gathered for food and music. We give thanks for the end of winter, and the promise of spring to come."

"*An t-Earrach*, to Spring," people repeated.

"This is our first council in many years," Alec said. "I am glad to see so many clans represented. I know you are here for the *ceilidh*. Before the feast and dancing begin we need to talk about a grave situation that may affect everyone in the glen. Ian MacDonald," Alec gestured to the curved row of benches to his right, "and I have returned today with bad news from the outside."

Ian moved over to make room for his wife Margaret, and her parents, Neil and Catherine Sinclair. Everyone looked at Ian, as he was an incomer, having only lived in the glen for two years. The folks in Kildonan knew him quite well, but others from up the river had never seen him before. He looked different than the Highlanders. His cheekbones were pointed in his long face, and his forehead was narrow. His hair was dark, like some locals, but it was short and trimmed carefully. He didn't have a beard, although he must have been close to thirty years old.

Alec continued and the group attention returned to his broad freckled face and fine golden beard. "You may remember last autumn when the Earl sent a new Factor to collect rent. He had other men with him who were writing and drawing on paper."

Neil said, "I did not like that man and his lowlanders poking around my land."

"None of us did, Neil. When Ian and I were at Golspie three days ago, we met several men from Rogart village to the south, who had all been Ross tenants. They said the new Factor, Patrick Sellar, convinced Edward Ross to stand aside as they put his tenants off the land. Sellar told Ross he could run sheep and make a lot of money rather than a small share of the harvest. A week later after all the tenants who would have defended Ross were gone, Sellar came back and ordered his men to evict Edward."

"What! They put him out of his own house?" Walter MacKay called out.

"Aye, Ross was put out with his whole family, women, children, and all, with no place to go, just like his tenants before him."

Everyone listening to this news was shocked into silence. Nothing this bad had been heard or even imagined.

Neil spoke again. "My family has been paying rent to the Earls of Sutherland since my great-grandfather's time. They can not do that to us here."

"They can do whatever they like," Ian replied, "because you are not in the class that can own land, none of us are. A few men own the Highlands, and we are all slaves."

"Surely the Countess, who is the mother of us all, would not stand by while we are treated badly by the likes of this Patrick Sellar," Neil said.

"The Countess is in London and has left Sellar in charge of our fate," Ian said.

"And how do you, a lowlander, know where the Countess Elizabeth is, young man?" Neil's bushy eyebrows were raised and his face was getting red.

There was a murmur from the Kildonan neighbors, as Ian's well known political views might start a quarrel. Plus the Glasgow lad talked so fast it was hard to keep up with him. Bella pulled Alec close and whispered, "Don't let them start arguing."

Catherine patted her husband's hand to try to calm him down.

"Father, please," his daughter Margaret said, "Ian is just trying to be helpful."

"Let's not start fighting among ourselves," Alec said. Several voices shouted agreement.

"Ach, I am sorry," Neil said to Ian. "It is hard to believe this could ever happen here. It must have been a mistake."

"And I'm sorry to sound rude," Ian said. "The men from Rogart told us they expected the Countess to come to their rescue, but she is staying out of Scotland."

Alec spoke again. "It is possible they will try to evict us too, as we have even more summer pasture than the Ross Clan. I'm sure there are a lot of questions and suggestions to be made."

From the back of the barn a man's gravelly voice boomed out. "Rotten news about my cousins to the south. Heard Edward was in a tight place, owed rent to the Earl. Know where they went, Alec?" James Ross wandered from glen to glen as he had no cottage or immediate family. Alec was not surprised to see him in Kildonan today, as everyone knew there would be food and drink for all at a *ceilidh*.

"We heard that the Earl and the Countess have arranged small plots of land along the coast for some of the favored tenants like Edward," Alec answered.

This statement sent an angry cloud of comments moving around the room. The coast soil was shallow, if it existed at all on the rocky bluffs, and the rain blew in from the sea without the benefit of hills to break it.

When it was quiet again, Alec added more news. "Ship passage has been offered to anyone who would emigrate. Some of the young Ross men have signed up to go to Canada or the colonies. Many lads have joined the English Army with the promise of new land when they return."

Bella's eyes searched the room for Robbie and Tommy. Still no sign of Tommy since they walked up the hill earlier, but Robbie had returned to play music. He was leaning against the wall opposite her, whispering something to Les.

Her attention was drawn back to the council as several men were calling for immediate revolt and a march on the castle. Alec called for quiet to finish his report. "The Earl has boats ready to send men out to sea after the herring."

This insult brought more outrage than the emigration plan.

"I will not spend my life in a damned boat," James Ross shouted.

"Better stand by the side of a river and catch a salmon than go out to sea for herring," declared Walter MacKay. Heads nodded in agreement to both statements.

Bella waited until it was quiet again to speak. "We need to be smarter than Sellar and think our way through this. I say we send a delegation to the Countess to remind her of our generations of loyalty."

The women finally had a chance to speak, with Bella breaking the usually male dominated discussion.

Mary MacLennan was shy to speak in front of a group like this, but with her home threatened she gained some courage. "I agree with Bella. We should do something before the wolf is at our door."

"I don't believe we will be evicted. It's just that lazy Ross Clan they are after, not us," Arthur Keith said from the doorway. James Ross glowered at him, but Keith just shrugged.

Ian stood to be heard above all the people talking at once. "We also heard the people in Farr and Assynt were put out. Last summer when I was in Glasgow, I saw an advertisement for sheep pasture in the Highlands. It promised a quick way to make money. That is likely what the lowlanders were doing here in September, picking out their pasture." He blushed as he finished, knowing that being from south of the Great Glen, they considered him a lowlander.

"We know that Sellar handed out a map to Kildonan pasture just a few days ago," Alec said, and avoided looking at Nathaniel. Other people craned their necks looking for the mysterious stranger who arrived that morning. Maybe he brought the map.

Nathaniel slouched on the bench, glad to be in the back row.

"We need a scouting party to get information," Walter said. A dozen men waved their arms to go at once. "I agree with Alec that we need a plan. I think sending a scouting group to Rogart, and as Bella suggested, a delegation to the Countess is the way to start. I am inclined to join the delegation, but will do whatever is necessary."

"MacLeod, would you lead the scouting expedition?" Alec asked. The MacLeods had a large family known for roaming the hills for weeks at a time.

Robert MacLeod nodded his agreement. "What exactly do we want to know when we get to Rogart?" he asked the assembled group.

"Anyone still living there?" John Gunn asked.

"Did anyone try to talk to the Countess?" A woman's voice asked hopefully.

"Find out if they knew when the soldiers were coming," Bella said.

"Did they try to fight back?" James Ross bellowed above the din of conversation. He pushed his way to the front of the room. "Round up all the sheep they've already brought north, and drive them back to England!" He jabbed his arm in the general direction of the border.

Keith joined him at the front. They clinked ale mugs in agreement and downed the contents, belching in satisfaction. They were both past their prime for rustling sheep, but could still cause trouble.

No one else joined them or encouraged the idea, so Alec grabbed the chance to speak again. "We heard eviction notices were posted on the tenants' doors in Rogart after the harvest last autumn. Most people did not believe the Countess would do such a thing, and so ignored the notice."

"If the Countess wants us to leave, that is what we will have to do," Martha Fraser said.

"No one here has received a notice, have they?" Walter asked. He looked around at the shaking heads. "We have been good tenants for generations. We've worked hard to pay our rent and our ancestors are buried here."

At the mention of leaving behind the remains of loved ones a low wailing began. Ross and Keith shook their heads in disgust and stormed outside. John slid the bow over his fiddle to match the lament. For awhile they were lost in communal grief, with heads bowed and tears shed. John played a higher note as Bella stood next to Alec and squeezed his hand, urging him to speak again.

"We don't have to wait until we are told to leave. I do not like the idea of stealing sheep, as Ross suggested, and think that should be a last resort." He looked over the assembled group and saw that many people nodded in agreement with Ross out of the room.

"Here's my idea. MacLeod will meet outside with anyone who wants to go up the river, over Cnoc Tuari, and down the back trails to Rogart. If people needing shelter are found, send a lad or two to guide them back here. See if there is anything left of the village, or if the Factor's men are still about."

MacLeod waved agreement so Alec went on with another idea. "Two or three men head for the coast. Go to the Inn at Golspie and listen to any talk about Sellar's plans for Kildonan. Those who want to write a petition to the Countess stay here for now, and choose a delegation to leave for Dunrobin in a week. The news from the scouts will help us decide what to do. Will that work?"

A chorus of "Ayes" signaled agreement. MacLeod answered, "Aye, it's a good plan, Alec. Anyone wants to go to Rogart, meet me outside after the council and we will decide when to leave."

Nathaniel noticed MacLeod earlier when Alec said his name. The man was tall like him, and had curly red hair. Robert's eyes were the same blue as his mother's. She always said he resembled the Scottish MacLeod side of her family. Maybe this was a distant Highland cousin.

When Alec called for a break, Nathaniel asked Walter to introduce him to MacLeod. "Sure, sure, lad. You look just like him, now that I see you in the same place."

Robert was standing by the door as men gathered around him to discuss their scouting plans.

Nathaniel wrapped the plaid around him and stood up. He and Walter joined the group at the door. "MacLeod, this is Nathaniel Reed, the lad that saved my son Jamie from drowning this morning. He believes he has kin in the glen, and I wonder if it's your family."

MacLeod shook hands with Nathaniel. "We have no Reeds in the Highlands, but you do have the MacLeod look about you." Everyone nearby laughed, as besides being tall and red headed, the MacLeods were fond of wearing the best clothes they could get their hands on. Despite Robbie's shirt and the old plaid, Nathaniel's leather trousers were a cut above everyone else's. And his hair seemed to be trimmed carefully, instead of chopped haphazardly as many of the men preferred.

The joke seemed friendly so Nathaniel said, "My grandfather, Donald MacLeod, left the Isle of Skye, met my grandmother on his way south, and never went back. My grandfather heard his youngest brother James relocated to a river valley in the Far North."

"Well, it seems like we are closer kin than you may think. My father James is still alive and waiting for your grandfather to return." He shook Nathaniel's hand more enthusiastically. "Glad to meet you, cousin, and hear that you have helped the MacKays. Have you been taught the MacLeod motto?"

Nathaniel remembered something about fast. "Run Fast?"

The crowd around MacLeod convulsed with laughter. When the uproar and backslapping let up, MacLeod, who had not cracked a smile, said, "Well, that helps too, but 'Hold Fast' is what we try to live by."

Nathaniel would have been embarrassed, but the men nearby seemed to get such enjoyment from his mistake that they all had to shake his hand.

MacLeod put his arm around Nathaniel and spoke quietly. "So, cousin, is it your father who has sent you to look at the pasture or your mother to look for long lost kin?"

"They both believe I am at school in Edinburgh. Coming north was my own idea to impress my father, taking initiative, he calls it. Now he will be angry to find out I left school without permission."

"A MacLeod, indeed," Robert said.

They sat on a bench next to each other as Alec yelled to get everyone's attention. "If we can just figure out who will go to Dunrobin, I think the other details can be worked out over food and drink."

"I would go to Dunrobin." The room became quiet as Nathaniel stood up. Everyone turned to look at him. Robert MacLeod seemed to have adopted the lad, and of course the dramatic rescue had been told and retold. "I can imagine you would not trust me as I am a stranger," Nathaniel said.

"He's my second cousin, if that makes him more, or less trustworthy." MacLeod said to a chorus of laughter.

"What do you have in mind, lad?" Walter asked.

"I have a horse and could travel quickly with just one other person. I believe I could get close enough to Sellar's men to hear what they are planning, maybe ask a few questions."

"Surely you would not come all the way back to tell us," Walter said.

"I would come back. But with a second man, he could ride my horse back quickly if there was pressing news and I could follow on foot." Nathaniel looked around to see who might volunteer.

Someone spoke from the cottage doorway. "I will go with Nathaniel." When they all turned to see who it was, Tommy stepped away from the shadows and into the light of the circle.

Chapter Eight

Let fear be far from all. Clan MacNab

THERE WAS GENERAL agreement to take a chance on Nathaniel, but before Bella could talk to Tommy about going to Dunrobin, he slipped out the barn door. Alec ended the council and Bella had to take charge of the feast set-up. Benches were moved to face each other in a long row, then plank tables were set between them.

Food baskets were collected from the pony carts, while Annie, Mary, and the women who lived nearby went home to bring back their contribution to set on the table. Everyone brought their own wooden bowl and carved spoon. People moved along the table, scooping a spoonful of potatoes, the mashed tatties, from one kettle, pease porridge, and garden kail from another with a sprinkle of Catherine's crumbled goat cheese to mix with the vegetables.

The trout Walter caught that morning were roasting on an outside fire. Bella put out the bannocks that had been baked haphazardly all day. Cream from the Fraser's cow was mixed with oatmeal and heated on the fire at the last minute. It was a feast of plenty for so late in the food year, and there was enough for everyone to fill their bowls twice.

The young people finished in a hurry and were tapping spoons in their empty bowls and eyeing up the possibilities for dancing partners. They danced together many times and knew who stepped on feet, or swung too hard, or was not fast enough to keep up with the reels. Although Rose would usually have been excited to dance and Tommy had practiced swinging her all winter, he did not appear when the food was served. Rose decided to stay near Margaret, in case she needed something, or labor started. That gave Rose the excuse to watch Nathaniel, although he soon went outside with a group of men.

As soon as the last person finished eating, the lads cleared the table and then carried the boards and braces outside to make room for line dancing. Married couples and older people moved the benches against the wall to sit and watch, as the younger dancers lined up facing each other, lads on one side and lasses on the other. They were short a few lads, so a search was made outside and some of the shyer boys were dragged in by the older girls and put in line.

Les was called on to choose the songs. He had been playing the pipes since he could bring up enough air to fill the bag. His grandfather, Colin MacLennan, had been a piper of renown and was a patient teacher to Les when Hugh was busy with the crops. Les scanned the line of dancers hoping to see Rose, who usually danced at the front. She was not in the line, nor was Tommy. His enthusiasm to play the pipes was waning.

He blew the first drone, hoping they would appear. Robbie was the fiddler for the first round, and he had left after the food. Had all his friends deserted him? The news about Tommy's birth was awful. It was hard to think about how he would react, if his own Ma said he didn't belong to her.

The MacDonan family had always seemed perfect to him, as he was often lonely for more laughter and even fighting. Now he felt grateful to have a simple, peaceful life, with just his mother and father. He saw them leaning against the wall by the fire heads together, his Da gesturing with his hands and his Ma nodding or shaking her head.

It was tempting to consider joining the scouts bound for Rogart. He had never been that far away from the Strath, so MacLeod would be a good man to go with for such a distance. Actually, he did not know how far it was, but if they would be gone a week, it must be many miles away. Les imagined himself guiding lost women and children through the forest to safety in their glen.

Nathaniel was leaving, and if he could do something heroic, maybe

Rose would agree to marry him soon. As soon as the first dancers were winded, he would go talk to MacLeod.

The boys and girls were jumping around without the music when Robbie finally arrived with his fiddle tuned and ready. Les chose the first reel, an easygoing strathspey. The fiddle set the pace as the pipes kept the tune and filled the barn with energy. The two lines of dancers skipped to the center, greeted with a handshake, strolled back and then met again in the center to swing.

The girls preferred the elbow swing as they had more control over the speed. One of the lads tried to grab a lass around the waist, but before he could reach around her she had him by the arm and flung him back to the boy's side. The adults watching laughed and clapped.

After a swing with their partners, the head couple in line swung each other and then a new partner in line all the way down to the last couple. Les became impatient for the dance to be over, so he sped up the tempo and Robbie raced to catch up on the fiddle. Les decided to wear them out quickly and then head outside.

At the end of the next tune, the young dancers collapsed on the benches and the adults lined up. His Da brought his pipes out and John Gunn tuned his fiddle. Robbie wiped his brow and headed for a cold drink. Les tucked his pipes under his arm and walked outside.

A group of men were huddled around the outside fire. MacLeod was easily visible being the tallest. Les noticed Angus Munro and the MacPherson brothers who lived up the river. He walked around the circle as George Bannerman's voice rose above the others, cursing Sellar and the Earl. Arthur Keith was suggesting to MacLeod that Hamish Gunn could not be trusted and should be left behind.

MacLeod had no patience for the ongoing feud. "Keith, your dispute with Clan Gunn should be put to rest. It has been 300 years, man. We have a common enemy who has just burned out our southern neighbors, Keith, Gunn, and Ross alike. If you want to go with us to look for survivors, you will have to shake hands with any Gunn who wants to go."

Keith grumbled but shook hands with Hamish.

"Well put, Robert," Angus Munro said. "We are heading for Rogart to try and help anyone wandering in the hills, whatever their name may be."

"Unless it's Sellar," a man shouted, followed by scattered laughter.

Munro added, "If the Factor's men are still about, we will need tight discipline to stay hidden. I say Robert MacLeod gives the orders."

"Aye," was echoed around the fire.

"Here is our plan then," MacLeod shouted above all the voices. "We meet at this fire mid-morning tomorrow. If you can obey orders from me, show up with a blanket and food for a week. We'll go up river and cross at the old log where the Craggie water comes down, then head up for the High Broch above Balnacoll. We should make it there by dusk. Anyone who cannot walk uphill all day should stay here."

"How much further to Rogart?" One of the lads thought it sounded harder than he imagined.

"Another half a day," MacLeod said, "but we are just going to see the situation for ourselves, not to start anymore trouble." He looked at Ross and Keith who were passing a horn of whiskey back and forth. MacLeod did not want to be stuck with Ross, an unpredictable old man, who didn't look to be in the best of health. Ross brewed whiskey as he had no land and probably sampled way too much of it. MacLeod was mulling over his options for potential runners when he turned to see Les MacLennan at his side.

"I would join the scouts," Les said.

"We could use some clearheaded lads. How far have you been in the hills yonder?" MacLeod nodded his head to the south.

Les tried to remember the streams he and Robbie had explored looking for salmon. "To the top of Lieath Beag," he said.

"That is the way we will go to Rogart. Answer me truthfully, could you find your way home if you were leading people in the dark?"

Les considered the dark. "If there was some moonlight I could, but not in the pitch black."

"That's a truthful answer, and the same one I would give. If I told you to wait by yourself would you do it?"

Les swallowed. "Aye," he said.

"Good man. I'll be heading home soon, but will be back in the morning, so have food and a blanket ready." MacLeod's attention shifted to someone else's question, leaving Les alone to wonder if he had done the right thing. It was too late to change now. He promised he would go and so he would. He turned back to the barn, ready to play again if his father was winded.

ROSE LEFT MARGARET when Ian asked his wife to dance a slow tune. She went out the hillside door to her favorite spot and found Nathaniel sitting on a ledge big enough for two. Rose considered the ledge her own and spent many hours of her childhood there playing with sticks, stones, and moss, building wee houses for the carved animals her Da made. When she began to read, it was her reading chair in dry weather and the place where she sketched trees and the hills beyond. As she learned to play the harp, it was a place to go where her brothers could not tease her about being clumsy.

Nathaniel looked up, smiled to see her, and moved over so she could sit next to him. She felt more comfortable with Nathaniel. He did not seem so much a stranger wearing Robbie's shirt and the familiar plaid. It was difficult to think anything good about the English or the Countess now. Yet here was a person born to an English father and raised on the borders, who did not regard them as ignorant savages, a phrase she had read about highlanders in general.

Dusk settled over the valley and perhaps tonight they would see stars again. Months of rain or snow sent her indoors at dark, but the light was stretching and the blue sky today was a promise of warmer days to come.

"We may see stars tonight," Rose began, looking up at the sky.

"I love watching them, especially the falling stars," Nathaniel said.

"Angels, losing their place in heaven," Rose turned to look at him. "We see them more in the summer, when we go to the high shielings."

"What are the high shielings?"

"The summer grazing land. Way up the stream behind us," Rose said, pointing behind them, "past the Auld Broch for half a day to the highest meadow. We take the animals and stay for weeks. The cows eat all the new grass and give the very best milk."

"You take a milk cow all that way?"

"Oh, aye. The cows love the fresh grass, especially after a hard winter. It is so lovely, Nathaniel. If you climb to the top of Morven you can see lower Scotland in the distance. The gloaming is so slow and peaceful, the sky is deep lavender, like the heather. On the longest day the sun only dips behind the hills. Everyone tries to stay awake to see it."

"Can you stay awake?"

"Only the past two summers. I sleep during the day to help me stay awake all night."

"Do your father and mother go to the high shielings?"

"Ma brings us food and usually stays for a few days, at least two or three times while we are there. She stays below if there is a woman who may need her. Rose glanced at him to make sure he was still listening. He was looking straight at her. "Da comes up sometimes too, but Mary MacLennan stays the whole time, to make sure everything gets done."

"What needs to be done?" Nathaniel only imagined them running through the grass and laughing a lot.

"Oh, we do weaving and make cheese and collect plants. There is lots to do, but we read and play games, too." Rose looked toward the door, thinking they should go back soon.

Nathaniel frowned. "I didn't know you could read. That is, we are told that Highlanders are illiterate."

Rose paused, deciding whether to be insulted or not. She took a breath and decided to be honest. "It's true many older people cannot read, or write. But now, with the Kirk of Scotland, we are taught to read the Bible for ourselves so we don't need a priest to tell us what it says. Or are you a papist and think we should be kept ignorant?"

"No, no. My family is Church of England. But tell me please what you like to read."

"Poems, and stories...." Rose was glad the light was dim to hide her blush. "About love."

"There is a fellow whose poems are all the rage in Edinburgh."

"What are the poems about?"

"Well, love mostly." Nathaniel recalled some of the bawdier songs and blushed himself.

"Oh." Rose looked around for her family. They were quite alone for the moment.

"Some are about auld Scotland. Wallace, Robert the Bruce, and all that." Nathaniel thought over what was so compelling about the poems. "He has written as Scots speak, not the way the English do."

"He is writing the Gaelic then?"

"No, more as they speak south of the Great Glen."

"I would love to read the poems. Who is the poet?" Rose would try to remember the name so her Da could find the book for her in Inverness.

"Robert Burns. It is sad though, he died in middle age. I have a book at home, but I memorized my favorites. Shall I recite one?"

"Please do!" Rose held her breath. This was the most romantic moment of her life. She glanced quickly toward the cottage, but it seemed like everyone was at the barn or outside below.

Nathaniel closed his eyes and began, not daring to look at Rose for fear he would become tongue tied.

> "O my luve is like a red, red, rose,
> That's newly sprung in June;
> O my luve is like the melodie
> That's sweetly play'd in tune.

As fair art thou, my bonnie lass,
So deep in luve am I;
And I will luve thee still, my dear,
Till a' the seas gang dry.

Till a' the seas gang dry, my dear,
And the rocks will melt wi' the sun;
And I will luve thee still, my dear,
While the sands o' life shall run.

And fare thee weel, my only Luve!
And fare thee weel, a while,
And I will come again, my Luve,
Tho' 'twere ten thousand mile."

Rose wiped tears from her eyes. Nathaniel was alarmed to have caused her distress. He put his arm around her. "I did not mean to make you cry."

She leaned against him. "It is just so beautiful and so sad at the same time. It begins with hope and ends with a longing."

"Yes, love found, and then lost, is the saddest thing of all." He kept his arm around Rose, and although his sadness was for his lost love to the south, the pain of their parting was easing up more than he could have imagined just yesterday.

Chapter Nine

Do not forget. Clan Graham

BELLA FOUND THEM a few minutes later, when she left the cottage hoping to find Tommy. "Rose, what are you doing?"

"Ma," Rose said, as Nathaniel withdrew his arm, "Nathaniel has recited the most beautiful poem."

"Ah, is that it?" Bella looked at Nathaniel. The only remaining light was cast from the cruisie lamp she held in her outstretched arm. They both seemed content to sit on Rose's ledge, and at least she knew where to find her daughter.

"Have you seen Tommy?" Bella asked them both.

Rose shook her head. "I have hardly seen him all day."

Nathaniel sat up straighter and leaned away from Rose. "I expect he will be looking for me. We need to plan our Dunrobin trip, if he has your blessing to go."

"I was surprised to hear him say he would go with Nathaniel," Rose said. "He has never been out of the glen before."

"He has always wanted to go with your Da, but I've kept him home." Anyone from Dunrobin would notice his striking resemblance to the Countess and her other sons.

"Here he comes," Rose said as Tommy walked around the edge of the cottage. "Tommy!" she almost cried with relief to see him. She jumped off the ledge and in four steps had her arms around him. "I have missed you all day."

Tommy squirmed out of her embrace as soon as he saw Nathaniel, despite his pleasure in the warm greeting. Bella stood by hoping he would look at her. Tommy looked at Nathaniel's clothes instead. "You look different up close, is that Robbie's shirt and Da's old plaid?"

"Yes, aye, your sister is helping me fit in better."

"She is good at that," Tommy said. He looked sideways and noticed his mother holding the light, but did not acknowledge her. "How about leaving at first light in the morning, Nathaniel?"

Nathaniel tried not to look at Rose. "What about the day after? It seems like I just got here."

Rose held her breath hoping Tommy would agree. If Nathaniel was around another day he might recite more poetry. She would never forget the Burns poem.

Tommy was already making plans. "We can go mid-day, time to get ready in the morning and go part way before dark. Do you still want to take your horse or shall we go on foot?"

"If we both had mounts we could get there and back quicker."

"Our old mare couldn't keep up with your horse. I would be better to run alongside."

"We could take turns riding and running," Nathaniel said.

"Which way are you thinking to go?" Rose asked.

"I don't know what the choices are, having never been to the coast before," Tommy said.

"Nor have I, you know," Rose said. They both looked at Bella.

"You are not going," Bella said to Rose.

"Your father is inside." Bella turned to Tommy. "You can ask his advice."

She held her breath waiting for him to deny Alec was his father, or her his mother. He frowned but didn't speak. Then he nodded to her and headed toward the door. Bella led the way with the lamp.

Tommy looked back to make sure Nathaniel was following, but he was bending to whisper something to Rose. "Good thing you stopped Rose from going, Ma. She seems to be sweet on Nathaniel and would just be in the way."

"Indeed," Bella replied. The ice was broken and warmth flooded her face. He just needed time to adjust to the change. That was reasonable and she would try to be patient.

Alec was on his way out, but stopped when he heard Bella's voice. "Ach, it's good to see you both. I wondered where to look for you."

"Tommy has a question, if we can all gather by the fire for a few minutes."

"Aye, that would be grand, and here's Robbie, in from the scout's fire. We'll all be together." There were still plenty of people around, but they were spread out, talking with MacLeod, or visiting in households nearby.

"Da," Tommy said, "we're planning to take Nathaniel's horse to Dunrobin. Which way should we go?" They had all pulled up short stools by the fire, and Robbie had the poking stick moving to get the peat blazing.

"Well, if you go by the Glen Loth trail 'tis upstream quite a ways to ford the river with the horse. Then there's a steep climb better for a pony. The Loth Broch at the top has a bit of roof, so you would have a sheltered place to sleep. It is difficult path this time of year, but the stream is lined with stands of rowan, birch, and the hazels, which will be just leafing. Lovely scene indeed."

"And to the coast, how much longer is it?" Tommy asked.

"Aye, there's the path along the river, easy enough to follow, isn't it?" Alec said to Nathaniel, who nodded. "The river path is more distance, but 'tis drier and mostly flat. The Earl's having a stone bridge built across the river at the Helmsdale harbor, and if the workers are gone for the day, you could walk across, or wait for the ferry."

"I doubt Scout would want to go in the river again, or up a rocky path," Nathaniel said.

"Take the longer route," Alec said, "your horse will do better, and there's no doubt which path to take. If you move quickly you can be at Dunrobin in two days, look about, get off the road for the night and head back."

"We best leave at first light after all," Nathaniel said.

Tommy looked at his mother. "Ma, can you pack us some food?"

"I would be happy to do whatever you need." Bella got up to gather supplies.

Rose jumped up and joined her mother, before she begged them to stay another day.

Robbie noticed that Nathaniel was wearing his own shirt and looked over to his bed against the wall. "Have we traded shirts then?" he asked Nathaniel.

"Sorry, Robbie. Rose promised you wouldn't mind, but we haven't had a chance to speak yet."

"You look more at home wearing a homespun shirt, and I have only dreamed of having a shirt as nice as this." Robbie got up and brought the shirt to the fire. "What is it made from?" he asked, fingering the fabric.

"Linen, with lamb's wool. My grandmother made it for me."

"I will just keep it here on the hook to look at and maybe I will try it on, but I would ruin it herding the cattle."

"Are you thinking of joining the scouts to Rogart, Son?" Alec asked.

"They will be a traveling village as it is, with everyone who wants to go. I am for the delegation, and I have another thought as well."

"Da," Tommy said. "Could I take your knapsack for my blanket and food?"

"Aye, it's in the side room, yet to be unpacked from my return this morning." Tommy found the bag and took it to the barn.

Alec turned back to Robbie. "Tell me your other thought."

Robbie stood up then and spoke to Nathaniel. "Sorry to leave you, Nathaniel. We need a word in private, so we'll step outside."

"No offense taken, but I am ready to sleep. Shall I stretch out here by the fire?"

"Nah, take my spot yonder," Robbie pointed to the nearby lower bunk, "and I will sleep in the barn, which I was planning anyway."

"I do not want to put you out of your own bed."

"Honestly, it is the best spot for you. Rose will stay at the Gunn cottage down the lane, while you and all the other men are here."

"You have convinced me, I will be asleep in no time. Give me a shove when Tommy's awake in the morning. And Mr. MacDonan, sir, I will do my best to make sure we stay out of trouble."

"Thank you, lad. Now get some sleep."

Robbie grabbed his own plaid and turned over the heather chaff mattress and fluffed it up as best he could. Nathaniel rolled into Robbie's bed with Alec's plaid wrapped around him. Robbie took a heavier blanket from the chest to throw down on a straw filled mat on the floor of the barn.

Alec followed him to the barn where Rose and Bella were cleaning up the food and wrapping biscuits and cheese in cloth. Alec decided to give Tommy the money he had saved for an emergency, as this seemed to be such an event. There would be enough coins to feed Nathaniel, too, and for lodging at the Golspie Inn for one night at least.

Bella added more peat to the fire, as the lamps had all burned down. She talked quietly to Tommy and Rose, as Tommy rolled up his extra clothes in the knapsack. Robbie got his blanket arranged on the floor and then he and Alec sat on it and leaned against the wall.

"Tommy," Robbie called quietly and waved them all over to sit on the blanket. Bella pulled another mat to sit next to Alec, and Rose leaned against her knees. Tommy sat cross legged across from Robbie.

"Remember that cave we found last summer, when we walked up the stream's north branch above the forest?" Robbie stared at him, ready to add more details if he had forgotten.

"The big cave where we scared each other?" Tommy asked.

"Well, I scared you, but I was just pretending to be frightened."

"So why did you holler when I jumped off that ledge?"

"You just surprised me." Robbie smirked as he waved off the idea of being frightened by his younger brother. "Well, anyway, my thought is this. That cave will be our meeting place if something goes wrong. I will make a couple of trips up there in the next few days to leave peat and meal. Mother, Rose, or Da can go with me different times so everyone knows how to find it. You would remember, wouldn't you Tommy?"

"Aye, I have thought about going back there on my own, when the light turns longer."

"I know the cave you mean," Alec said. "It faces southeast on a wide ledge just around a sharp bend, where the stream turns into a stepover. It has a narrow entrance, but widens just inside, so a dozen people could sleep in the back."

"That's it!" Tommy and Robbie replied in unison, and everyone laughed.

"Ah, it feels so good to laugh, a very serious day it's been indeed," Alec said. "The cave is an old MacDonan hide out from years and years ago. Who would have thought we would ever need to hide again." Alec passed his hand over his eyes. "I like your thought Robbie and am glad you can both find it again. I am desperate to sleep now, but we can talk more in the morning. Bella, are you coming to bed with me?"

"I'll be walking over to the Gunns's with Rose. She'll sleep there, so the lads from a distance can just lay down here in the barn."

"Sleep well then, Rose, and Tommy, get some sleep too." Alec stumbled up and headed outside for a last look around. The outside fire had almost died out, and only a few people remained with a fiddle player weaving sad, slow songs.

Just before he fell asleep, he heard Bella chant the smooring blessing as she spread the ashes over the coals. He just caught the end, "blessings on the earth, blessings on the hearth, blessings on us all."

In a few minutes, Tommy climbed on the bunk above Nathaniel, who was sound asleep. Bella took off her cap, untied her hair and pulled her dress over her head. "I will sleep in my shift tonight, with all the visiting men nearby," she whispered to Alec, as she crawled into their bed and pulled the double doors closed. They held each other gently, but as close as possible, both ready to cry, but hoping to fall asleep before the tears spilled.

Chapter Ten

Hold Fast. Clan MacLeod

Sunday, 21 March, Morning, Kildonan

BELLA'S SLEEP WAS interrupted by the same repeating dream. She escaped Sellar's men by going through the barn, out the back door, and over a small rise until she was above the cottage. She waited behind the grain dryer wall for Rose and Tommy, her pulse racing, beads of sweat gathering on her brow and an overwhelming urge to bolt seemed to take possession of her legs. She clamped her left hand over her mouth for fear she would scream their names, then crouched close to the ground to stop herself from running. There were times she had been afraid before—at a difficult birthing, during a flood or horrid storm, but never with this sense of urgency in her legs to just carry her away. She could now fully sympathize with the deer bolting from the hound. If Tommy and Rose did not appear before she counted to twenty, she would go back for them. There was no way she could go on without them. One, two, three, she began, aching for the sight of them around the barn. Four, five, six, and there was the rooster crowing. It caught her attention. Maybe they were waiting by the chicken hutch for her, but no, she opened her eyes as it crowed again, and found herself safe in her own bed.

Alec's hand was on her belly. "Are you well, love, you have been moaning and mumbling. I guessed a bad dream and was trying to wake you gently."

Bella rolled into his arms. "Keep me awake, I do not want to go back there."

"Where were you, lass?" His voice was gentle.

"Hiding behind the grain dryer, alone, waiting for Rose and Tommy to escape the cottage, as the men were coming with torches and hunting dogs."

"Ach, dear, I hope it does not come to that."

"No. The dream was bad enough."

They were both wide-awake now, but the anxiety of the dream was very real.

"Alec, we must be ready to leave suddenly and meet at the cave if we are separated. And I will go back for the children if they do not arrive. No counting to twenty in real life."

"Ah, is that what you were doing, counting. I thought you said 'sex' and was eager to please you."

"I have other things are my mind," Bella said with a rueful chuckle at Alec. She gave him a quick kiss, opened the doors, and rolled out of the bed.

No one was stirring yet and daybreak still seemed a ways off. Alec went back to sleep so Bella had a bit of time alone. She pulled her dress on, grabbed her shawl from the hook, and sat by the fire. After raking the ashes from the peat coals with the metal fork, she added bits of heather twigs and pine needles to feed the dwindling coals. She felt the need of the morning blessing at her hearth more than ever. Bella began her song with a whisper.

"As the sun rises on yonder brae,

Keep us safe and warm today.

Keep the fire burning bright,

'Til she's smoored in dark of night."

Once the beginning flicker was sure to continue, she added fresh peat and then put the kettle on the hook to boil water for tea. After a step out to the privy Bella returned to find Alec by the fire singing the blessing. She joined him and they sang the chant again together. Their voices woke Tommy, who rolled to the wall and then at once turned back toward them, "Is it morning already?"

"Aye, Son. It will be a grand day for you. Come and sit with your mother and me before everyone awakens."

Tommy was instantly alert. He dropped from the bunk, quickly pulled on his clothes and pulled up a stool between his parents. "Ma, Da. I could not think what to say yesterday, but thank you for caring for me so well all these years. You are my mother and father, I will always remember that, but now I feel this yearning that I cannot explain."

Alec added a larger block of peat to the fire and responded. "Life is like this fire, Tommy. It needs constant feeding and care. Wherever your yearning leads you, remember that your mother and I will always care for you, any time you have the need."

Bella's face was streaked with tears. "Alec, he is only going to Dunrobin for a look around and then will be back."

Tommy grabbed her hand. "Aye, Ma. I will be back in four or five days."

"Of course you will," Alec said. "I only want you to hear me say that I will be your father whenever you need me."

Tommy nodded, tears in his eyes. "I'm going out for a bit, maybe find a few eggs and then wake Nathaniel. I still want to get an early start."

"I think I hear the hens clucking already," Alec said with a wave, as Tommy grabbed the egg basket and ran out the door.

"I am struggling to find some good in him going off, Alec. I thought they were just going to have a look and try to get some news."

"We cannot hold him back any longer, but I will caution him to take care who he speaks to around Dunrobin. As for the good of things, our secret of all these sixteen years has now seen the light of day. The lad still loves us. We can just return his love and help him in the next part of his life."

"I hope he doesn't think the Countess will want to see him."

"If what we heard is true, she is not in Scotland. My guess is she will stay away and let Sellar take the hate they are spreading. But let us help

Tommy before he goes. I have some coins for him that I've been saving. Do you have a small purse he can tuck away so it won't be lost from a pocket?"

"Aye, I can find one. Will you make tea and refill the kettle?"

"I will do whatever you tell me."

"That is a promise I will remember," Bella said with an attempted smile.

Alec mixed a concoction of herbs for the tea, adding some thistle seeds to lift the depression everyone seemed to be feeling. He poured the boiling water into the teapot, set the cover on and then stepped out to the spring to fill the kettle. The sun had just crested the southern hills and the valley fog was beginning to lift. Another dry day, he hoped. He carried the full kettle back inside and hung it above the fire, adding more peat until the flames licked the bottom of the iron pot. The room was warming up quickly as the fire burned hotter.

Robbie came out of the barn rubbing his eyes. "Are they leaving soon, do you think?"

"Tommy is looking for eggs, and our English lad still snores in your bed."

"I woke up thinking yesterday could have been one of Uncle Neil's tales, but when I remembered Rose traded my clean shirt, it seemed all too real."

"If all we lose through this is one shirt, we will be very fortunate indeed," Alec said.

"Do you mean Tommy or Rose?" Robbie nodded his head toward Nathaniel, who had yet to stir.

"Change is coming to the Highlands, Son. There can be no doubt any longer. It is like a spring flood. You know there is more snow in the hills than the river banks can hold, but will it melt over time, or all at once flooding fields, killing cattle and even people caught by surprise."

"Were people killed at Rogart? You did not say that in the council."

"I do not believe anyone was outright murdered, but certainly the very old or sick people will perish from the cold if not given shelter."

"Do you think I should go with Tommy? I am a bit worried about him taking off with a stranger."

"I trust Nathaniel as far as that goes, but I do not trust the Factor at Dunrobin."

Before their conversation could continue Nathaniel rolled over and sat up quickly, almost knocking his head on the bunk above.

"Well, lad, that was a close call. A lovely highland morning to you," Alec greeted him with a chuckle. "Robbie's woken up with a lump on his head many a morning." Alec nudged Robbie, who managed a mutter of agreement.

"I'm off to the chores," Robbie said as he waved toward the bunk, and then strode back to the barn.

Alec finger tested the water. "Warm enough for a wash-up before your journey, lad."

Nathaniel swung his legs over the side of the bunk. "Thanks, I would like to clean up, but where?"

"Just above the byre is a stand of thick birch. Fill this horn to take with you, soap is already there, and a drying cloth. Here, save half the water to rinse off." Nathaniel filled up the horn, which seemed to be enough water to wash his hands. He raised his eyebrows and glanced at Alec, who was grinning and holding out a bucket. "You might need a bit more water, as tall as you are." Nathaniel smiled in relief and added warm water to the bucket and headed out the door.

Alec found himself alone for a change. A formidable series of tasks lay before him and all he cared to do was stir the fire. He wondered what his father would have done in his place. The MacDonans were long past raising an army to defend themselves. A charge on the castle, as some might like, would be quickly defeated by the troops the English King had stationed just outside Inverness. They could all be slaughtered or imprisoned and then the women and children would be abandoned. They were in a tight place, no doubt about it.

All thoughts led back to the people who were counting on him, and it was no use to sit and wish for the simple tasks of planting the crops and tinkering with stones. As if everyone had been waiting for him to decide to get moving, Bella and Rose walked in the front door as Tommy arrived with a basket of eggs and Robbie with milk from the goat.

"Is the tea made?" Bella asked.

"Yes, indeed. Everyone ready for a cup?" His family gathered before him as he poured each of them a cup. "To good health in the times to come," Alec said.

"*Slainte mhath*," they replied and stood quietly for a few minutes, sipping the hot tea.

"Ma," Tommy said. "I am relieved to say I felt like myself again while looking for the eggs." Bella smiled and tried to tousle his hair, but he was ready and jumped aside in time, without spilling his tea.

Rose picked up the basket and counted the eggs. "I'll cook six in the shells for you and Nathaniel to take as soon as the porridge is finished."

"Ach, the porridge," Alec said, reaching for the kettle. "I'll just get a wee bit more water and have it cooking in no time." He came back in a few minutes and hung the cooking kettle on the hook above the fire. Rose measured the cracked oats and scooped out a bit of the water to start the grain soaking. Robbie strained the milk into a pitcher and got a bowl of butter from the cool box.

Bella mixed a travel brew of tea. Nettles, rosehips, and raspberry leaves would nourish them for many a mile. The water had begun to simmer, so Bella poured grain in the water and gave it a stir. When the cooked oats were soft, Bella scooped them out and Robbie added milk to each bowl. Nathaniel was back and talking with Tommy as they went through the supplies in the knapsack again.

When they sat down around the fire with their bowls and wooden spoons and second cup of tea, Bella began the blessing. "We commit this moment to the spirit of love. May we travel and work apart for a short time and be reunited in health and joy. May our son and his friend be welcomed with kindness, as we welcome others. Amen."

They paused looking at the fire. "I shall cherish this meal with all of you for the rest of my life," Bella said.

"As shall I," Nathaniel added, as the rest nodded agreement. They ate in silence, content with the shared closeness and affection. When every drop had been scraped from the bowls, Robbie and Tommy collected them to wash outside, while Rose slipped the eggs in the water kettle over the fire.

Alec peered out the window. "I believe I will check for sleeping bodies and get everyone up and fed before MacLeod arrives."

Nathaniel and Rose were left alone by the fire, Rose gently stirring the eggs, and Nathaniel wishing they were staying another day. "I best see to my horse. Would you show me which hay I should use? When the eggs are done, I mean."

Bella was sorting herbs from her cupboard into a small bag, and offered to finish cooking the eggs. "All right then," Rose said. "I will do chores while you feed your horse." She stood up to leave, but first Rose kissed her mother on both cheeks. "Thanks, Ma." Bella squeezed her hands in return.

When they got outside there were already people milling around the fire, which Alec had kindled. Mary MacLennan put a kettle on a grate so folks could soak their grain and make tea. Nathaniel felt an urgency to speak to Rose as their time with a private word would be brief. "Rose, you are a lovely girl. I have enjoyed talking with you and appreciate all the help you have been to me."

"I am sorry I was so mean at first."

"You had a right to be. I was, or I still am, an ignorant fool. And now I am leaving. I cannot promise anything, except I will think of you often, and hope very much to see you again."

"I hope to see you again also," Rose managed to say before several people approached her wondering about hay and water for their ponies. She was soon bringing out buckets for water and several armfuls of hay and in the process lost sight of Nathaniel.

When she finished with the animals, Les was waiting for her, pipes under one arm and a knapsack over his shoulder. "Mornin', Les. Are you going to Dunrobin too?"

"No. I'll be off with the scouts when MacLeod arrives and gives the word."

"You are going to Rogart?"

"Or wherever we end up. MacLeod may have me wait by myself somewhere, as sort of a messenger."

Rose impulsively squeezed his spare arm. "I am very proud of you for going. Be careful, will you?"

"I am sure it could turn dangerous with the Factor's men about." Les looked toward the river path but no one was around.

"Are you scared, Les?"

"A bit," Les said. He looked down for a moment, then met her eyes. "I want to be of use, Rose, and this seems to be the right thing to do." Her hand was still on his arm. He let his pipes slide to the ground so both hands were free in case she let him embrace her.

"You are very brave. I wish I could go somewhere, but Ma has said I cannot."

"Well, you should not, Rose, but we will all be back soon enough." Les took both her hands in his. "Maybe we can talk about pledging marriage when I return."

Rose let go of his hands and looked away. "We don't know what will happen next," she replied and realized she was about to say the same thing Nathaniel had said to her, "so I cannot promise anything, but I will think of you often." She suddenly had to get away. She turned and ran up the slope to home.

Chapter Eleven

Gang (go) warily. Clan Drummond

ALL THE MEN who had spent the night nearby, or arrived that morning with Robert MacLeod, were ready to hike up the river. MacLeod's wife Lorna joined the group to tend to the sick or injured and be company for any women. Lorna was tall like MacLeod, but her hair was dark and her skin fair. She was dressed for hiking, her skirt cut above her ankles and men's boots on her feet.

As they were leaving, Les joined them, trying to blend in with the men to avoid saying another round of farewells. No use making more of it than it was, he decided.

Once they were out of sight, Alec spread the fire to save any peat that could be brought to the hearth. He was the only person around, as it seemed that everyone had gone inside or marched away. It was good to be alone with the sky above and the earth below. There was promise of life to come in the leafing of the birch and willow. The fresh grass and bracken dazzled the eye in vibrant shades of green with the slightest sunshine. The light was clean and with the sun now higher in the sky, their small community looked born again. Beneath the birdsong, the river on her way to the sea had a deeper message. "Alec, remember this moment," he said aloud, then turned toward his home.

Tommy was coming out the barn door followed by Nathaniel, Rose, and Bella. The lads looked ready to depart, knapsacks slung over their shoulders and Scout's saddlebags bulging. Nathaniel and Rose veered off to the pasture, walking very close to each other, Alec noted. He sighed with relief that Nathaniel was leaving before his daughter became any more smitten.

"You are lost in thought, Da," Tommy said, nudging his arm. "Do you wish you were going with us?"

Bella put her arm around Alec's waist and gave him a squeeze. Alec forced his brain to focus on what Tommy asked.

"Go with you? No. I only want to be here in Kildonan. I think I would prefer to never leave again." He noticed the big smile on his son's face. "You look excited and ready to walk."

"I am a bit nervous, but ready for something new, whatever it will be."

Bella put a small leather drawstring bag in Tommy's hand. "Keep this bag in your deep pocket. There are enough coins to buy food and lodging at the Inn in Golspie. Tell the innkeeper you are Alec MacDonan's son. He will take good care of you."

"I never thought of needing coins. I really am ignorant," Tommy said, pushing the purse deep into his trouser pocket.

"When you are going to the Inn or market, take a few coins out and put them in your shirt pocket when you are alone, so that no one sees you have a bag of coins," Alec said.

"Do you think someone would rob me?"

"Most people are honest, but there may be men desperate to feed their children." Alec imagined himself in such a situation and shuddered.

"But if they have hungry children, should I not spare them a coin?"

Bella answered when Alec seemed unable to speak. "Better to give a hungry family some of your food, than show you have coins."

"Go in peace." Alec put his arm around Tommy's shoulder, and Bella hugged him close. Rose and Nathaniel arrived with Scout, and after Nathaniel shook hands with everyone, the lads started down the path. Robbie came running down the hill to say good luck and give his brother a playful shove to push him on his way. Tommy turned once to wave where the lane met the riverside path, and then they were gone around the bend.

Rose burst into tears. Bella had been trying to brave but gave up and joined her. They sat on the ground next to each other and sobbed together.

Robbie looked at his father in disbelief. Alec rolled his eyes and put his arm around Robbie. "Let's go inside to console ourselves with a wee dram."

When the tears were spent and Rose went to her ledge to write in her diary, Bella started to clean out the barn.

James Ross stumbled around the corner. "Ach, missed the scouts' take-off, have I?" He looks relieved, Bella thought, not disappointed. He smelled worse than ever. His untrimmed whiskers drooped in his mouth, and he was missing another tooth. Bella looked away.

"They have been gone long enough for the fire to smolder." Bella nodded to the ashes smoking on the ground. "You might catch them."

"Hmm, well. Bella, is there a bite left to eat? My meal bag is empty."

"Alec is inside, ask him to give you any scraps, but we sent most of the cooked food with Tommy and Nathaniel."

"Ah, the lads to Dunrobin. I will catch up with them instead of the Scouts. Take in some sea air away from all this trouble."

Before Bella could think of a way to dissuade him, Ross picked up his bundle and made off down the path in a hurry. "James, wait. I will cook eggs," she called in desperation, but it was no use. He was gone as quickly as he had arrived.

Bella leaned her broom against the wall and went inside to find Alec. He was rolling up the bed covers and tying them into bundles. She held onto his arm to keep his attention. "James Ross has gone after Tommy. I could not stop him."

"That is odd. I thought he was determined to go with MacLeod."

"He claims to have overslept, but seemed wide awake to me."

Alec stacked the blankets on a shelf by the door as Bella moved the kettle near the fire. "Alec, he has been gone all winter and returned a few days ago. It was James that suggested herding the sheep back to England."

Alec joined her by the fire. "I wonder if he spent the winter in Rogart and was there during the eviction. That might explain why he was a lit fuse in the council."

"But why not say he was there? We were all guessing, and he would know what really happened."

"Maybe he left when the Factor arrived instead of helping people get away," Alec said.

The image of children crying and Ross abandoning them was too awful to consider.

"Alec, he stopped by a month ago complaining of chest pain. I dosed him with foxglove. He has a quick temper. I hope he does not spoil Tommy's journey."

"There is not much damage he can do just walking along the river, and then they will part company, if he can even catch them. They were both walking fast and had the horse to ride."

"I hope you are right. I do not trust Ross."

The water was hot, and Bella got out the herbs for a fresh pot of tea. Alec handed her their mugs.

"It seems so cruel," Bella said, "to evict everyone for no reason, when there is no place for them to go. What can the Countess be thinking?" While the tea was steeping they glanced out the window, both nervous now that something bad might happen if they did not remain vigilant. The village was quiet.

"I have been trying to put it all together, Bella. There must be wealth and power involved, or they would just leave us here to get by as we can. We are no burden to the Countess."

"Even if several families could not pay rent, surely with hundreds paying, a little less money could not put them out much."

Alec carried the mugs outside and sat by Bella on the ledge by the lower door.

"Last fall when I was in Inverness," Alec said, "I read a piece in the Edinburgh news. I had forgotten it 'til just now. The Earl of Sutherland has become the largest landowner in all of Europe."

"How is that possible, Alec? You mean even including France and Spain?"

"The day he turned twenty-one he inherited the family estate in northern England and the Earldom at the same time. When he married our Countess Elizabeth he became the legal owner of all her land, from the Dornoch Firth to the Atlantic Ocean, and he recently purchased land on the north coast as well."

"One man holding the deed to so much land, it seems indecent." Bella said with a frown.

They remained silent, sipping their tea. Bella spoke first, eyes on the ground. "I cannot help thinking if the Countess knew Sellar was sending men here, to take our land, she would put a stop to it. She could not want her son left out in the cold." She was lost in thought for a minute, then gasped. "Oh, I have the cloth patch the Countess gave me with her insignia, in case Tommy was very ill and I needed her help. I should have given it to Tommy." She stood up and paced in agitation.

Alec drained his mug. Time was flying by.

"Keep it close by. There may be a need for it yet. The delegation folks are meeting soon. Perhaps we could use it to get past Sellar. That may be the only way we could speak to someone important."

"I will stitch it to my hem so I will always have it with me."

Mid-day, The River Path

NATHANIEL THOUGHT THEY were halfway to the coast. "Scout needs a break and I want to consult the map," he said to Tommy. They agreed to rest on the sandy beach where the river curved at a stone outcropping. He tethered the horse to a large oak tree where there was plenty of fresh grass to eat underneath. Nathaniel opened the saddlebags, handed Tommy the food sack, and then reached into an inside pocket where he kept the map.

It wasn't there. He thought back to the last time he had it, in the cottage when he and Tommy traced the route from the Castle to the MacDonan pasture.

"Did you pick up the map after our hike to the Broch?"

"No, I never saw it again, but then I wasn't looking for it. We don't need it, do we?"

"I know the way. Let's eat."

Tommy unwrapped the cloth with the hard cooked eggs and tapped a shell on his knee. Nathaniel did the same and they split an oat biscuit between them. After they washed their meal down with the last of the tea Bella had poured in a travel horn, they both stretched out on flat ground, agreeing to rest for just a few minutes. The sun was still above the hills. Tommy figured they had plenty of time to make the coast as he drifted off.

James Ross hurried to catch them, having no food at all, but knowing that Bella would make sure her lad had plenty to eat. He finally spotted the outcropping they called "the Auld Man." It was a traditional place to stop, although the lads might not know that, it was worth a look down into the meadow.

Before he could step over the edge of the slight embankment to the river path, he heard a horse approaching. He jumped down and took cover behind some bushes. It must be the lads coming back for some reason, but no use taking chances these days. He let the horse and rider pass his hiding place. A lone man on a full sized horse was moving along with a purpose. Maybe he had some food to spare, the saddlebags were full.

"*Breagha an-diugh,*" Ross called out as he jumped back in the road and waved at the man. When he reined in the horse, Ross realized the man looked foreign and probably did not understand his Gaelic greeting. He could speak English if he had to, so he said, "Hello, lovely day," as he approached the rider. He was tempted to ask what the hell the man was doing in the glen, but first things first. "Have a bit of food to spare?" he asked, glancing at the saddlebags.

"If you can tell me how much farther to Kildonan." The rider adjusted his lanky frame on the saddle and pushed his riding cap back over his graying hair.

"Kildonan's a long strath along the river. Depends who you are visiting."

"I am looking for the place where the Kildonan stream enters the river."

"MacDonans' place. Looking for Alec, are ye?"

"Not exactly," the man said, handing Ross a cooked potato from a cloth bag. "So, how much longer to this MacDonan's? An hour, two, three?"

Ross looked at the sun to guess how long he had been walking and to stall for time. He devoured the potato and then said, "You had best turn around. You are one of those sheep farmers from the south planning to steal our land."

"I am Charles Reed, and I do plan to lease some pasture, if I like the look of it, but from the Earl of Sutherland, not some local peasant."

Ross stepped forward, drew a dirk from his boot and grabbed the horse's halter. "This land is not for lease," he yelled. "Go back to England where you belong!"

Reed jerked on the reins, the horse whinnied and reared up on his hind legs, nearly throwing Reed off. Ross let go of the halter and shouted threats in Gaelic.

Tommy stirred when he heard people yelling and a horse whinny. He jumped up and ran toward the sound.

He arrived on the path as Reed wrestled control of his horse and Ross hurled a final threat. Tommy froze as the stranger turned his horse toward him to get away. Reed stared straight at him and kicked his horse to go forward, as if to run over the boy. Tommy dove for the embankment and rolled down the hill.

When he got to his feet the horse and rider were gone. Ross was hurrying back toward Kildonan. "Wait!" he called to Ross, who kept going.

Tommy turned back to the river. He kicked a dirt clod and tried out a few new curse words. The strange encounter was a bad way to start an adventure. He hurried to wake Nathaniel and get far away from the place.

Late Afternoon, Kildonan

THE FOLKS PLANNING the delegation to Dunrobin and the petition wording were gathered along MacLennan's wall. Bella was surprised to see James Ross emerge from the river path. He was even more bedraggled than when he left. "Ross is back," she said and motioned with a slight nod. Everyone turned to look down the hill.

Hugh was passing out mugs of ale and samples of Mary's morning baking. "Why, I thought he went with MacLeod."

"No." Bella said. "He missed their take off, so tried to catch up with Tommy."

"Unlikely anyone could catch Tommy. He was running down the path," Walter said. They all chuckled, picturing Ross, a man at least sixty years old, trying to catch a lad as quick as Tommy.

Instead of stopping for a greeting, Ross kept going along the upward lane. Bella broke away from the group and caught up with him. His face was flushed, his brow wrinkled and his barrel chest was heaving. "James, you need a sit down. Will you rest here? I will bring you some tea and a bite of food?"

"All right. I'm done in." He collapsed in a rumbled heap at the edge of the pasture.

"Any sign of Tommy?" She tried to keep anxiety from her voice.

"No, no. Did not see them, so came back."

Bella went back to the group to fill a cup for Ross and grab a few biscuits. Mary raised her eyebrows in a question to Bella, who smiled and shook her head "no" ever so gently.

She returned to Ross. "I was a bit worried about you rushing off like that, with you having chest pains so recently."

"Should not have gone, but feel so helpless waiting around like an old woman. Would like to get that Factor alone and teach him a lesson."

"Well, drink your ale. I will brew up a remedy for you when our meeting is done."

"Ah, thank you, Bella. Might have a lie down right here."

Bella returned to the group on the wall as Hugh was explaining the plan. In the next few days, someone who could write proper English would draw up a petition stating the grievances mentioned in the council, the most important being the ancestral inheritance in the Strath of Kildonan. Virtually every rock, tree, dwelling, and meadow could be traced to an event in collective family history. Maybe the Earl did not understand their need.

The twelfth Earl of Sutherland had granted James MacDonan sanctuary in the valley following his father's murder in 1536. His descendants, family by marriage, and those who swore allegiance to the MacDonan chief populated the twenty-mile strath.

Every valley in the Highlands had an original clan. The MacKays held the land to the north, the Ross Clan to the south, and MacLeods to the west. Over the centuries, intermarriage complicated the clan hierarchy, and after the rout of the Jacobite Clans in 1745, the valleys were a mixture of people without a recognized chief.

It was agreed by the group on MacLennan's wall that the petition would recognize Clan MacDonan as the official landholders. Alec was designated the tacksman who sublet the land to others. Alec's grandfather had in fact collected rent from all the sub-tenants and paid the Earl rent for the whole strath. That allowed those who had a crop loss or family illness to be absorbed by the whole group. Since the present Earl had been sending his factor to collect the rent once a year from each household, they had been divided, and individual families might be legally evicted for not paying their rent.

"Now," Hugh was saying, "'tis just a matter of deciding how soon to leave. We'll be waiting for the Rogart scouts to return and the lads to Dunrobin and back. That's about four or five days from now."

"I am willing to do the writing," Bella said. "I want to deliver the petition and try to talk to the Countess." She reached for Catherine's hand. "There is another month before Margaret's time. Is that all right with you?" Catherine had lost several babies before Margaret was born, so was becoming increasingly nervous about her daughter and the birth of her grandchild.

"I can see you should go, Bella. Rose and I will manage if it comes to that. First bairns are late, so there should be plenty of time. I know plenty about birthing."

It took most of the afternoon to work out the details and other people arrived with names of delegates, so in the end a dozen men and women and an assortment of children planned to deliver the petition. They split up as darkness fell, agreeing to meet again in a few days.

Bella and her smaller family gathered around the evening fire, ready for an early bed. "I wonder where they are sleeping tonight." Rose said and twirled her braid.

"I was just thinking the same thing." Bella added and Alec nodded.

"I was thinking I wish I had gone with them.'" Robbie poked a few more flames from the peat. He knew the coast route well and wasn't sure Nathaniel would come back with Tommy.

"Will you go with the delegation, Son?" Alec put his hand on Robbie's shoulder.

"I would like to, unless you think I should stay."

"I can manage the chores well enough," Rose said. "I'm more worried about Margaret. Ma, I wish you were staying. Do you think the Countess would listen to you, if she were there?"

"Aye, I saved her life and rescued her son, she should hear what I have to say."

The River Path

TOMMY WENT BACK to the riverside where he left Nathaniel, who was just beginning to stir. Tommy stepped down to the water's edge, lay on his belly, and dunked his head in the cold, clear water. He drank his fill and went back to Nathaniel, who had gone back to sleep. When Tommy stood above him and shook the water from his hair, Nathaniel sat up wide-awake. "Damn it. What are you doing?"

"Just waking you up, let's go."

"I guess I fell asleep." Nathaniel rubbed his eyes and got up.

"Aye, we both did and lost a lot of daylight. Let's go."

"Let me get a drink first." He thought about splashing Tommy in return, but remembered the water fight the day before and how chilly the air could turn.

"I will fetch your horse and pack up," Tommy said over his shoulder as he headed for the tree where Scout was tied.

On their way again, Tommy ran along the path, while Nathaniel took a turn riding. They changed places when the runner was winded and then sometimes both walked to give the animal a rest. Tommy kept the incident with Ross and the man on the horse to himself. The whole thing seemed so strange that he hoped to forget it.

They made good progress and near the end of the daylight reached a place where the river widened and a few new houses appeared along the opposite bank. These dwellings were totally different than the cottages at Kildonan. Instead of a thatched roof hanging almost to the ground, these had high walls with thatch that ended abruptly at the roof line, as if it had been trimmed with a sharp knife. There were glass windows in every house; some had four or even five windows. The whole of Kildonan had only five windows.

As they walked along, the riverbank spread out below them. Hundreds of sheep were eating new grass within a walled field. A small stream crossed the path just as the last light faded.

"Let's stop here," Nathaniel said. "It's too dark to see our feet in front of us."

"I want to look at the sea." He peered through the gathering darkness.

"We can get up at first light. Hey, we are almost there. I remember this place." So they spread their blankets in a flat spot, ate the leftover tatties Bella had packed, and drank their fill of the cold, fresh water.

Evening, The Coast

WHEN CHARLES REED fled on his horse he was more annoyed than frightened. But by the time he got to Helmsdale, he had worked himself into a state of righteous indignation. "That despicable savage tried to rob and assault me," he muttered. He had even given the man food, and the lout was probably wondering what valuables he had in his bag. And that dark-haired boy, sneaking up behind him like that.

He rode hard from Helmsdale to the Brora Inn, just north of Dunrobin. He arrived after dark, rented a room, and went to the public house to order stew and a pitcher of ale.

The bartender brought his drink and food. "Where have you come from, sir? You look a bit road weary."

"Up the Kildonan Valley. Do you know it?"

"Never been there myself," the man replied. "Wild country up the glens, they say."

The bartender started to walk away when Reed said, "I was assaulted by some of the wild inhabitants."

"What's that you say?" He came back and stood by the table.

"A tough looking native drew a knife and grabbed my horse to rob me. Just as I was getting away his accomplice jumped me from behind."

"Have you been hurt?"

"Hurt?" Reed pondered the question. "I fought them off well enough and made my escape." He waved the man away to drink his ale and think it over.

Sellar never said there would be trouble. Quite irresponsible of him to allow a lone man to ride into hostile territory. If they thought he would be scared off, they were wrong. What little he had seen of the valley looked good for sheep pasture, and he would be back when the two-footed animals were gone.

Chapter Twelve

By Sea and Land. Clan MacDonald

Monday, 22 March, Morning, The North Sea

TOMMY TOSSED AND turned and only dozed off after watching stars until the wee hours. Nathaniel woke up when the sky began to lighten. He nudged Tommy, who turned over and groaned. "Is it really morning?"

"Race you to the sea."

"All right, hold on." Tommy sat up, jumped to his feet, and ran his hand through his hair. While he splashed water on his face from the stream, Nathaniel rolled up their blankets and tied all the gear on Scout's back.

Tommy took off on foot with Nathaniel right behind, leading the horse. The path grew wider and soon was paved with flat stones. It was broad enough for five or six people to walk side by side, or maybe even two pony carts. The smell of the sea was strong and Tommy began to run. Nathaniel and Scout followed close behind. The river widened below them, the ferry tie-up appeared to the side, and a gleam of sun off the water ahead caught Tommy's eye.

"It's the sea!" He began making long leaps toward the blue water, spread out before him just minutes away. The immense body of colorful moving water made the Kildonan River seem insignificant, and his own torment a drop in the water bucket. He stopped, stunned, and Nathaniel caught up with him.

"It is so big," Tommy whispered. "I cannot see land out there."

"'Tis a long way to Norway," Nathaniel said with a big smile on his face.

"Norway?" He scanned the horizon. Close by was the new village of Helmsdale, taking shape right before his eyes. Men were laying flat stones on streets that were roped off in straight lines. But there was no solid ground visible across the sea.

Nathaniel raised his arm across the water to the far northeast. "You can't see it, but trust me, it's where the Viking raiders came from. I just studied them in university."

"The MacDonans have Viking blood." He shook his head in confusion when he remembered that he wasn't a MacDonan after all. He stared at Nathaniel. Did he already know? Should he tell him?

Nathaniel gave a Viking roar and gave Tommy a playful shove. They both laughed and headed for the shore.

As they started down to the rocky beach, several boats left the harbor. One was quite large and rigged out with huge sails. "Where can it be going?" Tommy stopped to watch.

"Most likely to Edinburgh, full of fish and wool. The smaller one is heading back out for herring, probably been out all night and came in to unload their catch at the fish house." Tommy looked where Nathaniel was pointing alongside the harbor. Dozens of men and women were standing at tables chopping fish and throwing them in barrels.

"How do you know all that?"

"I slept here on my way north, at MacDonald's Inn right along the harbor."

"MacDonald? I wonder if that's Ian's uncle."

"The Ian who came back with your father?" Nathaniel remembered the other lowlander from the council.

"That's him. He arrived in Kildonan a few years back saying his uncle was at Helmsdale, and he was taking a long walk to see the source of the river. He met Margaret straight away and now they are married."

"Mrs. MacDonald said they have kin at Kildonan, it must be him."

The river widened more as they approached the harbor itself. Waves borne by the tides were coming up the river as the boats rode over them on the way out to sea. "The river looks rough here. How will we cross? I am used to boulder hopping or just wading."

"They are building a fancy bridge of stone, but we will take the ferry. It goes back and forth all day carrying people and animals."

"I remember Da saying he took a ferry. It costs money, I suppose." Tommy felt his pocket for the small purse. It was still there, he was relieved to discover.

"The ferry master will take trade, but I have enough coins to get us across. Let's go straight on to the sea, and catch the ferry on the next trip," Nathaniel said.

"Straight to the sea," Tommy repeated, running again until he reached the edge. He dropped his knapsack, stumbled over the round wet stones, and was up to his knees before he stopped, bent down, and reached for the bottom. He pulled up sand and rocks, dropped them, splashed his hands around and then splashed his face with the cold, salty water.

He spit out a mouthful. "What! It has a salt in it!"

Nathaniel was laughing next to him. "You did not know the sea and oceans are saltwater?"

Tommy turned red. "Well, sure I knew. I just forgot." He kicked the next wave as it came in. "Salt or not, I love the feel of the cold water on my feet. And this is the strange part," he looked sideways at Nathaniel, "I have been restless at home lately, not knowing my longing was for the sea."

"I am glad it pleases you so. The waves coming in here are just like the waves along the shore near Edinburgh, and even in England."

"It is so calm and peaceful."

"It looks peaceful now, but I have seen boats are tossed around in a storm, and sometimes people are drowned."

Tommy looked behind them and pointed to the edge of town. "I would like to see a small storm, where no one is hurt, from the hillside, yonder."

Nathaniel turned to look. "There is Mrs. MacDonald's place." He pointed to the middle two-story building along a row of houses joined together facing the sea. "Shall we ask if we can buy some porridge and tea? We have a long walk to Dunrobin ahead of us."

"Would you go ask, while I stand here 'til my feet turn blue?"

"Yes. I will be back soon if she has too many to feed."

"I have some coins to pay for food if she can help us."

When Nathaniel was gone Tommy turned in every direction taking in this new scene and memorizing every outcropping, dwelling, and stone wall of the harbor. Satisfied finally that he knew the place, and hearing Nathaniel call, he left the water to feed his growing hunger.

After eating as much as possible, they crossed on the ferry, and walked up the hill with a large contingent of disheveled folks with plaid blankets and knapsacks. They fit right in.

They continued south on a narrow trail as close to the sea as possible to satisfy Tommy. Most of the other people took the wider inland path so they had the view to themselves. They stopped in the afternoon to sit on a bluff with the sea below them.

Tommy had been trying to decide how to tell Nathaniel about his birth. Best blurt it out, he concluded.

A gust of wind blew his hair. He reached up to push it back and realized that his hair was black, his mother's reddish and his father's brown. Robbie looked like Alec, Rose had Bella's looks, and even Nathaniel resembled MacLeod. He didn't look like anyone.

"Nathaniel." Tommy paused.

"Ready to go?"

"No." Tommy looked out to sea. "What if your mother told you she was not really your mother?"

"I wouldn't believe her. She's my mother." Nathaniel looked at Tommy. "What an odd question."

"My mother told me that yesterday."

"You're joking again."

Tommy looked at the ground and ripped the grass in front of him.

"It's true. She told me after we came back from the falls. My Da was with her and did not deny it."

"Did she say who your mother is?"

Tommy turned his head south. "The woman who owns the castle we are going to, the Countess of Sutherland."

Morning at Dunrobin Castle

THE COURTYARD AT Dunrobin was bustling with activity. Sellar's agents were lined up at a long table with maps and deeds for prospective leasers, while at another table men kept track of writs of eviction delivered and glens cleared.

Sellar appeared occasionally to check over the progress and debate his next move. He was taller than most of the locals. His beak-shaped nose, deep-set eyes, and long pointed fingers made everyone work harder when he swooped down on them. His profession as a law advocate in Edinburgh gave him experience in the art of intimidation. Although he detested sheep, he considered the illiterate peasants, who did not even speak English, on the rung just below the animals. Better to be rid of all the worthless human baggage and bring some law and order, and profit, to the Sutherland Earl's estate. And if he could make a tidy profit above his salary from the Earl, well, that would be a satisfactory achievement.

Sellar was adding up imagined revenues when he noticed a somewhat familiar figure striding toward him. It was the English chap he'd sent up to Kildonan, although now his face was red and his fists were clenched. Sellar waved his assistant over to back him up if need be.

"Well, Mr. Reed, is it? Did you find the pasture in Kildonan to your liking?"

Reed had been rehearsing his speech. "I am here to file a complaint against an unruly mob of savages from Kildonan, who attacked me with no warning and put me in great fear for my life."

A small crowd gathered when Reed approached, and now a hubbub of alarm spread from mouth to mouth. Sellar wasted no time with such convenient news. "We will see to the matter at once. Could you identify the men who attacked you?"

This gave Reed pause, as really he had only seen the two men, but had convinced himself there were dozens lurking in the bushes below. "I could positively identify at least two of them."

"The ringleaders, do you think?"

"Certainly," Reed said, "the ringleaders. MacDonan territory. Dangerous looking fellows, may be headed this way." The last comment was an afterthought, as he had no idea if they were going anywhere at all. The lout said it was MacDonan land he was after, must be them.

The attention he was getting fed his imagination, and the usually contained man became carried away. "They said something about the Castle, but I didn't catch it all, as I had just made my escape."

Sellar turned to his assistant. "Take a written statement from Reed and have him sign it."

Within a few hours rumors spread through Dunrobin and to the nearby town of Golspie that Clan MacDonan was marching down the coast, threatening to burn Dunrobin Castle to the ground and hang Sellar.

Sellar could hardly wait to report this disturbance to his superior, William Young, who was the Earl's Land Commissioner. Young had been riding north from business in Inverness during Reed's announcement, so a rider was sent to meet him. When he arrived at Dunrobin a few hours later, a full-scale panic was underway. He hurried to his quarters and sent for Sellar.

Young's usual shrewd self-control was shaken. He was pacing back and forth, running his hand through his unruly blond hair. "Sellar, what the devil has happened? The place is in a bloody uproar. The cannon is being loaded."

Sellar chose his words carefully. "It is said that a mob of MacDonans are marching on the castle, and that you and I are the object of their rage."

"Have they been served with writs of eviction?"

"No." Sellar said. "They are scheduled for next week."

"What has them up in arms then? I assume they don't have any real weapons, but a haying fork can be deadly."

"An Englishman looking at pasture went out to the Strath. A mob attacked him and he fled for his life."

Young held up his hand for Sellar to stop. "Quite unlikely, don't you agree? No one has ever been attacked before, and they do not know they will be evicted."

Sellar hesitated, grasping for an explanation. "Reed's arrival may have tipped them off, and the Ross tenants are scattered all over the north by now."

Young turned on Sellar, almost shouting, "My orders were to herd the Ross evictees south to the herring sheds at Dornoch."

"They offered more resistance than expected," Sellar said. "Things got a bit out of hand and a few of them fled over the hills to the north."

Young tried to control his anger by lowering his voice. "Isn't Kildonan just to the north of Rogart?" He got a map out, and spread it on his desk by the window.

Sellar pointed out Rogart and to the north, Kildonan.

"Well, I suppose they could have heard about the trouble there and took it into their heads it could happen to them," Young said.

"Yes, the MacDonans are a hard and unruly people. There might be serious trouble when their eviction notice is served."

"What other names are on their rent rolls?" Young had the troublemakers on a list somewhere.

"I would have to get my ledger to be sure, but I believe an assortment of all the northern families—MacKay, Gunn, Sinclair, MacLeod—that lot."

"Hmm. Sounds dangerous. If a mob is truly headed this way, perhaps we can overwhelm them right off, arrest the leaders and frighten the rest into obedience. Any sign of their approach?" Young peered out the window. His quarters were on the second floor of the west side of the castle. That gave him a view of the courtyard and road to Golspie.

Sellar smiled inwardly now that Young was going along with his plan. "The Sheriff has sent deputies north to look for a mob, but they have not returned yet." Sellar joined him at the window.

"Sentries are posted, I assume." Young was beginning to worry. The castle must be protected at all cost. The Earl and Countess and their children lived in the east side. It was filled with ornate furniture, silver goblets, and the family jewels.

"Of course. We've rounded up a militia."

"Good. Here's what I am thinking, Sellar. This might be just the opportunity we need to hasten the evictions in Kildonan. If there is no sign of a mob in the next two days, send several armed deputies up the Strath on horseback with a message for the MacDonans and the rest of them. Let them come peacefully to Dunrobin, and we will hear their grievances and explain their options to them. For a reason I cannot fathom, the Countess has set aside the best land near the Helmsdale port for an Alec MacDonan. Perhaps that good news will break whatever resistance they might try."

"Brilliant, Commissioner." Sellar could not have convinced him of such a plan himself, so having him order it was perfect.

"That would save them planting a crop at the old place. They can just start off in their new location."

Sellar nodded agreement. "Very thoughtful of you, sir."

"Have the Sheriff send for a detachment from Fort George to back us up." Young was at his desk writing an order.

"It will take a week for them to get here," Sellar said.

"I will say we are besieged. That will speed things up."

"Right." Sellar almost rubbed his hands together with the excitement of it all, but checked himself in time. No use letting Young think he had any personal stake in all this. He might just lease Kildonan himself. Tell Reed to go home.

"Now leave me be, and I will write a writ of eviction, and a warrant for the arrest of the mob that attacked the farmer. What is his name?"

"Reed from Northumbria."

"Can this Reed identify anyone?"

Sellar recalled the report. Reed said two men, but that hardly sounded like a mob. "He said four men for sure, maybe more."

"Get the Sheriff for me and come back in the morning, unless there is more news tonight. Send my servant in on your way out, and by the way, good work, Patrick. This is all going faster than we hoped. The Earl will be pleased."

"Thank you, William."

The Sheriff balked a bit about saying they were besieged when really, nothing at all had happened. Young pointed out that by the time the infantry arrived they might well be under attack, and then it would be too late to send for help.

The deputies returned after dark reporting no sign of a mob, although with a bit of prompting from Sellar, the Deputy agreed there were so many folks out on the road that a mob could have heard the sound of their horses and hid in a ditch.

Messengers left that night from Dunrobin; one rode to Fort George asking for the army detachment. Another two left for Edinburgh to catch the next boat to London to deliver a message to the Countess. Her favored tenants in Kildonan were in revolt.

Chapter Thirteen

Quite ready. Clan Murray

Thursday, 25 March, Afternoon, Kildonan

LIFE RETURNED TO a slow pace in Kildonan for a few days. The dry weather held, the river rocks could be seen again and Bella had her spade out, turning the soil in the garden. The deep earthy aroma filled her nostrils. She scooped up the damp, loose soil, and let it sift through her fingers. Time to plant the tatties, as her mother would say when the ground began to dry.

Several people were shouting. Maybe it was Tommy coming home. He had been gone four days, enough time to get to Dunrobin and back. Maybe he'll bring good news and they could all stay home.

Bella wiped her hands on the grass nearby and went around the corner for a look.

It was Les back from the scouting. Lorna Murray, MacLeod's wife, was with him. They were moving down the river path with a very pregnant lass between them. The girl was tall and very thin, except for her huge belly. She had lost her cap and her long red curls hung in her face.

Lorna walked hip-to-hip with her, left arm around her back and her right hand supporting the girl's elbow. Lorna was a strong woman and could keep her steady.

Les was carrying all their supplies. He waved to Bella to hurry.

The girl stopped abruptly, brought her arms forward and dropped to the path on her hands and knees. Bella could see her rocking back and forth as she ran to meet them.

Lorna called to Bella, "She has been like this since we crossed the river."

Les was about to bolt for the hills, so Bella told him what to do next. "Les, go to my cottage, stoke the fire, and pull the kettle down." He took off and ran to a safer task.

"She is sixteen, her name is Irene Murray," Lorna whispered to Bella.

Bella knelt by Irene, who was panting and shaking. Her blue eyes were wide with fear.

"We will care for you as a daughter," Bella assured her.

When the pain seemed to diminish, Bella and Lorna helped her stand. "Just a few more steps and you can lie down. You are a strong lass and will have your wee one soon." Bella said. Irene began crying with relief at Bella's door a few minutes later.

"Keep going to the next room, there is a bed on the floor." They stepped through the barn doorway and made it to Robbie's mat as another strong surge began. Irene collapsed on the bed and turned on her side facing the wall.

Lorna helped Irene get comfortable as Bella knelt next to her. "Try to be calm now and rest for a few minutes. You made it here and will be safe." Lorna hummed a soothing tune while she gently pulled the sweaty hair away from Irene's face and stroked it to the back of her neck. Lorna's own black hair had come loose from her braid. There were no men around so she took off her cap, shook out her hair and stuffed the cap in her pocket. Despite the difference in their age and hair color, they both had the Murray Clan fine eyebrows and full lips, and Bella guessed, determination.

Bella gathered clean rags, a bowl of hot water, and a bar of soap. She and Lorna stepped outside to wash their hands and decide what to do. "We'll need more water to wash Irene," Bella said. "Ah, here's Mary. Would you send Rose to get water?"

"She has been to the spring already and has more water heating. We are both ready to help if you need us." Mary and Rose had heard the story from Les when he escaped for home.

In a few minutes Rose brought a smaller kettle of water and a clean bowl. She was surprised at how young Irene looked, close to her own age. She handed the bowl to her mother, who dropped a new cloth into the water as Rose poured warm water on top.

"Irene, I want to wash between your legs and then use my fingers to feel the bairn inside you," Bella said. Irene opened her eyes, another pain had lasted a long time, but she felt calmer now that she could lie down. When she looked up, the four women whose kind faces surrounded her could have been women from Rogart.

Mary shut the doors, built up the fire, and lit several cruisie lamps, as the room was quite dark. She put a lamp on the floor next to Bella.

"Irene, are you feeling a pain right now?" Bella asked.

"Not a grand one, but it never goes away."

"Mary and Lorna are going to help you turn around and sit up. My daughter Rose will sit behind you so you can lean against her." Rose smiled and Irene managed a slight grimace in return.

Rose quickly took her place, back against the wall, while Lorna and Mary each held one of Irene's arms, and with all of them working together, she managed to move quickly. As soon as she leaned against Rose, another pain started. "I'll wait 'til this one is over, so lean back and let your breath flow out," Bella said.

Irene closed her eyes and noticed that this pain was different. She felt something moving inside her, like a huge ball was pushing her inside out and it hurt in a sharper way, like a fire.

"It's burning." She tried not to cry.

"Tell me as soon as it lets up." Irene closed her eyes and began to moan and then grunt. "Let me wash you before you bear down." Bella picked the cloth out of the hot water and half wrung it out. "Here we go, just let your knees drop and your legs open all the way." Bella started at the top of her hairline and washed down and around her thighs, then folded the cloth in two and motioned to Mary to pour more water. This time Bella gently opened the vaginal lips and pressed the warm cloth against Irene's flesh. She folded the cloth again and pressed it against the skin below.

Irene stopped moaning and rested her head against Rose's shoulder.

"Take a deep breath while I slide my fingers just inside," Bella said. "If a pain starts I will try to be quick, but I would like to feel the bairn's head."

The fire was burning hot and the lamp was bright, and Lorna could see the sudden fear in the girl's eyes. "Irene, dear, look into my eyes. We're here with you. Do not be afraid." Irene turned toward Lorna, who had helped her all that way and had not left her side. She was ready to scream, but Lorna's kind face and steady love gave her courage.

Bella crawled as close to Irene's left knee as she could, leaned over and slid her two fingers inside. She quickly pushed past the bones and then the inner flesh until her fingers felt the internal opening. She spread her fingers out and felt a thin, tight band around something soft, like bread dough.

Thinking she must have missed the hard bones of the head somehow, she pulled her fingers back a little to try again. Mary began singing a lullaby and Irene relaxed more. Bella pushed her fingers deep again. She was astonished to feel the tight band loosen and a bottom with two wee balls move quickly between her fingers.

She pulled her fingers out as Irene said, "It has to come out, it's coming out!" She bore down hard. In just one long push, Bella could see the bottom cheeks push Irene's outer skin open. Bella was searching her memory for a time she had been with her mother and a bottom first birth happened like this.

It was at least twenty years ago, before Robbie was born. She had gone to a cottage high above the loch at Brora with her Ma. The poor woman had been laboring for two days with no result. They arrived just at nightfall. It was horribly smoky inside, and smelled strongly of manure, as the milk cow lived in the house with them. Something about remembering the smell triggered the whole scene and she knew what to do.

"Mary, come right next to me." Lorna picked up the lullaby melody as Mary knelt next to Bella. "The baby is upside down," she whispered. "I'll need your hands next to mine, just do what I say." Mary nodded, her heart racing.

Irene had pushed twice and now the baby was on its way out. Irene pushed again and the legs showed enough that Bella hooked a finger under one knee and then the other and gently pulled them down and out. "Wrap him with a cloth," she said quietly to Mary. Bella reached inside Irene again and gave a gentle pull on the cord. It was loose and a loop slid partway out with the body. She reached for his neck. The cord was not wrapped around it, but she felt a thin ridge of inner skin still holding the head inside.

Irene was ready to push again and Bella doubted she could stop her. She took a chance and as Irene pushed down, Bella's fingers pushed the ridge back over the small chin, the nose, and by the time the forehead reached the ridge it was gone. Bella kept her fingers inside, loosening, guiding, and smoothing the passage for the head to be born. "Lift him upwards," she said to Mary. As Mary lifted the wrapped body slowly towards her chest, Bella kept her fingers inside, making an air space next to the tiny mouth and nose.

"Lorna, press your hand on her belly," Bella said. As Lorna put a slight external pressure on the head, Mary lifted the body higher, Irene pushed, and Bella eased the head out into the world. He took one breath and let out a loud cry.

"OH MY GOD, it's over, my bairn, my bairn!" Irene was crying. "A boy, is it really a boy, oh thank you, thank you." She reached for her son as Bella laid him on her chest. "He's crying. What should I do?"

"Talk to him, stroke him, he knows you," Rose said. They were all crying now with the relief and joy of it. Bella wiped his face and neck clean of blood and fluid.

"Was he really upside down?" Irene asked when she could speak again.

"Aye," Mary said, "you are a lucky lass to get to Bella. Most women don't know what to do and the bairn and sometimes the mother dies."

"You gave me quite a surprise, we are lucky my mother taught me what to do."

"Bless your mother's soul," Mary said.

Lorna helped Irene get the bairn to her breast to start sucking, while Mary and Bella prepared to receive the placenta. The cord was plenty long so the bairn could stay attached for now.

"As soon as he is sucking well, the afterbirth will come out, it will hurt some, but not as much as that boy," Bella said. "We would be honored to bury the afterbirth in our garden, since you don't have a place..." Bella almost said, "to live," but stopped herself and said, "to put it." Irene swallowed hard, the reality of the eviction had been pushed aside by the pain, but she could not bear to think of that now, so just nodded to Bella.

"Ah, he is sucking really hard," Irene smiled and then grimaced with another pain. "Ouch, it does hurt again." Bella began twisting the cord gently, putting a bit of pressure on it and as the urge crested, Irene pushed, Mary held the night pot under her and the afterbirth slid out. Bella nodded to Mary, who immediately pressed firmly on Irene's belly. The placenta had come out whole, and the bleeding had slowed to a trickle.

Bella got up to stretch and get her birthing bag from the front room. She had woven some very fine yarn that she used to tie off cords. She had a small ball of it and brought it back to the room with a clean knife. She tied off the cord a hand length away from his navel and again a bit toward the placenta.

"My turn to hold him." Bella laid him on his side between Irene's legs, so she could watch, then slipped a small flat piece of wood underneath the cord. "Do you have his name, Irene? We will all say it as I cut him free." Irene nodded and whispered the name that had been chosen for a boy.

"Welcome, Duncan Murray Ross," they said as Bella quickly sliced through the cord.

"A powerful name for a wee lad," Lorna said. Duncan opened his eyes, alert to his new surroundings, as Bella rolled him to his back. They all gazed at the new being among them, while Bella made sure his body was perfect.

She put her head to his chest to hear his heart. "He has a strong heartbeat."

"He will be a strong man, like his Da," Irene said. The women all fell silent then, but Irene finally said, "I could do with a cup of tea," and the spell of words unsaid was broken.

"Rose will help you wash, just press hard on your belly before you move to stop the bleeding. We'll find a clean dress for you and moss pads to catch the blood."

"You must be starving dear, I will fix you some tea straight away and we'll put some meal in the pot," Mary said, as she and Rose helped Irene stand up.

While Rose and Irene were at the privy, Bella wrapped a seaweed poultice to protect the end of the cord at his navel. His light brown hair curled around his ears and he had those precious newborn rosebud lips. Lorna picked out a large cloth from the stack and sat next to Bella. She spread the cloth on her lap and Bella laid Duncan in the center. Lorna folded a smaller cloth between his legs and then wrapped him securely in a neat bundle. She held him next to her heart as Bella cleaned up the soiled rags and put them in the waste bucket near the door. Bella would bury everything beneath the rowan tree where her children's placentas had been buried.

Lorna and Bella sat close to each other looking at Duncan, who had gone to sleep. "Tell me about our Irene," Bella said.

"On our second day walking toward Rogart, we began to meet people coming this way. They had left to find kin as soon as the Factor's men appeared. They were mostly cottars and since they had no land to defend, they were traveling quickly. We met them at the top of a ridge and we could see the smoke of the burning cottages from there. It looked like the whole forest was on fire."

"How awful." Bella put her arm around Lorna.

"Aye, it was terrible. The young men were going to circle around north to reach the coast above the Brora water, then try to sign up for the colonies."

"The colonies!"

"They heard there is a ship leaving for Canada, taking young people who want to work hard."

"And Irene? Was she with them?" Bella started cleaning up the room. She pulled away the soiled blanket, turned the mat over and found a clean plaid in a wooden bin.

"No. We found her at the Broch along the Black Water. She and her mother had made it that far, but lost track of their family in the panic. Everyone scattered when the burning started and the men and lads were up in the high pasture rebuilding walls when it happened."

"Where is her mother now?"

"She went to look for her husband and two small lads. Irene's cottage had just been built for her and her husband when the Factor's men came. They were about to torch the thatch, so Irene climbed on the roof thinking they would not set a fire to a pregnant woman."

"Oh, no." Bella stopped making up the bed and held the plaid to her chest.

"Aye. They chased her about to drag her down, and she fell through the thatch. They gave her mother 'til they counted to five to get her out, and then they torched the thatch and roof beams."

"What cruelty." Bella shook her head in disgust.

"She said the men were quite drunk and were laughing in a disgusting way at everyone's panic."

"Did the fall bring on the pains?"

"It started with the fall, but she made it to the Broch before it was strong, and then when she rested it stopped. Les and I agreed to stay with Irene overnight while her mother went back to look for the family. We promised to start for Kildonan in the morning and her family will come here."

"Good decision, but it must have been awful hard for her mother to leave her with strangers." The clean bed was ready. Bella motioned Lorna to slide over and lean against the wall.

"Her mother hated to leave her, that's for sure, but I am a Murray after all, which made it easier. Irene tossed and cried out all night. I lay right next to her, although neither of us slept much. When she stood up in the morning to do her business, the pains arrived one after the other and we started off for your door."

"She walked all day," Bella said, "no wonder the birth happened so fast. Here, let me hold him again." She took the wrapped bundle and Lorna stood up to stretch.

"Les and I half carried her some of the time, but if she rested the pains slowed down. Well, we had to get here before dark so we kept going."

"You got here quickly considering your situation."

"Aye. Les was determined that he would not be anywhere near a birthing. He would have slung her over his shoulder and run for home, but for her huge belly." They both laughed at this image. Duncan woke up and began nuzzling Bella's chest. "She had best get back here quick," Lorna said with a chuckle.

Friday, 26 March

IRENE MADE A quick recovery and by morning was very happy with her new son. She felt confident her family would arrive for her soon. Rose convinced Les to meet Duncan, and Irene wanted to thank him in person. Rose dragged him into the barn by the arm. "It will not hurt you to say hello," Rose said.

He stood awkwardly next to the bed and said, "Hello."

"Hello, Les. Thank you for bringing me here. Without you telling me to keep going, I would have laid down and still been there, maybe with both of us dead." She touched Duncan, who was sleeping safely in her arms.

"Well, we were lucky to get here in time," Les said.

"Very lucky," Rose agreed. "Can Les hold wee Duncan for a minute?" Irene was ready to hand her bundle over, but Les declined.

"I would be scared I would drop him. I had better be going anyway."

"Where are you going now?" Rose asked.

"Back to the Broch, which is my post unless I meet MacLeod on his way back. He will wonder where I went as it is."

"My husband and family will be looking for me," Irene said. "Would you know my mother again?"

"Aye. I will bring her here myself, but if I see the rest first, I won't know them."

"My father and the small lads have hair like mine," she pulled long strands of golden-red hair to the side so he would notice. "My husband is Matthew Ross. His hair is long and dark, but his eyes are very blue."

Rose wondered if Les would really study people's looks.

"Don't worry. I will ask everyone I see if they are looking for you."

"Thank you, Les."

With a blush and a quick wave Les was out the door with Rose just behind him. "Must you leave so soon?" Rose was impressed with all Les had done. Maybe she would be satisfied marrying Les. Although

Nathaniel was new and interesting, he was unknown, while Les was
someone she had known all her life.

"Is not Duncan a lovely bairn?" Rose tried another question when he
did not answer.

Les was distracted already, planning what else to take to the Broch.
"I would not know, as I barely looked at him."

"Take my word for it then. And Irene, do you find her lovely?"

"I hardly looked at her either. She is a brave enough lass though."
He was walking quickly down the lane to his cottage.

Rose ran behind him. "Aye, she is very brave. I do not think I could
keep walking through all that pain as she did."

"I gave her no choice. She was desperate to lay down, but I told her
over and over, 'when we reach Bella's door you can lay down, and not
before!' It worked, she kept going."

"Les, you have changed since you left just a few days ago."

Les stopped, and took her hand. "If you see what they have done, or
if they do it here, you will change, too. I am sorry, Rose, but I am filled
with hate right now and cannot see the beauty in a new bairn or in our
future." He dropped her hand.

"I hope they don't come here."

"They are clearing the Highlands of people and we are in their way. I
am thinking of leaving. I may just ship off to Canada." Les looked around,
as if Canada was just beyond the next ridge.

"What are you talking about?" Rose followed his gaze.

He turned back to her and they continued walking. "The English
Earl wants us gone, Rose. That is very clear to me after talking to the
people fleeing Rogart. Some are headed for a ship the Earl of Selkirk has
commissioned to sail from the north coast in June. There is free passage
for any man who signs up to work for a few years, and after that he
receives free land."

"I never thought you would leave your Ma and Da." Rose would
have added, or me, but her feelings became more confused by the minute.

"I do not want to leave anyone, but I will send for them when I have my land. I will build them a cottage and they will be content."

"I could not go so far away from my mother and father." Rose meant to think it, but found herself speaking.

"So you would not go to the colonies with me?" They both stopped to look at each other, realizing it was their final moment to say yes or no to each other.

"It is so far. I just couldn't."

"That is as I thought." Les gave her hand a squeeze and then let go. "I will be leaving for the Broch in a bit. Will you walk up the river with me, for all the good memories it will bring?"

"Aye. Call at the door when you are ready. Lorna will stay with Irene."

In a little while he hallooed at the door and Rose came out quickly. She handed him a bundle of food, and Irene had cut a scrap of her dress for Les to give her family as a token that she was well. He was stocked with supplies from his mother, as she had been cooking all morning to feed the MacDonan household. He could probably feed six homeless people.

Their walk up the river was bittersweet. Les mentioned times when they were small children following behind Robbie and the older lads.

"If you leave, we will be without a piper in the glen," Rose said.

"My Da still has his wind."

"You are the best at the dance tunes."

"Maybe, but then I never get to dance. Someone else will take my place. A piper will be the least of your worries."

Rose wanted to cry with the sadness of his words and mood. He had always been cheerful before and thought only of the good. When he took his leave at the cross over, they held hands and briefly kissed goodbye. It was the kind of kiss she would receive from her brothers.

Sunday, March 28, Mid-day, Kildonan

THE CHURCH BELL began ringing an hour before the Kildonan parishioners were expected to arrive. The sound caught Bella by surprise, as she had lost track of the days of the week. It happened occasionally that she would hear the bell and think, "Oh, of course, 'tis Sunday."

But this time the bell had a hollow ring to it. Reverend Sage must know about the trouble brewing, but he had not come by with a hopeful word or blessing. Still, prayers for their safety were more important than ever, and although she had been making her own pleas and promises to God, perhaps their collective voices would be better heard.

She tried to pry Rose away from Irene and wake Alec from a nap without any luck and headed down the lane to meet Mary and Hugh. Their families always walked up the river and around the bend where the old kirk stood.

Mary was waiting by the gate alone. "Where is Alec?"

"He says his head hurts. Is Hugh coming?"

"He claims a stomach pain, but I think his pain is higher." She put her hand over her heart.

"We are all aching there, but I feel a duty to go. I think I will ask the Reverend to speak to the Earl on our behalf."

"You do that. I will be behind you, shaking as usual. My courage leaves me if I try to speak to someone like the Reverend."

"If I am mad enough, I would speak to the King himself."

Mary laughed at the image. "I'm sure you would. And in that case, I would be miles behind you."

Bella took her hand. "You are braver than you think." As they walked hand in hand along the river other folks along the Strath joined them.

When the church service was well under way, it became clear to Bella that the most pious of her neighbors thought God had punished the people of Rogart for their sins, and the only hope for Kildonan was absolute repentance by those who drank whisky, had wanton sex, or skipped church. The Reverend Sage could hardly disagree with them, but Bella was pleased to hear him say he would speak to the Earl and Countess on their behalf.

They started for home feeling a bit more hopeful of saving Kildonan.

WHEN ROSE FELT it was safe to go outside, that church was surely over, she took the kettle to get water at the stream. A group of people on the river path were walking toward their cottage. It was Les and MacLeod and with them a family that must be Irene's. She ran back inside.

"Irene. They are here! I will hold Duncan while you run to meet them."

Irene disengaged Duncan from her breast and handed him to Rose. "Come with me," Irene said as she stood up, dropped her shawl on the rocker and ran out the door.

She hardly recognized her family. They seemed more like a group of ragged tinkers, dragging sacks that bumped on the path behind them. She put her hand to her heart to steady herself. It was painful to think she had been living in luxury while they were suffering. She glanced back at Rose.

"Keep going," Rose said, squeezing her hand, "they see you."

Irene's mother dropped her bundle and ran up the hill to her daughter. "Irene, Irene child." Irene had her arms open and embraced her mother until the rest of her family joined them.

A dark haired young man, with a broad grin on his face, put down the small lad he was carrying and said, "My turn!"

He lifted Irene and kissed her full on the mouth. He was so happy to see her that Rose felt envious. Then Irene's mother was at her side reaching for Duncan, and Rose ended her daydream of Nathaniel being that happy to see her again.

"You must be Rose, and this is my dear grandchild," Irene's mother said. Rose reluctantly handed over Duncan and glanced at Irene and her husband. They were still kissing.

She looked around in confusion and saw Les staring at her. She attempted a smile and wave, but could not seem to move from the spot.

Irene came back to earth and introduced Matthew to Rose. "This is the angel who has been tending me for days."

"It has been my pleasure," she managed to stammer.

"And here is our son Duncan." Irene took the bairn from her mother.

Matthew held the baby tenderly and pushed the blanket edge away from his head. A smile of pure wonder spread on Matthew's face. Rose had never seen a man look at a bairn quite like that before.

"Well wee Duncan," he said, "I hear you were in a hurry to come out and see your Da. I am sorry I was not here to greet you." Duncan opened his eyes and looked at his father. "He looks just like me," Matthew said in amazement.

Everyone laughed, which startled Duncan. He began to cry. Rose was there in a flash. "Here, I will carry him." She put the bairn against her chest, and he stopped crying. She led the way to the cottage.

By evening Alec and Bella had everyone fed and had borrowed clothes from folks nearby so the travelers could wash and put on clean clothes. They all congregated in the barn to officially welcome Duncan with a ritual Bella offered to new families.

Those present sat in a circle around the young family. Bella passed a large ball of green yarn to Alec, Rose, and Robbie. While they were each holding a section, Bella took the yarn to the center and sunwise circled the new family. As she did so the MacDonans pledged their support and love to the Ross family. She brought the yarn ball back to the outer circle as the MacLennans and MacLeod pledged the same until they were all tied together.

After a blessing, Bella walked around the circle, cut the yarn in small strands and tied a piece to each person's wrist. Although they were now separate individuals again, the yarn would be a reminder of their pledge.

MacLeod's plan was to take the whole family with him to the glen above Kildonan where they could find shelter. Other Ross families were on their way with the other scouts to Strathnaver in the far north. They could squeeze in with the folks there through the summer, or until they could decide where to go. So far, the upper valley had been spared the eviction rumors.

Bella, Mary, and Rose walked up the path with them the next morning and said their tearful good-byes to Lorna, Irene, and Duncan. When they were out of sight, Rose began to weep. Bella put her arm around her daughter.

"It is very easy to love a bairn, is it not?" Bella said. "When you see a bairn emerge from his mother's body, it is a miracle. There was no person visible for all the time before, and then your heart opens to love a fragile human being so quick, it takes your breath away. Duncan will always be a special lad to you, and that is cause for joy as well as the sorrow of parting."

The three women made their way home. A light rain began to fall and by the time they reached home, the warm dark cottages were a welcome sight. Mary hugged them both and turned off to her door. When they reached home, Bella stoked the fire as Rose collapsed on her bed.

"I feel like I have done the birthing, but with no one to hold to my breast."

"Ah, my dear, be thankful your heart has been opened."

Chapter Fourteen

Either peace or war. Clan Gunn

Monday, 29 March, Mid-day, Kildonan

FOUR MEN RODE out from Dunrobin with a message for the people at Kildonan from Commissioner Young. The men were armed and ordered to defend themselves if attacked, but were under strict instructions from Young not to provoke anyone or start a confrontation or mention the mob.

They had a notice with Young's signature inviting the MacDonans, and whoever else might join them, to meet with the Commissioner at Dunrobin to clear up any misunderstanding. They spent the night in Helmsdale and set out for Kildonan in the morning.

Bella and Rose were weeding the garden when the men showed up on the river path. "Tell your Da there are four men on horseback," Bella said. Rose hurried around the corner and went inside.

The leader of the group got off his horse and walked up toward the garden, leaving the others to dismount and let the horses graze by the stream.

By the time the man reached Bella, Alec and Rose had joined her. Robbie came out of the barn and Mary MacLennan stopped pegging the washing to join them.

Alec opened the gate for him with an offered handshake and a somewhat stilted "lovely day" greeting.

"Aye, lovely day," he said. "George MacBean, it is." When he put out his hand for a shake everyone relaxed a bit. In another minute Alec would have to invite him in for a cup of tea, but he was hoping MacBean was just passing through and would keep going.

"Ahem." MacBean cleared his throat. "Commissioner Young," he said in a questioning way and glanced at Alec. Alec nodded, so he continued. "Well, Young has sent me with this invitation, as he calls it, to come to Dunrobin and meet with him about whatever your grievances may be."

"What grievances does he mean?" Alec asked.

"He did not exactly say, but with the evictions and all at Rogart, he may think you are concerned about Kildonan."

"We have not received any writs of eviction, or is that what your paper is about?" Alec pointed to the scroll in MacBean's hand.

MacBean almost dropped the paper. "Lord, I hope not." He quickly tipped his cap to the women. "Sorry, Ma'am." He handed the scroll to Alec.

"They evicted Edward Ross and all his tenants, if what I heard is true," Alec said.

"I heard that also, but I have been in the far north 'til just a few days ago. I returned to Dunrobin and was sent straight here."

Alec opened the paper and read it aloud. "The MacDonans and other tenants and inhabitants of the Strath of Kildonan are invited to Dunrobin Castle for a meeting with Commissioner Young on Friday, 2 April."

"It is our chance to bring the petition to the Countess," Bella whispered to Alec. "Mr. MacBean, is the Countess Elizabeth at Dunrobin?"

"I don't know if she has come back from London. One of the other chaps may know," he inclined his head to the men waiting.

"Would you all like a cup of tea?" Bella asked. MacBean smiled in relief and waved the men to come up the hill. He and Robbie met them at the pasture gate. Rose went home with Mary as Alec and Bella returned to the cottage.

Bella mixed the herbs for tea. "He seemed nervous to meet us, and we were anxious of him. I have never felt that before."

"These are such strange times, to think Young himself would send for us. MacBean seems a decent enough chap. Maybe he will give us some news."

"I wonder if he's seen Tommy."

"It sounds like he was hardly at Dunrobin before being sent off here, and I hope Tommy is staying clear of the castle anyway. It would be better not to ask."

"I am sure you are right, but I am worried since they have not returned," Bella pulled the kettle closer to the fire.

"Maybe I can get MacBean alone for a bit, he may say more that way." Alec glanced out the door. "Here they are."

The four men shuffled in the door and sat on the low chairs and bench Bella placed around the fire. Alec poured water from the kettle into their largest teapot.

"We are grateful for the hospitality," MacBean said. "These chaps have never been this far up the river before. They wonder how the fishing is this time of year."

"Well," Alec said, "there is always a wily trout to be sure. Of course, the salmon all belong to the Earl. He has printed his crest on each one, to make sure we remember who can eat them." The men snickered and felt more at home with a bit of a joke at the Earl's expense. "Nice spot here on the river," MacBean said. "Been here all your life, have you, MacDonan?"

"Aye, and my father, his father, and his fathers before him for twelve generations."

"That is a long time."

"Aye, and I hope for twelve more generations."

They sipped their tea in silence. They all had an inkling that the Highlands were about to undergo a change, but how exactly that would happen, and what it would mean to each of them, was still a mystery.

Hugh arrived with biscuits Mary baked. He was passing the food around and saying hello to the men when Alec saw his chance. "Step outside for a minute, would you MacBean? I want to show you a project I am working on."

MacBean turned to his companions. "Take your time then, lads. I'll call when we are ready to go." They waved him on as Bella refilled their mugs.

The two men walked up to the grain dryer Alec had dug out of the bank last summer. "Do you think I've got the smoke hole at the right angle?"

"Looks like it will pull a good draft to me. How was your harvest last year?"

"We have been a bit hungry the past month, but we made it through the winter and helped those in need. Cannot complain about that."

"No. Must have been a relief after the crop failure a few years back."

"Aye, that was rough." Alec motioned MacBean along the upper path.

"So," Alec changed the subject. "What do you make of the sheep they are talking about?"

"I have just seen herds of them further north. They survived the winter by huddling along the river with only the stone walls for protection from the wind." MacBean looked down to the river. "This land would be perfect for them."

"If the Earl wants a flock of sheep, our lads could care for them, and then give him the lambs and some of the wool."

"They are putting thousands of sheep in a valley like this." MacBean waved his arm at the pasture below. "They eat every blade of grass as fast as it comes up. There would be no room for oats or barley or kail, nor grass for a cow or goat."

"Then our only hope is that the Earl's greed is satisfied early."

"Well, they sent us with the notice for a meeting, although there's been a report of an Englishman being assaulted in Kildonan, so I didn't know what to expect."

Alec looked MacBean in the eye. "No one has been assaulted in Kildonan, English or otherwise."

"Must have been strangers along the coast path." MacBean said and looked away. "I will tell the Commissioner of the peaceful scene here and your hospitality. Well, we best be going, MacDonan. Perhaps I will see you at Dunrobin, although they may send me off again. I suppose you will all be walking so it will take a few days to get there."

"Aye. We have written a petition to the Countess and Earl that a dozen people in Kildonan want to deliver, so I expect it will be four days from now."

"I will tell the Commissioner to expect the MacDonans on Friday, shall I?"

"Friday," Alec said, and shook MacBean's hand.

They started down to the cottage and were met by Hugh and the other men who had rounded up their horses. "We appreciate the food and tea, thank you all," MacBean said.

Alec and Hugh watched them ride away. "What do we make of all this, Alec," Hugh said. "It was our idea to send a delegation, and now they have invited us. Fate seems to call us. I don't see how we can refuse."

Tuesday, 30 March

EVERYONE FOR THE delegation met at the barn the next morning. Alec read the message from Young and it was agreed to leave for Dunrobin that day. A few lads were willing to go in the army for a salary, or head south for the canal labor to pay any back rent owed, if that was the issue.

Twenty people set out by mid-morning. Bella, Alec, Robbie, Mary and Hugh MacLennan, Neil Sinclair, Walter MacKay, and John Gunn, from their immediate village, as well as at least one person and a few children from each family group along the lower Strath. James Ross showed up at the last minute to tag along, once he learned they were heading for the coast and had food. A goat was brought on a tether and Neil's pony pulled a small two-wheeled wagon full of meal, cooking pots, and blankets.

It was slow going and rain fell occasionally, but at the beginning it was an adventure. They had their petition and were in high spirits. Hugh led the way piping the tune of each Clan's signature march. Bella heard one of the lads say to his friend, "Come on, Sandy, we are chasing bagpipes!"

They made Helmsdale by nightfall and walked across the new bridge. It was paved with stone and arched smoothly over the river. The hillside path wound up a steep hill, so they stopped below it on a field next to the river. Being too late for a fire, they ate hard-cooked eggs and dry meal cakes.

Wednesday, 31 March, The Coast

WHEN MORNING CAME, a neighboring Gunn family brought them peat and an ember from a fire so they could cook oats. They followed a path at the edge of the sea that exposed them to the wind and rain. The trail went uphill sharply from Helmsdale. They reached the top of the bluff where not even grass could grow in the rock. The path wound up and down and over small creeks until they passed the small town of Brora in late afternoon.

At nightfall they were headed for a Sea Broch that Alec had slept in before. Everyone was wet and cold by then and the bairns were crying. Bella caught up to Alec when she handed off one of the small children she had been carrying.

"We need some shelter quickly. People will start to get sick."

"The Broch has thatch that leans against the seaward wall, we can crowd under it. We are almost there."

They rounded a corner. "Is that it?" Bella pointed to a walled stone circle about 100 yards ahead.

He nodded to Bella and then called back, "Shelter ahead." Everyone picked up the pace.

Walter, who was scouting in front, ran back. "Alec, there is smoke from the Broch."

He and Walter ran ahead, and when they entered the Broch, found Tommy and Nathaniel sitting around a small fire.

"Tommy!" Alec called out, but Tommy saw him first and in three steps embraced him.

"What are you doing here, Da?"

"I would ask you the same. We expected you home a few days ago."

"A lot has happened Da, but we are on our way home now. Come sit by the fire." He motioned to the hearth they built with rocks.

"Your mother is here, along with Robbie and about twenty other people." Alec turned to Walter, but he had already gone back to give the news. "We are taking our petition to Dunrobin, and now need to get the children under cover."

Nathaniel was moving their sleeping rolls and sacks to make room for as many people as possible. Tommy ran out to greet his mother.

"Tommy, I am so glad to see you." Bella tried to kiss him but he dodged, and then laughed.

"Come see the lovely spot I found Ma, with a view of the sea nearby."

"We were beginning to wonder what happened to you." She tried to keep the worry from her voice.

"Nathaniel is here too, Ma. Everything has taken longer than we thought, and I cannot keep my eyes from the sea, it is so beautiful. I walk ten steps and have to stop to look at it some more." Tommy squeezed her arm. "It takes me a long time to get any distance."

The rest of the group crowded inside the Broch walls and got the children around the fire to dry off and warm up. A makeshift covering was set up with blankets to extend the thatch roof so everyone had a turn at standing by the fire. The rain finally let up and a few stars were visible as they bedded down for the night.

The MacDonans were waiting to hear about Tommy's adventure in whatever privacy they could manage. They took their bedrolls away from the Broch to a point where a flat stretch of pasture faced the sea to the east and the distant glow of lamps burned on the castle walls to the south.

"How close have you been to Dunrobin, Tommy?" Bella asked.

"We have stayed away. There are so many people around, and more arriving all the time. Some MacLennans near the Brora Waters took us in on our way south. They are cousins to Hugh and said they know you, Da."

"Ah, aye. Good people. I have slept on their floor during a bad storm or two."

"That is exactly what Mrs. MacLennan said, 'Storm or no, you lads must sleep in the same spot as your Father. It will bring us good luck, which we all need these days,' so we really had to stay."

"Of course. You cannot insult a MacLennan's offer of hospitality," Alec said.

"Well, then the next day, Mr. MacLennan insisted we walk up the Brora Waters with him to the best salmon pool in the Highlands. We got back so late we had to sleep again in the MacDonan's corner."

Alec laughed until his stomach hurt. "Tommy, I don't think I have laughed since you left. Did they bring out any granddaughters who need a husband?"

"No, we never saw one."

Alec began laughing again. "And what amuses you so, Alec?" Bella asked.

When he could speak again Alec explained. "MacLennan was determined I should marry his oldest daughter, Elizabeth. That was before I knew you, dear, but all I said was that she seemed like a nice lass. When her dad was not looking, she got behind me, pinched my ear, and hissed that I should say I was already promised to someone else. Which I immediately did."

"Lucky for you. She probably would have kept you in that corner all this time." Bella gave Alec a friendly swat with the end of her shawl.

It was too dark for them to see Robbie rolling his eyes. He got up and rearranged his blankets and moved closer to Tommy, then urged him to continue.

"When we finally got back on the road to Dunrobin, we met people from all over the Highlands. The men who had been evicted from Rogart were trying to find lodging for their families, some with small children. People who live near Golspie told them they were under the Factor's orders not to shelter anyone, or they would be evicted themselves."

"Do some take them in anyway?" Bella asked.

"After dark we saw children being left at doors with a whistle, then the parents slept outside out of sight."

"What have we come to that a stranger in need is turned away," Alec said.

"People say they have to think of their own children," Tommy replied.

"And when we all say that, no child will be safe," Bella said.

They fell silent for a few minutes, the crash of the waves seeming to echo Bella's words. "Tommy, you were born facing the sea and I regret that I kept you away from it while you were growing up."

"I am young yet, Ma, and now that I am by the sea, I know I can come back anytime. Maybe I will even go out in one of the ships someday."

"So did you ever get to Golspie?" Robbie asked in exasperation.

"Aye, after we finally left MacLennans', we kept to the path closest to the sea. It was rough going, but we decided to stay out of sight. We stopped at this Broch to rest and then walked around Dunrobin at dusk. I never dreamt it was so big." Tommy spread his arms high and wide. "The walls around the castle are huge. We could see people walking about on the upper steps, but no one even noticed us. We slept hidden by the trees and next morning made for the Inn. I still had all the coins you gave me, so we paid for a morning meal, a wash-up, and stabling Nathaniel's horse."

"Was Robert Davidson at the Inn?" Alec asked.

"That's him. He said he knew you, too. He was very kind to us. There were no empty beds, so he sent us round to his sister's house to sleep that night."

"Did you hear any news?" Alec asked.

"The strangest thing we heard, and why there are so many people about, is that someone was assaulted by a mob along the coast. They say the mob is headed for Dunrobin to burn it down. Now they are handing out guns to the townsmen if they join the militia to defend the castle."

"The messenger from Dunrobin mentioned an assault," Alec said. "Maybe the Rogart men have met somewhere and will try to go back to their glen. We had best get on to the castle with our petition at first light, so we don't get caught in the middle."

Chapter Fifteen

Wisely if sincerely. **Clan Davidson**

Thursday, 1 April, On to Dunrobin

ALEC WAS UP first and woke everyone. In less than an hour, they had left the Sea Broch and were making their way south. A storm was moving in off the sea, bringing more rain. Although they would have all liked to cook food, there was agreement to get to the castle as soon as possible. They were making good time and could meet the Commissioner a day earlier.

Mary passed around oatcakes from her bag, and Bella told stories to the youngsters to keep them going. They walked for an hour and could plainly see Dunrobin ahead. The terrain became flat and groves of trees and shrubs were thick before them. The road divided into two paths, one toward the sea and the other, wider and well-used, headed off into the woods and led to the Castle main entrance.

A man galloped toward them on the Castle road. His speed was so intimidating they tried to get off the road and into the woods. George MacBean reined in his horse next to Alec and jumped off. "Over here, quick." He motioned Alec off to the side of the anxious group of people.

"What's wrong?" Alec said when they were a few steps away.

"I just overheard the Sheriff telling the army commander that the MacDonan mob had been spotted leaving yonder Broch. I cannot believe they have called the army out and think you are the mob about to attack Dunrobin."

"The army is here? All we have to fight with is a piece of paper."

"I cannot fathom it myself, but the troops marched from Fort George and are lined up down the road to defend the Castle. I hate to give such bad news, and have to go back before they suspect I have spoken to you. I am only supposed to see how many men there are and report back."

"So they plan to wait on the road then?"

"Aye." MacBean looked around, but no one had followed him.

"Say we are only a few men and are resting." The two men clapped each other's shoulders and MacBean was back on his horse and away.

Alec relayed the news and a council began immediately. "We cannot walk into the hands of soldiers with women and children," Walter said.

"We will look less like a mob if women and children are visible," Bella said.

"We might as well be the sheep that are to replace us, if we walk toward men with guns, who might shoot us for the sport of it," John said.

Tommy's voice rang out from the back of the group. "We could take the sea path."

Everyone turned to look at him. "Good thought, lad," Walter said, as they all began talking among themselves.

Alec raised his voice to be heard. "It seems to me our mission has just changed. We have somehow been declared a mob, for the Factor's benefit I would guess. We may still have a chance to have our say, but I think we can assume we were not really invited to Dunrobin to discuss our grievances. It would be best to take the children home and have a smaller group go on."

The family groups huddled together. Most of the people wanted to start for Kildonan immediately. Neil decided to head back with the pony and cart.

"I will go back with my horse, and the children can ride," Nathaniel said

"That would be helpful, lad," Neil said.

Bella imagined Rose seeing Nathaniel return. Maybe it was not a good idea for him to go back to the Strath.

As if Neil could read her mind he added, "Rose could stay with Catherine and Margaret. The lad and I can sleep at your place."

"Thank you, Neil," Bella said.

In a few minutes the MacDonans, MacLennans, Walter MacKay, John Gunn, and James Ross continued along the sea route. Tommy walked with Ross a few times to give the man a chance to explain his behavior on the river path. Ross ignored him.

Tommy's idea had been a good one, as their efforts to go undetected were successful. They walked close to the castle wall in twos and threes and no one saw them, as all the guards were posted along the road watching for an angry mob.

After skirting the castle, they crossed a small creek and arrived at the Golspie Inn around noon. Davidson was out front and spotted Alec and Tommy right off. "MacDonan, come inside, hurry." He led them all to the back of the Inn where no one was around. "Davie," he yelled, "bring food and tea. Sit down, sit down," he said to Bella and the other women. "Ach, Alec. The Factor is looking for you."

"The Commissioner invited us to discuss our situation with him, and now we have been declared a mob," Alec said.

Bella reached in her bag for one copy of the petition. She pulled out a rolled up piece of rough paper with her careful lettering covering the whole page. Signatures were scrawled on the bottom, including a few marks from those who could not write.

"We have a letter to the Countess Elizabeth. Do you know of any way we can post it to London?"

"I could try to send it, but it could take weeks, if she even would read it." Davidson was pouring ale as he urged everyone to drink up.

"I believe if she knows it is from the MacDonans she will read it," Bella said.

"I will put it in my safe if you want, and try to post it as soon as someone I trust is going to Inverness."

Bella whispered to Alec, "We have two copies. One by post, and one to read to the Commissioner if he will listen." Alec nodded as Bella handed a copy to the Innkeeper.

Davie arrived with soup and bread for everyone. A chorus of thanks and grateful waves were given. "Thank you, Robert. I believe yours is the only hospitality we will receive in Golspie," Alec said.

"Sellar is like a bird of prey, swooping in for what he wants without regard for anyone else. It makes me ill. They pretend we will all prosper when the sheep arrive, as if the sheep will pay for a bed at my Inn."

By the time they finished eating and washing up, a crowd had gathered outside, as word spread that the MacDonan mob was inside. Some people were curious, but afraid, and stood along the edges of the crowd, while others were ready to join an attempt to hang the Factor. But when the Factor appeared a few minutes later with Commissioner Young, the Sheriff, and a troop of soldiers behind them, those ready to make a noose melted into the bushes.

"Innkeeper! Bring out your guests," Sellar shouted.

ROBERT WAS ENCOURAGING everyone to escape out the back, saying Davie would show them a trail through the woods.

Alec left a handful of coins on the table and thanked Robert for his trouble. "We came here for a purpose that needs to be finished," Alec said as they walked out the front door.

Sellar and Young were on horseback next to each other with guards on either side.

Alec calmly addressed them. "We are here to present you with a petition stating our ancestral right to the land along the Strath of Kildonan. As you can plainly see, we are not a violent mob, but a group of farmers who love our land. Our rent is paid up and you have no reason to evict us." Those standing beside him nodded their agreement.

"Is that so, MacDonan?" Sellar said. "Well, here is Mr. Reed, who was assaulted by some of you peaceful farmers when I sent him up the Strath to look at pasture. Reed, do you see the men who attacked you?"

Tommy's mouth fell open as he recognized the man who had been struggling with James Ross.

Reed was sure he saw the man who grabbed his horse standing with the mob, but when he got closer they all looked alike. Not wanting to make a fool of himself, he chose two men who may have been hiding in the bushes.

"That's them in front, with the green blankets," he said, pointing to Walter and John.

They shouted at the Sheriff that they had never seen the man before when Reed spotted Tommy.

"That one, there. He tried to steal my horse." He pointed straight at Tommy.

Tommy turned around, assuming he pointed at Ross, who had been behind him, but Ross was gone.

Soldiers advanced on the crowd. Three guards surrounded Tommy and grabbed his arms before he knew what was happening. Alec tried to help Tommy, but the soldiers were faster and had a bayonet at Alec's chest in no time.

Tommy struggled to get away and broke free. He ran wildly toward the creek and sea beyond, but four soldiers jumped him and threw him to the ground. He landed on his chest and his arms were pinned behind his back before he could rise.

Bella was at his side screaming, "Stop it, you are hurting him!"

"Ma, help me. I didn't do anything wrong."

"Stand back," one of the soldiers yelled at Bella.

"Go ahead and stab me then. I will not leave my son." Bella was kneeling on the ground next to Tommy.

The local people and the soldiers were shouting at each other until the Sheriff shot his gun into the air and everyone froze.

"These three men are under arrest for assaulting Mr. Charles Reed and attempting to steal his horse and personal goods. They will be held over in Dunrobin for trial."

The Sheriff began to read the Riot Act, which declared their assembly to be unlawful and threatened them all with immediate arrest if they did not disperse. He added that anyone offering lodging or food to the mob would be arrested also.

Tommy, Walter, and John were being led away toward the castle. Bella stayed right next to Tommy and the soldiers did not try to stop her. "We will get you out as soon as we can. We will not leave you here." Tommy nodded in misery as he stumbled and was pushed along. He began to sob with the realization that he was going to jail.

When the soldiers and their prisoners turned into the lane at Dunrobin, Sellar rode up to block Bella's way. "Stand back, woman. I advise you to go back to your hovel before you join your son in a cell."

"I would join my son. Arrest me also." Bella said, but Alec was at her elbow begging her to come back to the Inn where they could decide what to do.

"Alec, I cannot leave him. Wait, I have the token from the Countess." Bella bent over and lifted the edge of her skirt. She bit the loose threads holding the embroidered patch and yanked. The patch came free.

Tommy had been moved along down the path to the castle. Bella ran after him, shouting to Sellar.

"I have a token from the Countess Elizabeth." Bella held up the patch, Elizabeth Gordon's personal symbol, an ivy leaf on a blue background within a gold circle.

Sellar stopped his horse and waited for her to catch up. He bent down and took the patch carefully, as if it was contaminated.

"Looks like you copied this yourself. Now get out of my way." He urged his horse forward, but did not return the patch.

When Bella spun around to follow Tommy again, a rank of soldiers blocked her path.

Alec was by her side. "We have no choice. We must find a way to prove his innocence. It won't help if you are in a cell." He put his arm around Bella and pulled her along back to the Inn.

The soldiers were still there and one of the officers was telling Robert that he could not shelter or give food to any of the assembled Highlanders or he would be arrested for aiding the enemy.

"The enemy! And do you know, laddie, that for generations the MacDonans defended Dunrobin against the Vikings, and just sixty years ago from the Jacobites?" The soldier shrugged and looked embarrassed. Davidson was sputtering and turning red as he flung his last question. "Then how can you call them the enemy?"

"Times are changing, old man. The sheep are the new Highland Clan," the soldier said.

"Well then, let the sheep defend the Earl of Sutherland!" Robert turned on his heel and stalked back inside.

"We are going home," Alec said to the soldier, "so do not bother the Innkeeper."

The soldier left a dozen men to make sure and waved the remaining troops back to the castle.

The remaining Kildonan folks retreated behind the Inn to pack their bags. Alec was gathering whatever bread was left into one knapsack.

Bella threw her bag on the ground and yelled at Alec. "How could you let them take him away?"

"There was nothing I could do. They held a sword at my chest. We walked into a trap, and I did not even see it." He sat down on a bench, arms on his knees and head in his hands. "I am sorry, love. I failed him."

Her anger deflated at his misery. "It was my idea to come here. We should have all stayed home." Bella put her hand on his shoulder. "What can we do now? I cannot bear to leave with him in jail."

Alec stood up and tried to pull himself together. Robbie was waiting with an idea. "We better leave while they are watching us. Then we can decide how to free them all when we are alone."

"Aye, we must leave here now." Alec took Bella's hand. "Come away now and when we get to the Broch I will hide in the woods and double back. Maybe MacBean will help us again."

Bella frowned. "But how can we prove they are innocent?"

"Do you remember Nathaniel's last name?" Alec asked her and Robbie.

"MacLeod isn't it?" Bella asked. "No, that's his mother's name. He said it that first day, Nathaniel...Nathaniel Reed. Wait, the man on the horse who accused Tommy was called Reed."

Robbie threw the knapsack over his shoulder. "I thought Nathaniel worked himself into our family too easily, rescuing Jamie aside. I never trusted him like Tommy did. I will find out what part he has in all this."

In the end, Alec convinced her that he would have an easier time helping Tommy and the other men by himself. The small group reluctantly left Alec alone at the Broch and hurried back toward Helmsdale by walking until past dark. There was plenty of stumbling and scraped hands, but they made it to the field near the ferry and slept in the open again.

THEY CROSSED ON the first ferry in the morning with several other people who arrived just before it left. Ross took his leave then, saying he would stay in Helmsdale. When they reached the high point of the river path and looked back across at the other side, they saw a contingent of soldiers, who must have followed them the whole way. Robbie waved his arms at them in disgust, and in a few minutes the soldiers turned around and disappeared back over the hill.

Mary held Bella's free hand as they trudged along. "I cannot think how that evil man could accuse our Tommy of something he would never do. Steal his horse, bah," Mary said.

"The only sense I can make of it is that Tommy resembles someone else, or the man just pointed at anyone to prove his story," Bella said. "But why Tommy," she went on, "who has finally seen the sea, and Dunrobin where he was born."

"Well Bella, he will be inside the castle, and he knows who he is, and perhaps will talk himself to freedom, even if he has to say he is the son of the Countess. That would surely get their attention."

"I am not sure what kind of attention he would get, Mary. I've been thinking about the Countess." They stopped for a minute and Bella looked down to the river. The broad stretch of deep water was changing as they went along. Narrow canyons created falls, and the pools spread out behind the rocks. They were heading uphill and would soon come to the beginning of the flat pasture land. The path split around both sides of a tree. Mary shifted her bundles and took the downhill trail.

Bella followed her, single file and then they walked side by side again. The younger folks had gone on ahead and they were at the end of the line. Bella continued. "When the Countess was just a young bairn, both her parents went away quite suddenly because her baby sister died. They say her father accidentally dropped her."

"My lands, where did you hear that?"

"All the castle servants tell the story. While her parents were in England, the Earl became deathly ill, then his wife got sick and died just days before him. So our Countess lost her mother and father at an early age. Maybe she was not taught to care for others, so can abandon both Tommy and her people quite easily."

"That makes sense, Bella, and I almost feel pity for the woman, but only almost."

They finally reached the cottage before dark. Bella was relieved to see smoke sifting through the thatch. Robbie had run on ahead so he could build up the fire and heat water. Bella gained a burst of energy the last few steps and threw open the door.

Neil was stoking the fire and filling the teakettle. She could hear

Robbie's voice rising to an unfamiliar pitch, "All right then, Master Reed, get up off the floor! You have some explaining to do." Bella ran across the cottage, afraid that Robbie had started a fight with Nathaniel. She reached the barn doorway as Nathaniel put down a book he was reading.

"Get up, I said." Robbie's fists were clenched and he was scowling. Ian had just arrived from the spring and stood next to Robbie.

"Give him a chance, Robbie."

"Like the chance his father gave Tommy?"

Nathaniel was up on his feet. "Tommy? My father? What's happened?"

Bella interrupted them. "Where is Rose?"

Her question was directed at Nathaniel, but Ian responded, "She is with Margaret. It looks like the bairn is coming."

Chapter Sixteen

I stand for truth. Clan Guthrie

"MARGARET'S BABY? NOW?" Bella stared at Ian in disbelief.

"Neil and I have been sent here to be out of the way and do your chores. Nathaniel has been helping."

Her head felt light and the room was spinning. She leaned toward a bench and sat down.

Robbie returned to Nathaniel's question. "I will tell you what I think happened. Your father sent you up to this valley to pick out his grazing land. You met him back at Dunrobin and told him it's grand and the best way to get us out quickly is to throw Tommy in jail. We will be too frantic to defend our homes."

"Tommy's in jail?" Nathaniel and Ian spoke together.

"What has he done?" Nathaniel asked.

"That is what you need to tell us." Robbie pointed a finger at Nathaniel. "Your father accuses him of trying to steal his horse."

"You keep saying my father, but he is in England." Nathaniel shook his head and held up his hands to stop the very thought.

"He was called Charles Reed by the Factor."

"My father's name is Charles, but it is impossible." He ran his hand through his hair and scratched his head. "I was with Tommy the whole time and never saw my father. What did this man look like?"

"Like you, only a gray beard, long legs and a scowl on his face. He had on a leather coat and fancy boots, like yours, and was riding a big horse."

"It could be him, but I swear," he said looking at Bella, "bring me your Bible, if you will, and I will swear upon my soul that I have not seen or spoken to him since before I left Edinburgh."

Robbie pushed past him to get the Bible. Nathaniel continued looking at Bella. "I would never hurt Tommy, or any of you. Please believe me." Bella held onto the bench with both hands.

When Robbie returned he held out the well-worn book in front of Nathaniel and said, "Swear."

Nathaniel put his right hand on the Bible. "I swear I came here innocently, on my own, and have no knowledge of my father's actions. If I am lying, may I rot in Hell."

"Did you see your father when you were with Tommy?" Robbie looked him in the eyes.

"No, I swear I did not. I would have hidden from him, as he thinks I am at university and would be angry to see me here."

Robbie sighed and lowered the Bible. "I guess I believe you now, but I still do not understand."

"My father thinks he can make easy money raising sheep in the Highlands. I was trying to help him by coming north on my own. He is an honest man, but might try to make himself seem more important. Tell me what he said about Tommy. We were together the whole time. Maybe I can clear his name."

When Robbie told about the scene in Golspie, Nathaniel was as baffled as everyone else. "I can only guess that he just picked Tommy out of the crowd."

"We thought that might be it too. He also accused Walter MacKay and John Gunn, and they were with us the whole time."

"What about their families?" Ian asked.

"Mary and Hugh stopped to tell Annie MacKay, and Martha Fraser is with Helen Gunn," Bella said. The spinning of her brain had ended and she felt a little better.

"Where is Alec?" Neil asked from the doorway.

"He stayed to get Tommy and the others released," Bella said.

"I have tea ready and food cooked. Come have some while it is hot." Neil took Bella's arm and made her sit down by the fire with a cup of tea. Robbie apologized for mistrusting Nathaniel, who said he could hardly blame him.

Neil sat by Bella and asked if she would be able to check on Margaret before she went to bed. "Catherine would be much relieved to know you are home."

Bella couldn't imagine taking another step, but she said, "Of course I will" to Neil.

Ian filled bowls and mugs and passed them around as they took their places on stools around the fire. Bella took a deep breath and led the blessing. "Thanks to God for the earth below our feet, and the fire that warms our food. Our prayers are with are loved ones far away. May we never forget this glen, this river, and this home. Amen."

"Amen," everyone answered. They paused a moment to say their own private prayers. Robbie and Bella felt the relief of being home around their own fire with a bowl of barley.

WHEN SHE FINISHED eating, Bella gathered her birthing supplies and put on a clean dress and apron. Ian offered to walk her over to see Margaret and he carried Bella's bag as they made their way down the lane to the river path. The moon was visible among the clouds, as well as glimpses of twinkling stars.

"You must be so worried about Tommy," Ian said.

"It was horrible to see him taken away, not knowing what will happen, or how he will be treated. I feel ill from the worry."

"If I had any faith in justice, I would say that surely they will believe he is innocent and let him go, but I am afraid Scotland has justice only for the wealthy these days."

"I hope you are wrong."

They walked upstream to where the river narrowed and the current became swift. Bella watched the flowing water. "My life feels like the river, cascading with no controls over boulders and around bends that I cannot see coming." They were quiet for the rest of the way to the Sinclairs's cottage.

Ian turned to go back. "Please give my love to Margaret. I wish there was something I could do for her, but I guess men are no use at a time like this."

"It will help her to know you send your love." Bella felt deep exhaustion again, but once she went inside, Rose ran to embrace her. She held on to her daughter until she felt able to face Margaret with a clear head.

"Ma, Hugh came to tell us about Tommy. I am so worried. Poor lad, he must be terrified. I hope Da can free him."

"Your Da will bring him home, I am sure of it. Now tell me about Margaret, where is she?" Bella lowered her voice.

"She is in her bed. She will not let us help her. She says it is not time, she is just feeling poorly, and we should leave her alone."

Catherine heard them talking. "Ah, I am so glad to see you, Bella, but you must be so tired, dearie. Can you just see my lass for a bit and then get some sleep?"

"What makes you think it is her time?" Bella motioned them outside to talk privately outside the cottage door.

Rose tried to keep her voice quiet. "I slept next to her. Anytime I woke up she was crying or gasping in pain. If I rubbed her back, she slept again. I got up early and when I went to check on her the bed linens were wet."

Catherine glanced inside. "She tried to change the cloth before we could see her, but she was crying, poor dear, and we made her go back to bed."

"Could you see if there was blood?"

"No blood. But, oh, the poor bairn, it will be too small," Catherine said, on the verge of tears herself.

"I will talk to her. You make her some raspberry leaf tea, Rose. I brought more leaves."

"All right, Ma. I am so glad you are here." Rose said as they went inside.

Margaret called out, "Is that Bella?"

Bella kissed Rose and hugged Catherine, who was building up the fire to make tea. Catherine handed Bella a cruisie lamp and opened the curtain for her. When Bella's eyes adjusted to the dark room, she saw Margaret curled up in the corner of the floor bed with a blanket pulled up to her chin. Bella put the lamp on a shelf, took off her cloak and boots and crawled on the bed to sit cross-legged next to Margaret.

"Tell me what is wrong, Margaret dear. It looks like you have been crying."

She had not combed her hair in a few days and it hung over her face in limp dark strands. Her usually cheerful round face was puffy and woeful.

Margaret nodded miserably and fresh tears filled her eyes. "I don't know how Ian and I will manage having a bairn with all that is going on."

"It is a hard time, no doubt, but let's talk about that in a few minutes. Do you think the baby is coming now?"

"It's too early, Bella. I would be shamed if the baby was born now."

"Now that you will be a mother, the health of the baby is more important than what people might say." Bella stroked the hair back from her face. "Are you having any of the signs I said to watch for?"

"My back keeps hurting down there, real low," Margaret whispered, ducking her head.

"What else?" Bella asked gently.

"When I woke up this morning, before I could even get up, liquid was pouring down my legs, lots of it. I don't think that I peed."

"Does your back hurt all the time or off and on?"

"Every once in awhile." Margaret wiped away fresh tears.

"Have you been up much today?"

"No. Ma said to go back to bed and she brought me tea and food."

Bella nodded encouragement. "Were you as hungry as usual?" Bella smiled, as Margaret normally had a great appetite.

"No, I only had a few spoons of porridge, but I drank all the tea. It is too early for the birth, is it not, Bella?"

"Bairns choose their own time to be born, through no fault of yours. Irene's Duncan was born early."

"Really?" Margaret took a deep breath.

"Near a month early. Could you stand a bit more light, if I start another lamp?"

"Aye. I felt like being in a cave, but I am better now that you are here." Bella lit a second lamp and the small room took on a warm glow.

"Let's have you sit up for a bit and wash your face, and then I'll check on the bairn." Margaret brightened and struggled to sit up with Bella's help.

"I'll ask your Ma for some hot water and a comb. Would you like me to make a braid in your hair?" Bella asked on her way to the door.

Margaret nodded, but when Bella left, she caught her breath as a new stronger pain started.

Catherine had a cup of tea ready for Bella and the raspberry leaf for Margaret. "How is it looking, dear? 'Tis too early for the wee one to live, isn't it?"

"Too soon to know for sure, but I will be staying awhile," Bella said.

"Let me know if I can do something to help, or if you get hungry."

"I want to talk to Margaret alone some more, but we need the curtain open to warm up her room. Maybe you and Rose can stay out of sight for awhile."

"Whatever you think is best, we will do."

Bella carried a pan of water into the bedroom, putting it on the shelf near Margaret, then went back to get her tea. When she came back, Margaret was washing her face and neck. Bella sat down nearby holding her cup, wondering where to begin, but Margaret was eager to talk now that she felt safer. "I know Ian will be a good father."

"Oh Margaret, I forgot. Ian walked me here and said to send you his love."

"Ah, he is a sweet man. I wish I could see him, but Ma sent him away."

"What do you like about Ian the most?"

"Ach, well, he is so funny. He makes me laugh at just the smallest thing."

"I know how you love to laugh, Margaret."

"Aye. I have laughed more since I met Ian, than the whole rest of my life put together. You know how serious my Ma and Da are. They used to make me go to the byre if I couldn't stop laughing. But Ian says he loves to hear me laugh."

As another pain gripped Margaret, Bella knelt next to her. "Do not fight it, rub your belly and groan like this." Bella began a deep-throated "uummm" sound that Margaret tried. It seemed to help as Margaret continued the sound in between breaths until it ended.

"So, Margaret dear, we thought you had a month more to go but this seems to be the time now."

Margaret's eyes widened, tears fell, and a flush came to her cheeks, "Oh Bella, but it is too soon since we're married to have the bairn."

"Margaret, it does not matter to me, and I will not think less of you or Ian, if you tell me you were having a roll in the heather before the date of your wedding. It happens to many couples," Bella assured her. Margaret stopped crying while Bella was speaking, but another pain began so she practiced breathing and groaning until it was over. "And, in fact," Bella said, "now that the water has leaked out, I would be very pleased to hear that you and Ian loved each other before your wedding day."

"You would?" Margaret asked, a hope building in her voice.

"Aye, because that would mean your baby is ready to come and I won't worry about it being too small."

"But what would we tell my mother?" Margaret asked.

Bella considered her question thoughtfully. "I would honestly say that although it is early, which is true from your wedding date, the baby seems plenty big enough to be born healthy, most likely because of how well you are being cared for by your mother."

"Ah, she will like that." Margaret smiled at the idea of Bella's truthful, but safe answer.

"And perhaps that will be enough to say without causing her worry that the baby is too small or that people will talk," Bella said.

"You are a cunning woman," Margaret said.

Bella smiled. "Will you be comfortable with Rose sitting with you tonight? I need to get some sleep and it will still be hours yet, maybe even morning, before we see your wee son or daughter."

"Aye. I am hungry now and feel like walking around, maybe sit by the fire for a spell."

"Good, eat as much as you want, sleep as much as you can and let Rose know if the pains never stop or you feel the slightest urge to bear down, and she will send someone for me."

Bella left as Margaret took another deep breath and tried her humming. The pains were far enough apart that there might be a chance for a few hours sleep. When she stepped outside Catherine was waiting. "How is she?"

"She is feeling better, but the bairn is coming. It is early, but she is very healthy, thanks to you. The bairn is big enough to thrive, so that I think it is better early and smaller than late."

Catherine was impressed. "Well, that is good then, whatever is easier for Margaret and my grandchild."

"Where is Rose?" Bella had not seen her inside.

"She went home to get clean clothes and say hello to Robbie. She said she would be back soon to stay the night," Catherine said.

"I need to go home to sleep. I will send Ian back to sleep in your barn. Rose will sleep next to Margaret, but send Ian to get me if there is a change. All of the upset in the glen may have started her time early." Bella put her arm around Catherine. "Margaret is a strong lass and will do well."

"That damn Factor, all the trouble he is causing and now this. He better not send those men up to Kildonan with their torches and bother my daughter. I would chase them off myself."

Chapter Seventeen

I am ready. Clan Fraser

Saturday, 3 April, Early Morning, Kildonan

SOMEONE WAS RUBBING her shoulder and calling out, "Ma, Ma, wake up."

"Let me alone, let me alone." She rolled over and pulled the plaid over her head, her body rebelling from leaving a pleasant dream.

"Ma!" Robbie shook her this time. "It's Margaret, the bairn is coming. Ian has come for you, Ma. Wake up!"

With the mention Margaret and Ian, she was finally awake. She sat up. "Is it morning, Robbie?"

"Aye, Ma. Rose said to hurry. There is warm water for washing."

"Ah, thank you, Son. Get my hairbrush and my apron for me, will you, and I will be off in a few minutes. Any news of your Da or Tommy?"

"None."

"Come to tell me right away, won't you?"

"Of course, Ma."

In a few minutes Bella and Ian were retracing their steps of the night before. It was well past daylight, and when Bella realized she had slept a long time, she felt more confident that she would have her wits about her.

They were past the cluster of cottages the hugged the hillside when Ian glanced up to the cattle pasture far above them. Everyone had been watching for a glimpse of bright green grass that signaled a fresh supply of food this time of year. Most of the milk cows that calved last year were running dry, and those about to give birth needed immediate nourishment.

Although the people in Kildonan produced most of their own food, the only way to buy supplies and pay rent was from the sale of cattle. Each autumn the grass-fed cows were herded to the coast and sold to the highest bidder at a market. Any day now someone would spot the colorful sign of spring and start moving the animals.

Ian was hoping to be the first this year to make the call. Maybe that would elevate his incomer status a bit. He stopped and stared at the top of the hill. Bella was about to continue without him when he said, "There are men on the hill carrying torches. What the hell?" He turned to Bella. "I think they are firing the heather! Go on without me, I've got to stop them." He ran for the upper path.

"Fire, fire!" Ian shouted as loud as he could. They were away from any houses, but a few men were working in a field and ran after Ian as he headed up the path. It soon became obvious that it was a group of the Factor's men, who were spreading out to burn the dead bunch grass and the dried heather that grew in the cattle pasture.

By the time Ian got to the top of the hill, the burning debris was billowing smoke with patches of flame where spent bracken caught fire easily. It was impossible to reach the men through the smoke or put out the fire.

The arsonists were pleased with their work. The ground fire would spread rapidly and destroy food for the cattle, while making way for a later ground cover that the new sheep would thrive on. The men had more fields to burn and then they could report back to Sellar to be paid well for an easy job.

Bella arrived at Sinclair's cottage a few minutes later. Catherine was outside waiting and watching the scene on the hill behind.

"You have seen Sellar's face, is that right, Bella?"

"Aye. All too close."

"If he shows up here, point him out to me. I will strangle him, if it takes my life to do it."

"He sends others to do his dirty work, with the army to protect him."

Bella gave Catherine's hand a squeeze as they went inside. "We have to put our hate aside for now and get the bairn born safely."

Bella could hear Margaret from the door. "God help me, I cannot do this anymore. Rose, help me. Someone help me, please."

Rose was trying her best to calm Margaret, but she had run out of things to do or words to say. When her mother walked in, Rose almost cried with relief. "Ma, 'tis one long pain and she wants to bear down."

"Good, Margaret, you are doing well. It is time to push your baby out," Bella said calmly.

A birthing mat had been set up on the floor. Margaret had been lying on her side, while Rose rubbed her back, but with Bella's arrival Margaret wanted to sit up. Rose climbed behind her as she had with Irene and let Margaret lean back on her. "I need water," Margaret managed to say and her Ma was right there with a cup for her to sip from. Then Catherine rinsed out a cloth and washed Margaret's face. "That feels good, Ma."

"Soon you will have a wee bairn in your arms sucking on your breast, looking in your eyes. You are strong lass. You just do what Bella says," Catherine told her. Margaret nodded as another pain gripped her and her cry became high pitched and frightened.

"Let the sound come from deep inside you," Bella said. Margaret remembered how that had helped her earlier, and she growled a guttural sound that surprised them all.

"Good. Growl all you want. I am going to feel inside you, and then we will know how soon it will be." Margaret nodded.

"Let's get you out of your clothes. You will be more comfortable." Bella moved the night dress up to Margaret's chest and Rose helped pull it over her head. Bella crawled on the bed next to Margaret and carefully pushed her two fingers in as far as she could, and then spread them wide feeling for the bairn's head. There it was, deep inside Margaret, the bairn's head moving around as she touched it. Her fingers found a thin edge of the womb around the head, and as she rubbed, the edge disappeared and the head moved quickly down to fill the whole space and begin its descent.

Bella pulled her fingers out. Her huge grin was infectious. "Margaret, everything is perfect. Take a breath, grab Rose's hands, and as soon as a pain starts, bear down."

It was already coming. Margaret had her head down and was pushing as hard as she could. She grabbed another breath and pushed some more.

Catherine was at Bella's side with a clean blanket ready. Bella held onto Margaret's left leg and encouraged her to breathe and push again. The head was showing more each time. Another pain began, and Margaret began to whimper. Bella took Margaret's hand and moved it down between her legs to touch her bairn's head. "It's almost born, just one more push, good, good. Now stop." The head was completely born.

Catherine was crying. "Ah, my lass, Margaret, you are giving me a grandchild." Margaret took another breath and as the next wave crested, the urge to push overwhelmed her. As she bore down, the head turned sideways and the shoulders emerged. A red, slippery, crying boy with black hair slid into Bella's waiting hands.

Catherine slipped the blanket under him as Bella turned him on his back, loosened the cord and lifted him on to Margaret's chest. "You have a healthy boy, Margaret. Well done."

Margaret had been quietly saying, "It's over, it's over," but when her son was placed at her breast and stopped crying to look at her, she held him near her heart and carefully stroked his head. "He is so beautiful. I never imagined he would be so beautiful. He looks just like Ian. Oh, someone go fetch Ian, please."

Catherine was not about to leave Margaret's side and Bella was waiting for the placenta to deliver. They both looked at Rose.

"I will get him," she said. "You were so strong, Margaret. I am very happy for you." She kissed Margaret and touched the bairn's head and then climbed out from behind Margaret.

"Wait," Bella said. "Ian ran up the hill to put out a fire, so he may not be back yet."

"How could there be a fire up the hill?" Rose asked her.

"Let's get Margaret cleaned up and the afterbirth out, then we will see what has happened on the hill." Bella was wary. She had forgotten the fire and did not want to alarm Margaret.

"I will just step out to look for Ian," Rose said and went out the door.

She was back moments later. "There are strange men coming to the door! One has a paper in his hand."

"STAY WITH MARGARET," Bella said to Rose, as she and Catherine hurried to the door. They stepped out and Catherine pulled the door shut behind them.

There were four men, one with a long paper with what seemed to be a list, and another had a handful of smaller sheets of paper. They stared at the two women, as both had blood on their aprons, and Bella's hands were spotted with blood.

"Butchered a sheep, have you?" one of them joked and the others twittered. "Well, if this is Neil Sinclair's cottage, we will just hand over your eviction notice and be on our way."

Bella stepped forward with her bloody hands outstretched. "This is human blood, you fools, and if you do not leave our glen right now, yours will be the next blood on my hands."

With that encouragement Catherine picked up a rock from the wall behind her and lobbed it toward the men. They had already started to back away after Bella's threat, and when Catherine picked up the rock they turned and ran. The rock missed so she grabbed another. The last man in the lane threw the eviction notice on the ground. "Be out in forty-eight hours, you witches!"

Catherine threw her rock and then filled her apron with more and chased them down the lane cursing them and throwing rocks, until they dropped the roll of papers and ran to the river where they had tied up their horses.

She slowly came back to the door. "Bella, I have never tried to hurt a soul in my life, so cannot imagine why it felt so satisfying to throw rocks at those men."

"You are a mother bear, whose cub is in danger. Let's see to Margaret before Sellar himself appears for you to strangle."

"God forgive me for saying such a thing. Please don't mention it again." Bella nodded agreement as they went back to the birthing scene.

Rose had already caught the placenta in a bucket and was washing Margaret before tying the moss-filled undergarment around her waist with lamb's-wool knitted bands. Margaret's full attention was on her son who had latched onto her nipple and was sucking with enthusiasm.

After Bella and Catherine carried out the rags and placenta to bury, Catherine poured water over Bella's hands and arms while she washed up. "Are we to have no peace, Bella?"

"No. I think our peace is over."

Catherine sighed. "I don't know whether to wish for the old days when all our men could be killed defending our land, or be content to go meekly and live."

"It appears that we must go at any rate, as those men will surely be back with more than pieces of paper."

"What did they say about being evicted? Was it really just forty-eight hours?"

Chapter Eighteen

Courage grows strong at a wound. Clan Stewart

Monday, 5 April, Early Morning, Dunrobin

TOMMY WOKE UP in the cell as morning light sifted through the basement gloom. When a door opened at the top of the stairs, he rolled over to nudge Walter, but his blanket was dropped in a pile on the spot where he had been sleeping on the floor. Tommy sat up and was chilled to see that he was alone.

The three of them had been led here together and pushed into this cold, damp dungeon. Despite all their attempts to talk to the guards when they were taken to the privy or tossed bread and water, no one cared about them or the truth.

Some of the prisoners in other cells had been led away and not returned. There was a rumor that they were sent off to the British army, but no one knew for sure.

He got up and grabbed his own blanket, threw it around his shoulders and tried to prepare himself for whatever was coming. A gray-haired man Tommy had not seen before rushed down the stairs, glancing behind him furtively. He made his way to the cell and put his hand over his heart in a friendship gesture, and then his finger on his lips for silence. The mystery man looked around again. Satisfied that the men in the other cells were asleep, he slowly turned a key in the door, opened it carefully, and motioned Tommy to follow him.

The man led the way up the stairs. When they got to the top, he held up his hand for Tommy to wait. He tiptoed along the narrow corridor to the side of a sleeping guard and hung the key ring on a hook in the wall. When he got back to Tommy, he led him up another staircase in the opposite direction. They emerged on the sea side of Dunrobin, crossed a field, passed through an abandoned house and went out a small door on the north side of the wall.

His rescuer finally spoke. "Sorry to leave you so long, lad. I could not risk taking you three at a time, and your pals were awake when I got there. They are waiting for you along the tree line. Your Da's near the MacLennan cottage where you spent the night. He said you would know the way."

"Aye. Thank you so much. Who are you?"

"Someone who has always cared about you, lad. Your Da will tell you the story, but you had best be gone before we are both caught."

"I hope we meet again," Tommy said and then turned and walked quickly toward the nearby trees. Walter and John were there as the man promised. They rapidly made their way through the woods along the coast where they hoped not to be seen.

Several bursts of running combined with stealthful passing of open areas brought them past the Sea Broch and close enough to the MacLennan cottage to walk single file in the woods along the main road. Anyone coming on horse would be heard and they could quickly hide further in the trees.

When they were in sight of the cottage, Tommy heard his father whistle off to the side. He stopped quickly and headed in that direction with Walter and John close behind. He returned the whistle with a bird call until he could see his Da along the edge of a stream. A stone outcropping concealed him as he crouched down again. As soon as they rounded the corner, they dropped to the ground next to Alec. Alec clapped his son's shoulder and pulled him close. "Tommy, did they hurt you?"

"Just starved and froze us, but we are better already." He glanced at his companions, who were nodding agreement. They were already eating the meal cakes Alec had brought from Mrs. MacLennan and passed the bag to Tommy.

"Da," he said before taking a bite, "who was the man who helped us escape?"

"He is your true grandfather, James Gunn. He was the Earl's keeper of the hunting birds, the Falconer of Dunrobin, and he now tends the garden. He saw you being dragged into the castle and heard your name. There had already been talk among the servants that you were all innocent, so he thought you had a chance to get away.'

"My grandfather. And I didn't know it. But how did he know where I would find you?"

"Well, he is a Gunn after all. His family is spread out along the coast and have been helping us the whole way."

"I was too wrapped up in myself to even notice them."

"They noticed you and were pleased. The innkeeper's wife in Golspie is a Gunn, as is Anna MacLennan, who is helping us now."

"I wish I could go see them again, now that I know who they are."

"We cannot risk it, for their sake as well as ours. I have been sleeping behind the house, but hiding here during the day waiting for you. Soldiers have come by and searched the house for the people from Rogart, and we have had some close calls."

"What will we do now?"

John and Walter finished eating and handed Tommy another cake and some ale in a cup. "Let's go home," Walter said.

Alec nodded. "We have a plan worked out. I have a food package and some other clothes for Tommy. His long hair stands out, so I thought I would give him a trim, a new cap and a Gunn plaid. Ready to be a Gunn, Tommy?"

"Aye, cut away." Tommy held out the side of his hair, while Alec trimmed it with his knife. When Tommy put the new cap on and wrapped the blue and green plaid around his shoulders, he felt like a different person. "Call me Tom Gunn," he said. "I am no longer young Tommy

MacDonan who has never seen the sea, or the dungeon of Dunrobin."

"Tom Gunn, it is then," Alec said, "but it will be hard for me to remember that your name is shorter."

"Just look at my hair to remind you." He tugged at the short ends hanging below his cap.

"All right, Tom. I will try." Alec turned to Walter and John. "Tom Gunn, aye, men?"

"Aye, Tom it is," Walter said.

Alec unwrapped the clothes bundle. "Walter, you put this coat on and John, here's a different hat, maybe we can blend in with the other travelers." In a few minutes they were ready to go. Walter and John started out walking together carrying their food, a sack of baked potatoes. Tom and Alec followed them a few minutes later. They stayed along the edge and walked single file, ready to jump in a ditch or take cover behind rocks if necessary.

They agreed to take the Glen Loth path over the hill to avoid Helmsdale. Alec had seen MacBean again. Sellar was moving his gang to Helmsdale to be closer to Kildonan.

John knew the turn-off well, so he and Walter started up the trail, waiting for Alec and Tom around the first bend. There were a few scares when some soldiers went past, but they heard them coming and hid behind trees in time. Within an hour they were together and on their way.

They hiked up the hill until the light was gone and made a camp just off the path. The baked potatoes were cold by then, but were much better than the crusts of bread they had received the night before in the dungeon.

Monday, 5 April, Morning, Helmsdale

SELLAR CURSED THE men setting up his staging area by the harbor. He told them he wanted a view of the new bridge Telford was building so he could keep an eye on the people crossing. When he arrived late in the night and discovered they set up the tent near the sea, not the bridge, he made them move everything in the early hours of the morning.

His insomnia returned with word of the prisoners' escape. It was clearly an inside job as they were simply gone, the cell door left ajar. The militia was on the road doing a house-to-house search along the coast. If nothing else, the locals would be terrified and unlikely to offer shelter to anyone.

As soon as one of the tables was set up, Sellar spread out the map of Kildonan. He was estimating the time it would take to get there, evict everyone, and return to Helmsdale when the Sheriff appeared with a disheveled native in tow.

"Sellar, I remember this man from the mob in Golspie. He was sleeping under the bridge. Maybe he knows something about the prisoners."

Sellar put down his pencil and looked the man over. He had the shakes, smelled bad, and was sniveling. Sellar's lip curled in disgust. "Who are you?"

"Just a poor man looking for a drink and a bite to eat."

"Are you a MacDonan?"

"No, no. A Ross. James Ross."

"Were you evicted from Rogart?"

"No home to burn down. Wander here and there. Follow the whiskey trail. Can you spare a wee dram?" Ross licked his lips and looked around the tent.

Sellar called to his assistant. "Get the man a drink and a piece of bread." He turned to Ross. "Sit down over there." He pointed downwind. "After a dram and bread you tell me all you know about MacDonan, and there will be seconds."

When Ross revived a bit he told Sellar that Alec had stayed near Golspie to get the men released. He had not heard they escaped but guessed they would take the shortcut to Kildonan and avoid the bridge.

Sellar asked about weapons. "No weapons stashed away. All they do is talk. Refused my ideas for rustling sheep and burning the Castle." Ross realized he was babbling and shut his mouth.

The Sheriff was all for arresting Ross on the spot, but Sellar said, "Give him some food and get him out of my sight." When Ross was gone with a sack of food they assigned a deputy to follow him. The deputy came back to report Ross had started toward Kildonan.

Morning, Kildonan

NATHANIEL PROVED HIS loyalty two days before when he and Robbie ran up to the burning pasture with buckets of water, to no avail. Now Nathaniel was wrestling a harness around a cow's neck. "Robbie, where are we taking them?"

"I think the churchyard is the only place that hasn't been overgrazed. They can eat the grass coming up on the graves."

"Is there water by the church?"

"No, I didn't think of that, ach." Robbie rubbed his head, which was starting to ache. "We will have to take them anyway. And the river is nearby, I will figure out how to get them water later. We can halter the goat and tie her to the milk cow. She will follow the rest of the cattle."

"A procession," Nathaniel said.

"Our royal animals," Robbie said, rubbing his head again. They set off from the barn down the lane to the river path.

Nathaniel looked back and saw Bella and Rose on their way to the Sinclair household. He and Rose waved to each other until Robbie called him to walk faster.

Rose sighed when they were out of sight. "Nathaniel could have gone home by now, I wonder why he didn't." Bella squeezed her hand but was silent while they continued on to the Sinclair's cottage. Ian saw them coming and ran to meet them.

"Morning, Bella. Morning Rose. We have a grand baby boy. I am grateful." Bella gave all the credit to Margaret. Rose noticed Ian had that same joyful look about him that Matthew had when Duncan was born. She wondered if her own Da had been that happy to see her.

Neil waved to them and called Ian over to help sort out their cattle and sheep, which were temporarily in the garden. When Bella mentioned Robbie's idea of the churchyard, they decided to take their animals there also.

Catherine welcomed them with open arms, "Ah, the midwives, back again! Well, come see my beautiful grandson." Rose had never been called a midwife before, and she blushed with pride.

After admiring the baby, who was curled up next to his mother, both of them sleeping, Bella checked Margaret's bleeding. She was alarmed to see a steady stream of blood that had soaked through all the moss and into the blankets below.

Chapter Nineteen

Aim at difficult tasks. Clan Malcolm

MARGARET'S FOREHEAD WAS warm to the touch. Her cheeks were flushed and when Bella tried to wake her, she was slow to respond. Bella rubbed Margaret's belly and felt for her womb. She found it—soft, large, and spongy.

"Rose, get the bottle of shepherd's purse from my bag and some water in a cup." Bella picked up the baby and stroked his cheeks, until he woke up looking for his food supply. "Margaret, wake up, your baby is hungry," she said loud enough to startle Margaret awake.

Catherine came in. "Is something wrong?"

"She is bleeding too much. I need your help. Bring me a stack of clean rags."

"She was fine yesterday, what did we do wrong?"

"It's not your fault. We just need to work quickly now."

"Here's the herbs and water." Rose brought the cup to Bella.

Bella held the cup to Margaret's lips and said, "Drink it all quickly, Margaret." She grimaced at the taste, but Bella firmly repeated her instructions. Margaret emptied the cup and fell back on the bed. Bella took the rags from Catherine and stuffed a layer under Margaret. "I am going to press on her womb. A lot of blood is going to come out, but that is what is needed. Catherine, you hold the bairn."

Margaret began to cry softly, but yelled out when Bella pressed firmly on her belly. Blood gushed between her legs onto the layers of rags. "Ma," Rose said, "I'm scared."

"The blood is clotting, see the darker pieces," Bella said, "I think the clots just blocked the opening and fresh blood pooled up that is coming out now. We need to get the womb to contract and keep it hard." Rose swallowed and tried not to throw up her breakfast.

"Bella, stop! That hurts too much," Margaret said.

"I am sorry, but I need to do this 'til I am sure you are safe."

"What's wrong?"

"You were losing too much blood. Do you feel dizzy?"

"Aye." Her hands were clenching the side of the bed.

"Are you hot or cold?"

"Cold, very cold."

"Get a blanket." Bella nodded to Rose. Rose quickly tucked a wool blanket around Margaret.

The baby began to cry. Catherine looked at Bella. Bella said, "Let him cry, we need Margaret's attention on her baby. Margaret! Your baby is crying. Keep your eyes open. His life depends on you. Do you hear me, Margaret?"

"Hmmm?" Margaret's reply was weak and she closed her eyes again.

"Rose, get some cold water." Bella checked Margaret's pulse. It was sporadic. Rose returned quickly. "Press on her womb, let up a bit and then press again 'til it stays hard." Bella moved a blanket roll from Margaret's head to under her knees. She wrung out a cold cloth and pressed it to her wrists, rinsed again and pressed it to her forehead.

Bella slid a clean rag under Margaret. "It looks like the bleeding has stopped. Let up on the pressure."

"It stayed hard."

Bella rinsed the cold cloth and reapplied it to her wrists and forehead. Then she checked Margaret's wrist pulse, which was stronger.

"Margaret, talk to me!" It was a command.

Margaret opened her eyes and tried to sit up, but her eyes closed again and then the sound of her baby crying reached her. She opened her eyes and was alert again. "I want my bairn."

"Much better," Bella said at last. "I want you to have another dose of shepherd's purse, then turn on your side and feed your hungry bairn." Catherine had retreated to the corner of the room with him as his cry had turned to a wail. "Anytime you wake up, or stand up," Bella said, "rub your belly 'til it gets hard."

"I will. That was horrible. I thought it would be so much more peaceful to just drift away."

"I'm sorry. I should have come back again last night."

Catherine brought the baby over as they helped Margaret turn on her side. Bella put fresh pads under her and pulled away all the bloody mess. She tied a tight woven band around Margaret's belly to keep some pressure on the womb. The bleeding stopped, and the baby nursed for a long time. Bella and Rose stayed another hour and then headed for home.

As they rounded the corner by the MacLennans, shouts broke the peaceful sounds of the river. They hurried up the rise and saw the MacKays's cottage roof smoking.

Chapter Twenty

Boldly. Clan MacAlister

As far as they knew, Walter was still in jail with Tommy, so Annie was alone with their two children, and Walter's mother, Janet. They dropped their bundles by the garden wall and ran down the lane. The scene before them was chaotic. Annie and the children were outside. She was trying to get Jamie to hold the baby and stay by the wall so she could go back for Janet. Two men pressed their torches to the thatch edges. "Damn it, 'tis too wet to burn," one of them yelled.

A man on horseback was supervising. "Go inside and find a dry area. We may have to burn them from the inside out after all the blasted rain."

The two men went inside and yelled back, "Old woman still inside," to Sellar. Annie was trying to go back in the cottage, but Jamie was clinging to her skirts and the baby was screaming.

"Get busy, she'll move fast enough soon," Sellar said.

Bella and Rose arrived as Sellar turned his horse to the next cottage. "Rose, grab the children," Bella said. Rose scooped up the bairn in one arm and grabbed Jamie's hand. She pulled him away from the house into the garden.

Annie and Bella ran into the house and straight to the old woman's bed. Janet MacKay was crying, "*O teine*, oh fire," but began coughing at every breath. Annie took her under her arms and Bella by her knees and they carried and dragged her through the doorway as the ceiling collapsed behind them.

They continued to the garden, all of them coughing now, and laid Janet on the old potato bed. Bella picked up the shawl they had dragged behind her and covered her as best she could.

The bairn was wailing and Jamie struggled to get away from Rose to reach his mother. Annie stepped toward him and when Rose let go, he rushed to her side. Rose handed the bairn to Annie.

Helen's screams drew their attention. They all turned to see the men moving around her cottage, pressing the burning torches through the middle of the thatch. The thatch caught, igniting the drier birch branch frame.

"You cowards. You despicable criminals. May you rot in Hell!" Helen was following them, her children hysterical behind her.

"You have a chance to remove your belongings. I would suggest you do so," a calm voice behind Helen said. She whirled to see a sharp-nosed, well-dressed man, arms folded across his chest, a riding crop dangling from one hand.

"Who the devil are you?"

"I am the Earl's Factor. It is my eviction notice that you ignored at your own peril. Now, if you have any possessions you care about in your hovel, get them out before it burns to the ground."

Bella arrived at that moment and swept up Helen's children, as Helen ran back in the cottage and began throwing out blankets, a cooking pot and their meal chest. The chest sprang open, spilling oats on the ground. One of the men kicked at it as he went by, spilling more grain until Rose closed up the chest and dragged it to Annie's garden.

Red and orange flames erupted from the roof as Helen appeared with the family Bible under one arm and a basket of bowls and cups in the other. The women moved her salvaged belongings to Annie's garden, which now seemed to be the safest place for everyone.

People all along the Strath were outside and those closest to the burning cottages began moving their possessions to their gardens. Very few men were home that afternoon due to the crisis with the grass burning, the scouting party, and the prisoners, as well as regular chores that took them away. The men at home were trying to get their animals out of the byres and away from the fire.

Helen's chickens, trapped in their pen at the edge of the cottage, were squawking to be free. No one dared get close enough to the fire to open the latch. "Ma," Rose said, clutching her mother, "they will be at our house soon. We have to go home. What about Margaret? Surely they will not evict a woman who has just given birth. They cannot be that cruel, can they?"

Bella nodded toward Sellar. "That is the man who arrested your brother and burned out the Ross Clan. I believe him to be capable of even murder. Janet may die from exposure as it is. But, aye, we must go home and then on to Margaret."

"Where is Da when we need him? Why is he not here to stop them?" Rose stamped her feet in frustration.

"Your Da could not stop them. We have only our bare hands. They have knives, torches, and guns and the Army. You go home and throw whatever you can out the door. I will be there soon."

Rose took off along the upper path passing the Fraser sisters, who were throwing blankets and furniture out in their garden. "'Tis the end of the world," Martha Fraser called to Rose, as she pulled her spinning wheel through the mud. Rose could not think of a possible reply so ran even faster.

Bella approached Sellar, who was standing back from Gunn home, as if admiring his work.

"Mr. Sellar," Bella said.

"Ah, the fugitive's mother, I believe," Sellar said.

"Fugitive?"

"Your boy that is supposed to be in the Dunrobin dungeon will be found quickly enough if he has made it back here already."

"Tommy has escaped?" Bella's voice lifted. "But wait. He is not here. I would know it. Do not burn all these homes to look for him, please!" She could hardly stand begging a man like Sellar, but too many lives were at stake to let her pride overrule common sense.

"Mr. Sellar, please. I assure you my son is not here. Please call off your men. There are old, sick people here and a new bairn born. They will not survive without food and shelter."

"Then you should have all packed up and moved on when my men brought your eviction notices. Half the people here are behind in the rent rolls, and his Lordship is tired of supporting a hillside of lazy fools." Sellar turned his back on Bella.

The thought that Tommy was free was tangled with the terror of their situation, along with a new fear that Tommy would suddenly walk down the path and be recaptured. She spun around to the river path, but Tommy was not there. Annie and Mary were tending the children and Janet as best they could, so Bella headed along the upper path for home.

When she walked inside, Rose was on the floor weeping. "Ma, what can we do? I feel so awful. Those poor people, and we are next. I wish I were a man. I would punch them with all my strength."

"A bit hard to punch someone while you are on the floor," Bella said as she began unloading her herb cabinet into a blanket she took from the bed. "Rose, we are going to the cave as we planned. We need to take food and blankets and an ember from our fire. Tommy has escaped from Dunrobin and will surely try to get back here."

"Tommy's free?"

"That's what Sellar said. They are looking for him. You must get up right now and drag the meal chest to the door. Get up and do it. They will be here any minute."

Rose lifted herself to her knees and wiped her face on her skirt. She got to her feet and made her way to the meal chest. "It's so heavy. I don't think I can budge it."

"Get a sack from under the table and scoop meal into it, we may have to leave the chest."

"But it is Granny's meal chest. We can't leave it." Rose grabbed the leather strap on the side and pulled as hard as she could, but the chest didn't move.

"Imagine it is one of those mean men coming. Drag him across the floor." Bella had made a trip outside and was back for the next load.

Rose planted her feet and gathered her anger and pulled again. The chest slid a bit this time but still would be too much for even both of them. She got a sack and began scooping meal as fast as she could.

"Where will we put it to stay dry?" Rose had the sack full.

"Take it to the grain dryer and put it under the canvas. Bring in the milking bucket and scoop up as many embers as you can from the fire. Carry the bucket above the dryer and leave it under the rock overhang."

"All right, Ma." Rose did as she was told, and on her way out the door with the coals, Bella threw a couple of shawls over her shoulders.

"Hide these too." Bella stepped out the door with a bundle of Alec's tools for the next trip to the dryer.

The Factor's men were closer, at the Frasers' now. Martha and her sister were standing by in shock as their roof caught flame. The Factor's men were laughing at the sisters' passive demeanor.

"What, no screeches from these hags? Too old and dried up to screech," one of them yelled. The other men guffawed at the joke and touched another torch to their byre thatch.

The sisters had not moved their milk cow to the churchyard, and the poor creature began to bellow horribly. The sound brought the sisters out of their stupor, and they ran as one to the back of the byre.

"Let the old cow burn," the Factor yelled and two of the soldiers stepped up to block the sisters' path.

The man who thought he was so funny added, "We will be hungry when this job is done and our supper will be cooked for us." His cackle was infectious and the men passed the whiskey jug around again.

In ordinary circumstances, the men would all be horrified to listen to a trapped animal bellow until it burned to death, but something about the whole scene and the Factor's attitude that these people were less than human, less than themselves, gave them permission to ignore whatever moral principles they thought they lived by.

Sellar barked his orders to the soldiers. "Drag these old hags if you have to, but get them out of my sight."

"Where shall we take them, sir?"

There were too many women and children standing around weeping for the Factor's enjoyment. "Three of you round up all these strays and march them back to the coast. Drop them off on the south bank of the river. The Earl, in his generosity, has a spot for them there."

"A spot where, sir?"

"On the stretch of moor above the river. Just get them across the ferry and then come back here."

"How will they get there? We don't have enough horses."

"They will have to walk. Now off with them, and with your questions."

Annie had left her children with Helen Gunn to bring the Fraser sisters to join them. When she heard the Factor's orders she was even more furious. "We will not just leave without the rest of our family. This land is still ours, even if you have burnt our homes."

"The Earls of Sutherland have always owned this land, and now you are trespassing. So either go quietly to the place the Earl has provided for you, or you will be arrested and put in jail."

With that dismissal, the Factor turned his back on the women and set his eyes on the next cottage. It was up the hill a bit and he noted with satisfaction that the occupants were already moving out, both there and along the Strath as far as he could see.

When they got near the cottage he realized it was that annoying MacDonan woman. He would make sure her fugitive son was not inside before they torched the thatch and he slipped out the back.

Bella had a bundle over her shoulder, the braided rug rolled up under one arm and the iron kettle by the handle. She had just cleared the doorway with Rose behind her carrying her harp with Nathaniel's shirt draped over it, when Sellar appeared.

"Well, Mrs. MacDonan, we meet again, and now I have the pleasure to inform you that you are evicted and must vacate this hovel immediately."

"This is not a hovel, Mr. Sellar. It has been the MacDonan home site for three hundred years. I regret that the Countess does not have the courage to stand at my door and tell me to leave, but sends a lackey to do her dirty work."

"I have heard too much of your prattle. Now get away from the door before you get hurt."

"Very brave of you to threaten defenseless women, while you have an army behind you."

Sellar turned to the men and waved them forward to surround the cottage.

The iron kettle was heavy in her hand, and Sellar was a few steps below her. If she dropped the rug and gave the kettle a hefty swing she could strike Sellar in the head. She remembered the knife in her hand weeks ago when she wondered if she could hurt someone who threatened her home.

She began to swing the kettle.

Chapter Twenty-one

I shall never forget. Clan MacIver

A SCENE FLASHED before her eyes: Sellar was on the ground bleeding, she was kneeling next to him trying to repair the damage she had just caused. She and Rose were taken to the jail Tommy just escaped from. She saw herself trying to justify harming another human being to a judge and then to God. She put the kettle down.

"Bah, torch the place," Sellar yelled to the men. "We'll smoke out the brat if he is here."

Bella realized Rose was standing next to her. They looked at each with tear-filled eyes. Bella looked at the kettle on the ground. Rose picked it up and they walked past the mossy ledge to the upper path.

One of the men with the torches, who had not been drinking and laughing with the others, waited at the high point of the slope behind the cottage for Bella and Rose to pass. Bella stopped in front of him, thinking he looked familiar. "Are you not Flora Bannerman's lad?"

"Aye," he whispered, eyes downcast.

"When you next see your mother, tell her you burned out the woman who helped her birth you." Bella began to follow Rose up the path, but the lad said, "Wait, he promised if we did this he would spare Strathnaver. Go to my mother. She will take you in. I am sure of it."

Bella paused, not sure what to say to the poor lad, who thought he was protecting his own home. She looked down the hill and saw the MacKay, Gunn, and Fraser families being led away by the soldiers. They were defeated. There was nothing she could do to help anyone. She turned to the lad, "I would not believe anything promised by Sellar."

Then she followed Rose along upper path, away from the destruction.

Sellar barked his orders. "Torch the thatch, damn it!" It seemed several of the men were losing their enthusiasm—too much whiskey, maybe. They would take a break after this one and get some food in their stomachs for the next round. When the MacDonan roof was fully engulfed in flames and the fugitive did not appear, he signaled the men to head back down toward the river.

Sellar decided that since all the sniveling women and crying brats had been cleared out, they would set up in the first garden to regroup. The smoke was bad and several of the men were coughing, but they would have to get used to it.

They had no sooner passed out the rations and begun to eat when a low moaning reached his ears. "Now what?" Sellar motioned to one of the soldiers to investigate. He came right back.

"Sir, it's the old woman. She's on the ground in the corner."

"What! They didn't haul her to the coast?"

"I don't think she can walk, sir."

The conversation stopped except for one man who said to the others, "She could be my granny for all that."

"Shut your mouths, all of you!" Sellar yelled, his voice just barely under control. He turned to the soldier who found her. "Is there a blanket over her?"

"Yes."

"Leave her be then, someone will fetch her when we are finished. We will just move to the next yard over." He stood and began to pace around the men. "Now listen here, men, you are doing well. Do not let yourselves feel sorry for these people. They haven't paid their rent in years and they were given a warning to move to the coast. They could have taken the old granny and she would be in a better place right now."

He looked to see if they were listening. They were all moving over to the next garden. He followed them, still talking. "We are making progress here in the Highlands, so those of you who help us clear out this glen will be more prosperous in the end. Now finish your rations and we'll move on to the next place. We can finish up this bunch and be on our way back to town before dark if you get moving quickly. No more talking with these people. Just do your job and you'll get your pay before you leave. In fact, if we get done quickly, I will pay you a bit extra."

Upper Strath

LES SPENT SEVERAL days in the Halladale valley to the north, helping MacLeod settle the homeless Rogart folks with other families. It was the longest time he had ever been away from home. It felt liberating in a way he had not expected, as no one had preconceived ideas about him. He knew he had changed and now was anxious to get home to the familiar faces he loved.

He began walking south at daybreak, and the rising sun drew up the overnight rain into a ghostly mist. By noon he reached the top of the hill where the Kildonan River flowed east to the sea.

The air was harsh with the reek of smoke, far more than could be expected even from all the household fires. Les picked up his pace until he was running down the river path toward home.

Top of Glen Loth

ALEC AND TOM smelled the smoke as they began their descent from Glen Loth. Plumes of black smoke dotted the valley. A straight path across the river would take them home quickly, but it was impossible to ford in the spring, so they followed the trail north for the log bridge upstream. Walter and John were behind them, as John had twisted his ankle and was moving slower.

"Da, we better hurry. The smell scares me."

"Go as fast as you can, Tom. I will try to keep up with you."

Late afternoon, Kildonan

AFTER SHOVING THE kettle and spinning wheel under the grain dryer cover, Bella and Rose started toward Margaret's home. The MacLennan's cottage was burning, so Mary joined them. She was alone, as Hugh had gone fishing that morning.

When they turned the corner they saw Catherine throwing furniture outside, ranting the whole time and looking about the hillside for anyone to help. She waved frantically when she spotted Bella. "Help, Bella! Help me get Margaret and the bairn outside."

"We're coming straight to you," Bella shouted back. She had a few blankets and Rose carried the braided rug. When they went inside, the bairn was screaming on the bed while Margaret was trying to put warm clothes on over her nightshirt.

"Did you rub your belly before you got up?" Bella asked.

"Aye."

"Any more heavy bleeding or feeling dizzy?"

"No."

"Good. Rose is going to bundle your boy in the rug and carry him outside. She will hold onto him no matter what. We are all going to the MacDonan cave above the stream."

Rose laid the rug next to the bairn. She lifted him gently and wrapped him snugly, singing a lullaby. He stopped crying as she sang, and when she pulled him to her chest, he sighed and shuddered with the last sobs.

Bella helped Margaret put on shoes, then slipped her arm around Margaret's waist to support her as they walked outside. Catherine had released the chickens, which were running around and flapping their clipped wings, unable to fly. A pile of their clothes and cooking utensils overspilled the garden bed several yards from the door.

When the Factor, his hired arsonists, and the soldiers arrived, they averted their faces from the scene before them. Catherine was behaving like the madwoman they had joked about earlier. She was cursing every man she could think of, from God himself, to her worthless husband and son-in-law. The Earl and Factor got special mention as she compared their private parts to those of a rat's.

The young woman, barely able to stand, was only half dressed and her clothes were on backward and bloody in places. They were struck dumb for a minute until the lass from the last cottage came out carrying a crying newborn wrapped in a rug. Something about the pitiful look of the people made them angry instead of compassionate, so they began to complain about the people still being there, when they should have already been gone.

The sight of blood threw them into a panic to get this horrid job over, so they could go home and forget about the lot of them. The first one threw his torch before Sellar had even given the order. Catherine had gone back in for her meal chest. Her thatch began to burn without even a warning.

She charged out of the cottage straight at Sellar, who was standing at the edge of the garden. Her arms were raised, her hands outstretched aiming for his neck, a wild look in her eyes. He was glancing at the next cottage to be burned and did not see her coming until the last moment. Two soldiers jumped between them and pushed Catherine back.

There was a thud as Catherine's head hit the stone wall. Margaret cried out, "Mama," as she and Bella rushed to her side.

Sellar turned on his heel and yelled, "Torch the place and on to the next," as he strode down to the cottage below. A bank of clouds had been blowing their way and a cold rain began to fall.

"Catherine, can you hear me?" Bella was kneeling next to her, checking her head for blood, while Margaret sobbed.

Rose held the baby close. "I'm going for help." She hurried away from the destruction toward the path to the cave.

"Dear God," she prayed, "help us in our time of need." If only her father or brother would appear, she would not feel so all alone.

ROBBIE AND NATHANIEL had dropped off the animals at the churchyard and made another trip to the cave with a creel basket full of peat and a bundle of clothes and blankets. As they rounded the corner back on the Strath, blowing rain hit their faces along with the stench of burning thatch.

"Damn it. We took too long," Robbie shouted, as they began to run. Robbie spotted a familiar figure ahead.

"Les!" he called. Les stopped to wait for them to catch up.

"Are they burning us out?" Les asked.

"It smells like it. There are supplies at the cave, the one we hid in last summer. Can you find it?"

"Aye."

"Meet us there," Robbie said. They took off running toward home.

Rose saw them coming toward her as she passed the Munro's cottage. She had thought to stop there, but kept going. If she been inside the cottage, they would have run right past her.

Nathaniel stood out in her vision but she could not risk the distraction of making eye contact with him, especially in front of Les. She grabbed her brother's arm. "Robbie, hurry to the Sinclairs's. Mother is there and needs help with Margaret and now Catherine, who is injured. I have the bairn and will wait at MacPherson's. Tell them that is where I will be."

"What about my mother?" Les asked.

"Your Ma is with them, but your cottage is burned. Ours too," she added, nodding to Robbie. He swallowed hard and motioned for Nathaniel to come on.

Nathaniel put his hand on Rose's shoulder. "You are a brave lass." She looked away, afraid she would cry at a compliment that was not true. She was very scared indeed.

James MacPherson welcomed Rose and made her sit by the fire to have tea as if it was just an ordinary day. He admired the baby, who was finally asleep again after being jostled awake. He told Rose about the holiday his wife had planned. James was the oldest man in the glen, and at 88 his mind was slipping a bit, although he could still tell stories from the old days. His wife Elizabeth, who was just 76, he explained again, was taking him to visit their grandson in Beauly. "Not the best weather for travel," he said, "but Elizabeth has packed us plenty of food and a wee pint to keep us warm."

Elizabeth came in from releasing their animals and burying their valuables in case they could come back one day. When she stepped inside and saw Rose, she said, "My land—what a busy place. I just saw your father and brother run past."

Rose was out the door in a flash yelling, "Da, Tommy!" as loud as she could. The bairn woke up, crying and searching for his food supply. Tim Munro heard her yell and called ahead to Alec, "Rose is here!" When Alec turned around, he saw Rose waving them back to the MacPhersons's.

Alec started to return, but Tom continued toward home.

"Tom, come back," Alec called, "maybe they have all left for the cave." Tom reluctantly turned around.

They reached Rose's side in a couple of minutes and she thrust the rug into Tom's arms. "Hold tight, 'tis a bairn inside," she said to Tom, whose astonished expression would have been amusing just yesterday.

"Da," she said with a quiet urgency as she pulled Alec aside. "Ma needs help, she's at the Sinclair's. Robbie and Nathaniel have just gone that way, but Da, the Factor is there looking for Tommy. You cannot let him go any further."

"The Factor! How many men does he have?"

"A dozen at least. They have guns and are burning every cottage in their path."

"They have burned ours?"

"Aye."

"Then I am too late."

"There was nothing anyone could do, although I wished you were there, Da. Catherine tried to attack Sellar. The soldiers pushed her away, and she hit her head on the wall. And Margaret's just had her bairn and has been bleeding, and I have her boy, who will be hungry as soon as he wakes up." Rose stopped to catch her breath.

"What should I do?" Alec found himself asking his daughter for advice, a desperate state for a man to be caught in, but he could clearly see by her expression that she had an idea.

"Make Tommy take me to the cave. I don't really know the way and need his help. There's food and peat and we are all meeting there. You go on and help Ma and pretend you don't know Tommy has escaped if the Factor asks you."

"So the Factor is here looking for Tom. Walter and John are behind us on the trail. Are they to meet Annie and Helen at the cave?"

"The soldiers took them, Da. Their homes are gone, and poor Auntie Janet almost burned up."

"It is the catastrophe I was afraid would happen."

"Aye, Da, but just give me a squeeze and then go quick."

As they hugged, Tom's patience for holding a bairn was at an end.

"Da, let's go."

Alec put his hand on Tom's shoulder. "Son, I want you to take Rose to the cave."

"No, I want to go home. I have to go home. I have to see Ma."

"Our home is with each other now, and we all have to do our part. I need you to help your sister and this new precious bairn, who will not survive out in the rain. Your Ma and Robbie will be following soon. Will you do as I ask, Tom?"

"I want to go home so bad."

"We all do, Tommy," Rose said, "but I need you right now to help me, as we are saving Margaret and Ian's bairn."

Tom looked toward home but there was no sign of Bella on the path. "All right," he said, kicking the dirt, "let's go." As soon as they left, Alec continued on alone at a fast pace.

Chapter Twenty-two

With strong hands. Clan MacKay

BELLA AND MARY rolled Catherine onto a blanket and dragged her away from the burning cottage. Margaret stayed next to her holding a shawl to keep the rain off her face. Catherine had a pulse and began to moan, a good sign she would regain consciousness, Bella thought. She was relieved a few minutes later to hear Robbie's voice yell, "Ma, Ma. Where are you?"

Bella stood up and waved. "Over here, Robbie."

"Ma, you're all right?" Robbie asked his mother. Then he and Nathaniel had their first look at a burning cottage. Robbie was on the verge of tears when Bella answered.

"I am alright, but Catherine has hit her head. Rose left with the bairn."

"We met her. She'll wait for Margaret at MacPhersons'."

"Margaret cannot walk yet. Can you figure out some way to help her get to the cave?"

Robbie and Nathaniel were looking around for some way to carry Margaret, when Neil and Ian came back from taking the cattle to a high pasture that had not been burned. They were both panicked to see their home gone and Catherine on the ground.

"There is no time to waste," Bella said. "Ian, help Robbie find a way to carry Margaret. Neil come and help with Catherine."

Margaret draped the shawl over her mother's chest as Ian helped her up.

"Margaret. Our son. Where is our son?" he asked in alarm.

"Rose has him. We need to catch up with her."

Robbie found a chair that had been thrown in the garden and strapped a loop of rope to both arms. "We'll put the rope over our shoulders, you sit in the chair. Try it, Margaret."

Margaret sat down carefully and pressed in on her belly. Robbie and Ian each took a side and lifted the chair. Nathaniel pulled the rope around each of their shoulders and tied it off behind them. "I think we can do it," Ian said. Robbie agreed.

"What about Mama?"

"You go on, dear," Neil said. "I'll stay with your mother. Go to your bairn. He will be hungry."

Nathaniel debated staying or helping with the chair. "Wait with us a few minutes. They can manage for now, but we may need to carry Catherine as well," Bella said.

Les left with his mother to hide some of their salvaged possessions among the trees so they could carry whatever Catherine needed. Neil was bending over Catherine, urging her to wake up by making all sorts of promises he would probably never keep. Hearing his voice had an effect, though, and she began to stir and tried to sit up.

Bella took charge. "Catherine, roll onto your side very carefully, and we will help you sit up. Here, grab Neil's arm. Don't pull her Neil. Hold her steady while she moves."

Neil braced himself as Catherine held his forearm and slowly came to a sitting position. "Now, are you dizzy?" Bella looked into her eyes.

Pausing only for a moment, she answered. "No, I am fine. Help me up all of you. Do you think I've just had a bairn? Let's get out of here before I do get my hands on that Factor. Gave him a scare, didn't I, Bella?"

"Aye, you scared everyone, Catherine."

"Good Lord, I forgot my grandson. Where is he? We haven't even named him yet, and my lass Margaret. Where is Margaret?"

"They are on their way to the cave," Bella said.

Catherine was on her feet, rubbing the back of her head. "I believe I have a bump, but I am as ornery as ever, Neil, so just take my arm and we will walk away from this madness."

"Whatever you say, dear." Neil had one arm and Nathaniel the other as they all made their way down the lane to the river path.

People were streaming out of the glen, most of them following the river path upstream, hoping to find shelter with kin.

Alec passed several weeping families as he hurried along the lane to the Sinclair's cottage. His only thought was to get to Bella. He met Ian and Robbie, who were carrying Margaret in a chair. He told them that Rose and the baby were just ahead on the path to the cave with Tommy, who was staying out of sight.

Alec picked up the pace, and he and Bella saw each other at the same time and ran to embrace. "Alec, give me any news of Tommy. The Factor said he is a fugitive."

"He is here, with Rose, headed for the cave."

"Tommy is here but won't come this way?"

"No, he won't come this way. We met Rose at MacPhersons'. She insisted he take her and the bairn to the cave so Sellar wouldn't see him. He was desperate to come home and see you. I had to order him to go and thankfully he did. They have both changed so much this week. Rose gave me my orders, and I obeyed my own daughter."

"Just give her a wee one to protect and she is at her strongest. Alec, how did Tommy get away? Did you help him? Is he well?"

Alec stroked Bella's hair and held her back a bit to look into her eyes.

"'Tis a long story, dearest. I will tell it all while we are walking, but he is well. I want to see what Sellar has done to our home with my own eyes. Can you stand to go back?"

"No, there is no use in going back. Just look at anyone's home and you will see ours."

They gazed back at the smoke still pouring from most of the rooftops and a few people struggling along the river path. Alec put his arm around Bella's shoulder and pulled her close to him.

"Was it possible to save anything?"

"Rose and I put blankets and food in the grain dryer, and some of your tools."

"Where was Robbie?"

"He and most of the men in the glen took the animals away to safety. The Factor's men burned all the pastures while you were gone." They stopped for a minute to look up the brae. The earth was scorched and tree trunks blackened.

"I am so sorry I was not here to help." He touched her face and wiped tears from her eyes.

"My heart is broken, Alec. I have a sinking feeling, as if we are all about to drown. I could not stop them. They put all of us out in minutes. Annie, Helen, and the children were taken toward Helmsdale while we were helping Margaret."

They turned to take the upper path. Bella stopped and turned toward the MacKay's cottage. "Oh, God, I forgot. Janet is lying in the garden back there."

"What? On the ground?" Alec tried to see the garden from that distance, but it was too far.

"They burned the cottage around her. Annie and I got her out as the roof fell in. We had to leave her to help Helen and then ourselves." Bella buried her face in her hands and wept.

"Do you think she still lives?" He put his arms around her shoulders.

"She was alive when we left her. If she is alive, poor soul, she will not last much longer." Bella's voice broke.

They looked around the Strath. Sellar and his crew were nowhere in sight.

"I have to go to her. You can come with me or not, Alec."

"I could not live with myself if I did not go with you."

They climbed to a higher path to watch for Sellar, and then dropped down behind the remains of their own home. The roof beams had fallen in and were still burning, the thatch was a reeking mess, and an assortment of their furniture was tumbled about in the garden. Bella tugged Alec forward when it seemed like he wanted to linger.

The path wound down to the Gunns's and then to the MacKays's garden. Bella rounded the garden wall and knelt next to Janet MacKay. She touched the old woman's face and called her name softly, but got no response. Bella touched her neck to feel her heartbeat, but there was none. Her eyes were closed as in sleep, so Bella pulled the blanket up higher to cover her completely.

Alec was standing behind Bella. "I will get some stones."

"So cold after a life of warmth," Bella said, as she tucked the blanket around the body and through her tears gave a blessing for a life well lived. Alec handed her the fist-sized stones and Bella placed them above her head, on her chest and at her feet in the Clan tradition.

"That is all you can do. Come on, love," Alec whispered. Bella stood, took Alec's hand and they walked away.

Retracing their steps brought them to their own home again to gather the bundles Bella had left hidden. The embers in the metal bucket were still glowing, and the sack of meal was dry. Alec sorted what was left, and packed his knapsack with food to take to the cave. The final moments were brief.

Traces of their life were visible below the torn down smoldering thatch. There was a corner of the braided rug. The rocking chair was its own small fire, as when oak finally caught, it burned a long time. Shattered window glass spilled over the remains of the table where she had rolled out bannocks on the first day of spring.

Bella's head was throbbing. Her tears were spent for now and she was left with nothing to hold but Alec's hand.

Chapter Twenty-three

This is the valor of my ancestors. Clan MacLennan

Late Afternoon, On the Path to the Cave

MARY AND LES packed as much food as possible and were at the turn-off point to hike up to the cave. Hugh had left early in the morning, telling Mary he would bring back a salmon or two and had not returned.

"I cannot bear to think about Da going home to find us gone and everything burned. What will he do?" Les asked his mother.

"I don't know. Maybe we should wait for him here."

"Well, you could stay while I make a trip to the cave with the food and come right back, but I don't want you to be alone if the Factor's men are still around."

"We had best stay together. Let's sit on the ledge out of the rain for a bit."

They settled below the huge rock that marked the path to the cave. It was north facing so they were out of sight and out of the wind.

"For all Father knows, I am still with the scouts in Halladale."

"That's true."

"Did he say where he was going for salmon?"

"The deep round pool below Cnoc Tuarie."

"That is across the river and up the stream a long way. He will have to come past us on his way home. I have an idea. We continue toward the cave, stop every so often, and I will play MacLennans' pibroch. When Da hears it he will know there is bad news and will follow the pipe sound, not just straightaway head for home."

Mary nodded and touched her son's face. "You do that, dear lad, 'tis a fitting time for a lament."

"I will start now in case he is nearby." Les put his bundles on the ground and pulled his pipes from his shoulder bag. He adjusted the pipes for the deepest sound, placed his feet in a strong stance and took a deep breath. The opening drone carried across the valley to the other side of the river and up the slope behind them.

Everyone who heard it paused, knowing that a clan piper was mourning the loss they all felt, but could hardly voice. When Les fingered the chanter and the MacLennan's Lament melody began its story, they knew it was Les MacLennan playing.

His father was coming down the side of the brae just across the river and heard the pipes. He met Walter and John on the path. "Ach, the news is bad," Hugh said. "The smoke we smell is Kildonan burning."

"Go ahead then, Hugh," John said. "I am limping badly and we're going slow. Walter, go on with Hugh, send a lad back to help me."

"We are almost at the river, I won't leave you now." Walter slipped his arm under John's shoulder and John tried to hop faster.

Hugh continued on with the large salmon he had stalked and wrestled from the deep pool.

He crossed the river and headed straight for the path up to the cave. Les carried the pipes now and stopped every few minutes to sound another drone. Mary looked down the hill at each switchback and finally saw Hugh coming up the hill with a huge fish under his arm.

"There he is," she called back to tell Les, who had already seen him and began a higher note in recognition of his father. Hugh caught up with them, put down his prize, hugged Mary, and shook Les's free hand and was told the sad news. He asked if there were other people nearby who could help John the rest of the way, but Les volunteered now that his parents were reunited. He turned the pipes over to his Da and took off downhill.

The steep, seldom-used deer trail along the falling water became heavily traveled that day. Near the bottom Les met Robbie, Rose, and Nathaniel and behind them Margaret, who was walking for a bit with Ian carrying their son. Robbie had a stack of blankets and food for the Sinclairs as they slowly made their way up the hill. Les told them about John's injury, and Robbie promised to come back and help them after this trip.

"Do you know about their families?" Robbie asked Les.

"I can barely keep track of what I have heard," Les answered, shaking his head.

"Tell them the Factor is in the glen looking for them and they should come straight to the cave, so they will not try to go home."

"All right, Robbie."

By the time Les reached the bottom, he met Bella and Alec and was able to give them a report of everyone's progress. While they were talking, James Ross came along behind them.

"Ross," Alec said. "Where have you been, man? And what are you doing here now? Didn't you see the Factor's men burning out my family?"

"No, didn't see them. Tried the coast. Too windy. Looks like Kildonan's gone, it's a shame."

"I'm off," Les said quickly, leaving Ross with Bella and Alec.

"Aye, it is over," Alec said to Ross and looked to Bella to decide what to do about him.

"We are going up to the old MacDonan cave," Bella said.

"Guess I will follow along. Not much left here."

Bella led the way up the forested slope. The trail wound back to the running water so she and Alec stopped to drink. James was struggling to keep up with them and finally stopped at the last corner to catch his breath.

"Ross left us after Tommy was arrested to go north along the coast," Bella said. "He must have followed Sellar's troops but never offered to help us."

"I have a mind to let him find his own way."

Bella looked back at Ross. He dropped to his knees and clutched his chest with a strangled "aarrgh" of pain. Bella rushed back with Alec right behind her.

"God help me, God damn it!" He gasped and writhed on the ground, trying to get up again.

Bella knelt by his side. "James, I have foxglove in my bag. Alec, help him lay down."

Alec pulled a blanket out of his bag and threw it on the path. "Here man, calm down. Bella will save you."

"Bella," Ross struggled to speak. "Tommy's not to blame. I grabbed the reins and drew my dirk at the man. Tommy didn't do anything wrong…" He managed one more breath before his head went limp.

Bella leaned back in horror.

"The bastard, the bloody coward! All this time lurking in the bushes while others suffered," Alec said and ripped the blanket out from under his head. "If he is not dead, I will kill him with his own dirk."

"He is quite dead," she said after checking his pulse. Bella stood and backed away. "I never want to see his face again, or waste one of our blankets covering him up."

Alec looked over the side of the trail. "There's a lot of brambles just over the side. He'll roll quite a ways and no one will see him unless they look carefully."

"I don't want to touch him again," Bella said, looking over the side.

"I can drag him. It will be my pleasure."

Alec pulled him by the feet to the edge of the trail and rolled the body over the side. It stopped twenty feet below among the ferns and heather, with only a foot and some gray hair visible.

"He's gone." Alec wiped his hands on the bracken.

Chapter Twenty-four

Learn to suffer. Clan Duncan

THE GLOAMING WAS upon them as Bella and Alec continued to the cave. They stopped further up the path to drink from the stream. Voices drifted up the hill behind them and then Walter's owl call reached them. Alec answered with a whistle. As darkness fell, the air took on a deeper chill, and they had to walk with one foot in front of the other, staying close to the hillside, touching trees and large rocks to stay on the path.

Alec began his own call, hoping for an answer from someone above them. Finally Tom's whistle and the glow of a fire led them up a ravine to the left and then across the now quite shallow stream. They wound around a corner and back under the hillside. Tom came down to meet them with a small lamp. "Ma, Da, you've made it." He took one of Bella's bundles under his arm and held her hand as they walked up the final steps to the cave entrance.

"Hand me the lamp, I will go back for the others," Alec said.

"Da," Robbie said as he came toward them. "I will go with you."

"Good. I doubt your mother will let go of Tom again."

A smoky fire had been kindled near the cave entrance. Ian was trying to get it blazing with peat blocks that had been carried to the cave in recent days, but it needed a little more spark. Bella unpacked her metal tin with the peat ember from their fire, spilled the contents on the ground, and pushed the cinder with her shoe until it was under the bigger chunks.

"Give it a blow now, Ian."

"Just in time. Thanks."

Mary MacLennan was making the rounds collecting cooking pots that had been salvaged and food donations for whatever supper they could manage to cook. Hugh was sharpening a branch to skewer the salmon for roasting. Rose had a half-dozen cruisie lamps going along a ledge so it was possible to walk into the cave without stumbling.

Once Bella caught her breath, blocked the image of Ross going over the side, and hugged Rose, she asked about Margaret.

"Margaret is only bleeding a little, which is a fine miracle considering what she has been through. The bairn is sucking constantly and has hardly slept since we got here. They have plenty of blankets so are as warm as possible in a dank old cave like this."

"Is there washing water yet? I must wash my hands."

"Aye, the shelf is over here." Rose led her a few steps to a spot with a lamp, where the cave floor sloped down to a wide crack.

"The water is cold, but we have a bar of soap, and I will pour for you."

Rose poured water for Bella as she tried to wash death and the day's events off her hands. She soaped up repeatedly, until Rose finally said, "I think they are clean, Ma. Here's a cloth for drying. Do you need to rest a bit?" Although Rose was ready to be comforted herself, she had never seen her mother look so tired or discouraged.

"Where can I go?"

"Over here." She took her mother's hand. "Robbie made beds for us yesterday, and there is already a blanket." Rose led her to a nook in the wall that was packed with fresh cut bracken with a wool blanket covering. Bella collapsed and fell asleep as Rose covered her with a shawl.

Rose sat next to her mother, yearning to lie down next to her to receive comfort. She looked up and saw that Tommy was standing above her.

"I wish we could all lie down and sleep, and when we woke we would be home again," Tom said as he reached out his hand for Rose and pulled her up. "The food is almost ready. Do you know if we have bowls and spoons?"

"On our shelf, just to the side here," Rose reached over for the wooden bowls nestled in a stack on a rock ledge. "I better make sure Margaret has a bowl."

"Let Ian take care of her. You come eat with me." Tom took her hand and they made their way to the fire, where Mary was spooning cooked grain. The salmon was being turned on the stick and would be ready later.

"There is plenty, dears, so eat up while it's hot. Margaret already has hers," she said with a smile to Rose.

Tom and Rose sat along the wall by the fire, eating quickly at first and then more slowly as the initial hunger pangs were satisfied. "We did not even say a blessing," Rose said.

"Not much to be thankful about."

"Well, I am thankful you are here next to me, Tommy, and we have a roof," she looked up, "of sorts, over our heads, and a warm bowl of barley to get us through the night."

"I've changed my name to Tom Gunn. Call me that if you can remember. I'm sorry, I don't mean to sound ungrateful for the food."

"All right, Tom." Rose almost giggled. "That sounds so grown up."

Tom looked at her. "I grew up in jail."

She squirmed a bit, not sure what to say to him anymore. "What did you get to eat in jail, or should I not ask?"

"Probably more than we will have the next few days." He stared in his empty bowl.

"We have to go somewhere else. We cannot live in this cave for long." Rose scraped her bowl clean. "I guess in the morning Ma and Da will decide what to do."

"I need to figure out how to prove I was not trying to steal that horse."

"But what happened? I still do not understand why a stranger would even accuse you or anyone."

Tom told her about dozing off and waking to find James Ross riling the stranger's horse. "I hardly thought of it again, it happened so fast. When we were standing in front of the Inn, Ross was behind me and muttered a curse when the Factor rode up. When the stranger, ach, Nathaniel's father, pointed at me, I turned around and Ross was gone. Next thing I knew I was on the ground."

"Ma was so upset." Rose grabbed her braid at the thought of it.

Tom turned his face away. "I hated her to see me like that."

"But what could you do?" She risked putting a hand on his shoulder.

He sat up straighter and looked at her. "Nothing then, nothing now."

"What about Nathaniel talking to his father? Maybe he would withdraw the charge if someone spoke up for you," Rose said.

"If he accused MacKay and Gunn when he had never set eyes on them before, I doubt he would say he was mistaken about me."

"I suppose you are right."

"Ah, my big sister says I am right." Tom chuckled for a moment. "The sad thing is, I wish I were wrong."

Walter arrived carrying the cruisie lamp. Robbie and Les were behind him with John's arms over their shoulders. Alec came in last. Mary and Hugh were by the fire and looked for a spot for them to sit down.

Rose and Tom quickly moved out of the way so John leaned against the wall. Alec told them just a few minutes before that the soldiers took their wives and children away, and that Walter's mother was dead. As soon as John sat down, great sobs shook his body. Walter walked to the back of the cave looking for his family despite what Alec told him.

Walter soon returned to the front of the cave. "Who saw them last?"

Alec looked around. "I think Bella did." He turned to Rose. "Where is your Ma, lass?"

"She is sleeping, but I was there with her and saw it all."

"Why were they taken away? Couldn't they have made it to the cave too?" Walter was crying himself now and wringing his hands.

"I am so sorry," Rose said. "It all happened so fast. After your homes were burned, Annie and Helen were in the garden with Aunt Janet and the children. Our cottage was next and we ran home to save what we could. It sounds horrible now, I know, but we thought they would wait for us, and we would all come here together." Rose began to cry. "We didn't have time to think about what was next," she said between sobs, "we ran from one house to the other trying to save lives."

Alec had his arm around his daughter's shoulder. "You did the best you could."

"I do not mean to blame you, Rose. I am just too upset to think right. And my dear mother, who never hurt a soul, just left to die."

Rose wiped her eyes and snuggled closer to her Da. "Annie and Ma rushed into the burning cottage to bring her out. There was just no place to put her, except in the garden. Then after our cottage was burned, we left to help Margaret and her new bairn."

Walter looked at Alec. "I think those men are not human."

Rose whispered, "Helen cursed them, and Catherine tried to strangle Sellar, but the soldiers pushed her and she hit her head. We did the best we could, but it was not enough to save everyone."

"Ach, you are too young for such burdens, and I sat in a jail cell while my home was being burned and my family taken away," Walter said.

Chapter Twenty-five

Joined to one another. Clan Cameron

HUGH BUILT UP the fire to heat water for tea and washing, while Mary scooped bowls of porridge for the men. Les took a turn with the salmon roasting, the smell drifting through the cave. Neil came to the front of the cave to ask everyone to join in a naming ceremony they wanted to have right away, not knowing if his grandson would survive the damp and cold.

The focus on the newest life among them brought everyone together in a way that nothing else could. They gathered around Margaret, Ian, and the bairn. Alec woke Bella and kept his arm around her, while Rose led the naming ceremony for the first time.

"Although we have not yarn to bind us, we are bound together now by our misfortune and loss. This brave family and their tender infant need our help, as they never have before. I would ask each person to pledge their love and protection to…" Rose looked at Ian.

"Our son, Allan Sinclair MacDonald."

"We so pledge our love and protection," the group said between tears.

"Protection is a bigger pledge than ever, but I will do my best," Tom said.

"It is all any of us can do," Catherine said, "and I appreciate whatever any of you can do to help my grandson survive."

"Yes, indeed," Neil said. "Fortunately I had a small flask of my best toasting brew with me for, well, for such an occasion. I think a wee nip would help us all warm up and have a good night's sleep." Neil had a sniff and a sip, then passed the bottle around the circle.

"Thanks, Neil," Alec said. "While we are all awake and a bit warmer, we should start making plans for the morning. I know John and Walter will be anxious to look for their families, but the Factor will be keen to recapture them, and Tommy. Tom, that is."

"I could not sit in this cave, while they could be abandoned or hurt," Walter said.

John said, "If someone could splint my foot for me, I will walk as best I can to follow them."

Bella took a deep breath and held on to Alec. "The Fraser sisters are with them, if that helps ease your mind at all."

Walter and John looked at each other. "That is some small relief," Walter said. "Do you have any idea, Bella, who took them away, and where they were going?"

Bella shook her head sadly, but Hugh said, "When we were walking back from the coast, I noticed that a camp of some sort had been set up on the hill above the ferry crossing."

"Could you tell who was there?" Alec asked.

"Now that I see what has happened to us, I would guess evicted people from other glens. There were just a few animals, no dwellings as we know them, but canvas-covered sticks that women and children huddled under. A few fires were going under the shelters, and there were some soldiers standing around. There must have been thirty or forty people."

"Maybe that's the Earl's idea of our homes by the sea," Ian said.

"When Tommy and I arrived at Helmsdale," Nathaniel said, "I heard some men talking bitterly along the shore. One of them pointed up on the bluff and then spat on the ground. I really did not want to talk with anyone, so we kept going."

"There is no use pretending we are going to stay in this cave very long," Hugh said. "How many times can we feed everyone, Mary?"

"Four or five pots of oats and a little less barley."

"Considering that it is a two-day walk to the sea, or to Strathnaver, that gives us meals for two or maybe three days. We may be able to find unspoiled grain back at home, but I don't think we can count on it," Hugh said.

Les had been listening toward the back of the group. He stepped forward. "The closest people along the Naver have taken in Rogart folks. I think it would be three days to find a house with extra room, and then we don't know when they will be evicted." He looked at his parents. "Some of us have plans to leave tomorrow."

"What is your plan, Les?" Alec asked.

Les moved forward to stand next to his father and mother. "I want to go to Canada."

There were surprised murmurs around the circle. "I will send for Ma and Da as soon as I have the money. A ship is leaving from the north in June and free passage is guaranteed to men and women who are willing to work hard."

Hugh held on to Mary as she spoke. "It breaks my heart to think of him leaving, but with our land gone there is nothing to keep him here." Hugh nodded in agreement.

"I plan to go with Les," Robbie said. He shrugged apologetically at his parents, who had no idea he was thinking of leaving the country. "They expect us to pick up a weapon and fight in a war, but we cannot own one handful of earth."

"Well put, Robbie," Walter said. "If I were young and without a family, I would join you."

Bella looked at Rose, wondering if she had secret plans. It was hard to see her clearly with those spots moving in front of her. And Tommy, would he go with his brother?

The voices were so far away she could not understand words anymore. She felt her knees buckle and gratefully slid to the floor.

Chapter Twenty-six

By faith and fortitude. Clan Shaw

ALEC REALIZED BELLA was falling and caught her head in his arms. Rose was right next to him. "Da, carry her to the bed. It's just behind us."

Mary was a step ahead moving people out of the way, and giving orders. "Hugh, get some water and a cloth. The poor dear is exhausted, and I don't remember her getting supper."

Neil brought his flask over. "There's a drop or two left, Mary. Give it to Bella as soon as she stirs. She has helped everyone all day, we had best help her now."

Tom was waiting by Rose. "What should I do?"

"See if the water has boiled, then pour some off into a bowl and add some oats. Then get someone to make tea."

"Right," Tom said, and quickly located a bowl and the sack of oats.

Mary was applying a cool cloth to her head and Bella was starting to move her hands as if trying to hold onto someone. Alec took her hands and said, "Bella, darling, we're here to take care of you. Just open your eyes, and we'll bring you food in a few minutes."

She opened her eyes to see a circle of her loved ones hovering over her. "I think I fainted."

"Yes, dear," Alec said, "you have been running all day and slept through our meal. I'm sorry I did not wake you to eat."

"I loved being asleep. I want to go to sleep some more," she sighed and closed her eyes again.

"Oh no, you don't," Mary said. "You must drink some tea and eat some oats first, then you can sleep 'til morning."

"If I must."

"Aye, you must," four voices said at once.

Once Bella was given her tea and oats and settled back to sleep, the dreams for the future continued.

Ian announced their plans. "As soon as Margaret can travel a distance, we intend to make our way to Glasgow. My family will love Margaret and our son and will provide for us until I find work. We would like Margaret's parents to join us when we are settled."

Neil shook his head, and Catherine began crying.

Ian told them that he had enough coins hidden away above the cottage to take Margaret and their bairn in a hired horse and cart to Inverness, where a MacDonald cousin would loan him money for passage on a boat south.

Walter and John agreed they would have to risk being caught by Sellar, as they had no other choice. "I don't think he ever looked at us when that man on the horse pointed at us. It would be the guards in the jail who would recognize us, and I doubt they are out walking the countryside," Walter said.

Nathaniel had stayed in the background but now stepped forward. "I am sorry to say the man on the horse is my father."

"I don't understand. Did you come to the Highlands with your father?" Walter asked.

"No, I came alone."

"He swore on our Bible that he had no knowledge of his father's actions," Robbie said.

"Even though Nathaniel is sure his father would not listen to him," Alec said, "he is probably our only hope of convincing the Sheriff to drop the charges against everyone."

Tom decided his own confession might help. "There is another chance, I did not want to accuse anyone, but when Nathaniel and I fell asleep on our way to the coast, I woke up to shouting so I ran up the hill. When I stepped onto the river path James Ross was yelling and waving his dirk, while the rider, your father," he looked at Nathaniel, "was trying to get away."

He turned back to the others. "All I did was jump out of the way before he ran me over, but I could understand after we were arrested how he might think I was in with Ross. I regret not telling anyone what happened sooner. I was confused and wanted to forget it. When you," he nodded to John, "and Walter were arrested too, I felt terrible because you were standing next to me and that's why he pointed at you."

"That was not your fault, lad," John said.

"No, if any of us are to blame, it is Ross. The man has no control of his anger," Walter said. He put his arm around Tom. "This is a sad day for us all."

"Well," Alec said, "Ross died from a bad heart on his way to the cave."

"Ross is dead?" Tom sat down and leaned against the wall. "Then it is just my word against an Englishman. Well, I would not expect Ross to admit to a crime anyway."

"He confessed to Bella and I before he died, and although the Sheriff is not likely to believe us either, at least we heard the confession, and now we all know what really happened."

As people comforted each other and talked about their future, a plan was gradually formed to send a few men back to Kildonan at daybreak to look for food that could be brought back to the cave, so those who needed rest could stay longer.

Robbie and Les said they would leave in the morning. They would continue up the stream trail, climb over the large rounded hill, the Munro, and down the Dunbeath Waters to the coast north of Helmsdale, out of Sutherland territory. They would try to find work and a place to stay until the boat left for the Red River Valley in Canada.

Nathaniel, who hoped his horse was still grazing by the church, would leave in the morning for Helmsdale with John and Walter. John could ride Scout most of the way to rest his foot. If Annie and Helen were not on the moor across the river, they would try to find them.

"I feel like we are walking into the darkness without a light. How will we ever find each other again?" John asked.

Ian joined the conversation. "My uncle, Leland MacDonald, has an Inn and kitchen in Helmsdale. He and his wife Bess will help us as much as they can. It might be a place for Kildonan people to leave messages for each other."

"That would be very helpful," Alec said and others agreed.

The rest of them were planning to stay in the cave another night, until Bella got her strength back and Margaret could travel safely.

Sleep was early for everyone that night. Rose was hoping for a chance to talk to Nathaniel before he left. He smiled at her a few times, but with fifteen people in close proximity, it was unlikely they would have a minute alone. She gave up her dream of endearments from Nathaniel and snuggled up next to her mother. The men took turns keeping the fire and stretched out wherever they could.

Mary cried herself to sleep; the thought of her only child leaving for an unknown country was unbearable. Hugh tossed and turned next to her on a flimsy collection of old blankets and wondered how they would all survive.

The bairn woke up crying a few times, which woke Catherine, who was next to her daughter. Catherine got up often to get Margaret water, or help her to the edge of the cave to relieve herself in the bushes, while Ian held his son and kept him warm.

Chapter Twenty-seven

Love endures delays. Clan Lumsden

Tuesday, 6 April. The Cave

AT SUNRISE CATHERINE started coughing, and Rose woke up to take a turn helping Margaret. When the bairn was quiet again, she walked to the front of the cave. Nathaniel was there, adding peat to the fire.

"Mornin', Nathaniel." Rose picked up the tea kettle.

"I will get water with you, if you don't mind," Nathaniel said.

"That would be lovely."

They walked up the stream a bit, as the sky was turning lighter and the path was visible. The rain had stopped but a brown fog hung over the valley below. The smell of loss was in the air.

"I don't fancy walking down into that smoke," Nathaniel said.

"Nor do I. It would be tempting to just stay in the cave if we had enough food. No one would bother us up here."

They reached a spot where a flat sloping rock was dry and sat together by the side of the stream.

"Once John and Walter find their families, I need to go and face my father."

Rose looked at him. "How will you know where he is?"

"I expect he has gone home, since looking for pasture didn't go well. From what Tommy said, he only got halfway to Kildonan before he turned back. I think he would give up after that."

"Where is home?"

"Along the border with Scotland, on the east coast, an area called

Northumbria. It took me two weeks to get to Dunrobin, but I stopped often. I could get home sooner than that."

"So I will probably not see you again." Rose felt tears coming, but tried to hold them back.

"I do want to come back here, to see all of you, but don't know when."

"I don't even know where we will live."

"Since Ian mentioned his family in Helmsdale, I was thinking that, well, if I am able to come back, that I would ask them about you."

"I could leave a letter for you, if I knew where we were going," Rose said looking at the stream and the overflowing kettle.

"A letter would be good." Nathaniel felt his nerve failing. Best say it quickly. "Rose, would you wait for me? That is, not promise yourself to anyone until I have a chance to come back and ask you to marry me?"

Joy bubbled from deep inside her. She smiled and took his hand. "Aye, Nathaniel. I would wait for you a long time."

"Rose, you are dear to my heart." Nathaniel kissed her hand and then her lips.

Her lips were soft and warm. She kissed him in return. In a moment their arms were around each other and they were kissing deeper. Before she had time to think they were reclining on the rock, arms and legs wrapped around each other.

She struggled to sit up. "Someone might come for water," Rose said. Her eyes were wide and her breath was quickened. Her emotions were too close to the surface to risk another kiss. She was afraid she would beg him to take her along. That would be running away from her family and the trouble they were in, something she could not do.

WHEN THEY RETURNED to the cave holding hands, Robbie was at the fire, poking it to life. Nathaniel put the kettle on the flat stones at the edge, smiled again at Rose, and went into the cave to pack his belongings. Rose busied herself with fixing the tea and sorting the food stores.

Robbie and Les were gathering the few possessions Robbie had brought to the cave ahead of the evictions.

"I have my fiddle, a knife, some fishing string, and a couple of hooks, my bowl, cup, and spoon. Well, that's about it, except for the clothes on my back and my blanket and cap." Robbie looked at Les.

"I have what I am wearing, my blanket, and my bagpipes."

"Not much to carry, then."

"No, not much to eat, either."

"Do you have any coins at all?"

Les fumbled in his pockets. "Aye, when I left with MacLeod I took all the coins I made from the cattle sale last year in case we ended up at the coast. It might be enough to get us a place to sleep and food for a week or so."

"If we can get to Dunbeath in two days, then to a bigger town in two more days, we would have enough to keep us alive 'til we find work."

"What sort of work do you think we could find? All we know is farming."

"Well, we can build walls, we could lay stones, thatch roofs, tend animals…"

"While we were walking toward Rogart, MacLeod was saying the flat stone in Caithness is being sent all over the world for paving streets," Les said.

"Did he say if there is a port nearby?"

"He said a town called Wick, on the northeast coast, is where the ships come in from Europe."

"Let's go to Wick then. Maybe we could load the stone." Robbie was getting enthusiastic about the possibilities.

"What did your Ma and Da say about your leaving?" Les lowered his voice as Alec was sleeping nearby.

"What could they say? They will miss me terribly, but there is nothing for any of us here now. They agree I might as well try to make a life somewhere else."

"I am afraid my Ma's heart is broken. At least yours has Rose and Tommy still near her."

"Aye, although I don't know how long Tommy will stay with them. Anyone young should just leave the Highlands. It would serve the Earl right if there was no one left to do his bidding."

The water was boiling. Robbie found the tea leaves Rose had left in a bowl, pulled the kettle off the fire with the edge of his blanket, added the leaves and set it in the dirt. Les took the cooking pot to the stream to fill with water and get some oats going.

The smell of the fire drifted back into the cave and several people stirred enough to wake up. Any hope of being back in their own beds was dashed quickly. Alec had been awake for awhile and had listened to Robbie and Les discuss their plan. He got up and walked outside, and met Les coming back with the kettle full of water.

"Need a hand, Les?"

"No, I can manage. The water is very good to drink this high up. There are two rocks just around the bend that make a great place to catch water, in your mouth or in the kettle."

"Thanks for the tip. I will give it a try."

Alec turned the corner and hiked up the stream until he saw the two rocks Les meant. It was a natural canal along the edge that poured water into a shallow pool. Despite the cold morning he put his whole head under the stream and shook the water off several times before his mind felt clear. Then he opened his mouth under the rush of water and drank until he felt he was floating. Finally satisfied with the cleansing inside and out, he made his way back to the cave.

Bella was sitting by the fire with a cup of tea in her hands. Rose was next to her, arm hooked at her mother's elbow.

"I am feeling better," Bella said.

"Good, just take your time. We are going to rest one more day before we set off."

"I do not know how I can bear to see Robbie walk away."

"Maybe you will need to close your eyes then." He put his hand on her head tenderly.

"That would be even worse, to not see him as long as possible, so I will have to keep them open."

Alec knelt next to her. "Bella, I heard him talking with Les. They have a reasonable plan to get to Wick and I think they will make it."

Bella blinked back her tears. "I didn't think to take our coin box when," she couldn't bear to say it, "when..."

Tom was dishing up their oats. "I still have coins that I could not spend in jail. I will give them to Robbie."

"Even a few shillings would help," Alec said.

"After I fill Ma's bowl, she has to eat first," he said, eyeing Bella as if she might get up to start serving others. "I will empty my purse and you decide what to do, Da."

"Thank you, Son."

Robbie sat by the fire with his family. Alec handed him half the money they had left. "Here lad, all we have left to give you is a handful of coins. Not much compared to half the land along the stream in Kildonan. I never thought all we worked for these past generations would come to so little."

Bella took Robbie's hand. "Are you sure you want to go? Maybe we will find good land again. The coast has its own beauty and you have many talents that could earn you a living."

"I don't want to leave all of you, or Kildonan, but I think I can make a life for myself somewhere else. All the evicted people will need food and shelter. One less person will make your needs lighter as it is. When I buy land in Canada I hope you will all come to live there."

Bella wiped her tears away. "I will think of you playing your fiddle and being loved by all who hear you."

Les went outside with his parents to say his goodbye in private. "Ma,

Da, ever since I walked up to the loch with MacLeod I have felt a keen desire to see more of Scotland and the world beyond. I am sorry to leave you both, very sorry. I will miss you every day. I will write to you at the MacDonalds's and will send for you as soon as I can, or come back and get you."

Mary cried while he was talking, but managed to stop herself to say good-bye. "You are the best son we could ever hope to raise. I will miss you every day, too. The world is changing and there seems no place for us here, so I am glad you have the courage to find your own place in the world."

His Da held back his tears. "You know you are a MacLennan and what your heritage as a piper means. Take good care of yourself and find a bonny lass to marry in that new land."

"I will do my best," Les said, hugging them both.

They all gathered back in the cave. Rose packed some oats for them and put a coal from the fire in a small metal tin. "You will have to soak the oats in cold water, but at least you can build a fire against the cold."

"There are probably dozens of stray goats and cows in the hills, so I think we will have fresh milk," Robbie said.

"If you can catch one," Tom said with a grin. The two brothers playfully pushed and shoved each other a bit, and sooner than anyone expected, Les and Robbie waved goodbye to the rest of the people, touched their families and were gone.

Bella and Alec stood at the edge of the stream and watched until they were out of sight. "Come dear, sit with me by the fire and let me hold you in my arms," Alec said. He took her hand and they found a spot out of the smoke. Alec leaned against the wall and Bella curled up against his chest to grieve.

Five minutes later Hugh went looking for Tom. "Lad, run after Les and Robbie. We are going with them. Mary cannot bear it. Ask them to wait and we'll be along shortly."

When Mary was ready to leave she sat for a minute by Bella and

Alec. "I am sorry to leave you my dear friends," she said, as they all began to cry. "You understand I cannot be without Les, don't you, Bella?"

Bella nodded and kissed Mary, stroked her face, and said, "Aye, my dear. I know Robbie will be better with you along, and I am relieved about that."

Mary unrolled a black and white knitted sweater. "I have been working on this all winter to surprise you, Bella. I hid it away so you would not see it and so it survived. 'Tis a wee bit big now, so pull it over your clothes, it will keep you warm."

The knobby wool was soft and the stitches even and perfect. Bella snuggled into the comfortable garment and hugged Mary. They embraced as Hugh and Alec shook hands and consoled each other as men do.

Tom ran up the hill and soon caught up to his brother and Les.

"Your parents are going with you, Les. Your Ma missed you too much in just five minutes. At least you will have someone to cook for you. I was afraid you would starve."

"Why don't you come with us, Tom? Get away from your past, come with us to a new country," Robbie said.

"It is tempting to just walk away, be Tom Gunn, no one would know who my parents are or care. But I think I have to face my problems, not run away. Maybe in a few years I will join you. Be sure to write to us at the MacDonalds's and tell us about Canada."

Mary and Hugh arrived with bundles over their shoulders. Les ran to greet them and took his Ma's basket from her. "I am happy you want to come with us. We can all start a new life together."

Tom said goodbye again and went back down the path as they continued upwards.

When he returned to the cave he found his mother waiting along the stream.

"I am back, Ma."

"I thought you might be tempted to go with a second chance." She took his hand.

"Only a little tempted. For now I am staying with you and Da." Tom squeezed her hand and then went back to the cave.

The wailing of the newborn changed Bella's focus, as Margaret and Ian, carrying wee Allan, made their way to the front of the cave. "I am so sorry Robbie is gone," Margaret said. "I already love this tiny boy so much, I cannot think about ever being parted from him." Ian nodded.

"We can only hope to see him again, in better circumstances," Bella said.

"We are going to walk up the stream a bit. Alec said there is a good place to drink. Would you come with us?" Margaret held out her hand to Bella. They walked up the hill and Bella held Allan, while Margaret and Ian washed and drank their fill. After Bella drank, they sat on a boulder together to listen to the water ripple its way to the river and the sea.

"It seems we need to follow this water and make our way to the shore," Bella said.

"Aye, we have to go, as sure as each drop cannot choose its destination," Ian said.

"It feels like this journey will be the end of our lives, but it will also be the beginning of who we will become without our land," Bella said.

"Now that I have lived here, I understand how much you are part of the land. The Strath will be a lonely place without you all, as you will be lonely for this valley wherever you go."

They all watched the water cascade over the rocks, as if its very purpose was to reach the sea.

Bella took a breath and felt some small part of herself healing. "While we have all this water Margaret, I would like to give you and Allan a bath. We can wait 'til we are just women in the cave, and make sure you are healing well."

"Thank you, Bella. I am feeling very unclean, and Allan still has dried blood on him. I am checking his navel, though and it seems to be healing well."

"I have neglected you. I am sorry."

"I am well tended. I just need your touch when you are ready. And Ma, she was coughing in the night and seems worn out as well."

"We will devote today to mending our bodies as best we can, and start out fresh tomorrow," Bella said. She stood up and reached out her hand to Margaret.

Chapter Twenty-eight

Bravely and justly. Clan Elliot

ALEC AND TOM planned to search the remains of Kildonan with the group leaving that day. They hoped to return with eggs or milk from one of the cows. Bella bandaged John's foot, deciding it wasn't broken, but badly sprained. Walter and Alec helped John hobble down the path, while Nathaniel and Tom ran ahead in hopes of finding Scout and meeting them by the river.

When they got to their old home sites, everything was a smoldering mess. The rain had effectively put out the flames, but every roof had caved in and burned the furniture and clothing. Only the stone walls remained to mark the outline of their former homes. Tom, Walter, and John had not seen the damage yet and were completely shocked.

When they got to MacKays's at the far edge of the community, there was Walter's mother's body, covered with the blanket and stones as Alec and Bella had left her.

"This is worse than I imagined. Alec, I need to bury my mother. Will you help me?"

"We will find some shovels. Even if the handles are burned, the metal will still be good," Alec said. "And the digging should be easy if we can bury her right in the garden. The churchyard is too far away."

"Aye, in the garden, where she toiled so many years. It is fitting."

So the men took turns digging as deep a hole as they could with the blades and sticks they could find. Walter gathered rocks from the house foundation and when Janet MacKay was safely in the earth, they covered her body with dirt and marked the place with rocks around the mound.

"She lived sixty-five years and had a good life, but death is never easy. God bless her soul," Walter said as he placed the last stone on the grave.

Nathaniel arrived with his horse and tied as many of their belongings as he could behind the saddle. John climbed up and the extra blankets were draped across his legs. When they were ready to go, they said goodbye to Alec and Tom and promised to meet on the bluff, where they hoped to find Annie, Helen, and their children.

Nathaniel and Tom shook hands, clasped shoulders, and renewed their vows of friendship. "We will meet again, Tom."

"I will try to stay out of trouble," Tom said.

Alec and Tom watched them until they turned the curve along the river, then started back to their cottage.

"I might look for some eggs. Or maybe I can catch a chicken for supper. We might as well eat them now."

"You might catch one, since they are used to eating out of your hand."

"What will you do?"

"I think I will look for a few things your mother buried by the grain dryer and maybe sift through the ashes for our coin box."

"Let's not stay long. It is too sad."

Tom managed to find a few eggs in the bushes, and the goat came down the brae when she saw Tom. He tied a rope around her neck and led her over to the grain dryer, where Alec was sorting through the tools Bella had hidden. Alec wanted to take them all to the coast in hopes of someday returning to his craft. He wrapped everything in a worn blanket and left the package on the garden wall. A few coins that he found scattered on the cottage floor went in his pocket.

On their way back along the path they stopped at every garden. A few leeks were left at the Munros's, so Alec pulled those for their dinner. Most of the gardens had been trampled, but there was parsley here and there so he added handfuls of the curly sprigs to the food sack.

By the time they returned to the cave with the goat in tow, it was late afternoon. Tom tethered the goat to a bush nearby and went for the food kettle to milk her. Her milk supply was low, but at least there would be enough for Margaret to drink and pour a bit on their morning oats.

Margaret had been as properly bathed as possible in a cave. Catherine had been sleeping or coughing most of the day, so Rose and Bella had done the bathing. Ian and Neil collected strips of bark and bracken to fashion carrying devices for their belongings, so their arms would be free to help Margaret and Catherine.

Bella was delighted to see the parsley and leeks. "Heat more tea water, Alec. A leek poultice for Catherine's chest and a strong cup of parsley tea may cure her. We need her well enough to travel."

She lowered her voice. "Did you look over the side for Ross when you went by?"

"No, I am just going to pretend he is somewhere else. I suggest you do the same, dear."

"Did you see anyone else along the Strath?"

"No one at all. Not even the Reverend, who should be seeing to the needs of his people."

Bella chopped half a leek, scraped the bits in a bowl, and added hot water. Neil helped move his wife closer to the fire. Catherine was hot to the touch and had chills. Bella applied to the warm poultice and covered her with as many blankets as they had.

Margaret took short walks with Ian at her side, while Rose held wee Allan by the fire. He reminded her so much of Irene's little Duncan she was cautious about becoming attached to him, as Ian and Margaret would be going far away with him soon.

Tom came to look him over, but declined holding him. "You love bairns so much, Rose, you better get one of your own."

"I have to get a husband first!"

"It seems like you have or had a couple of suitors, but with Les gone to Canada, I guess that leaves Nathaniel."

She looked up quickly. "Has Nathaniel told you he wants to marry me?"

"Not exactly, considering all the upheaval, none of us can really make plans. I know he is keen on you though, he said that much."

Rose blushed and focused on Allan again. She planned to keep her proposal from Nathaniel, if she could call it that, her own secret. If he never came back, no one would know how heartbroken she would be.

The rest of the daylight passed quickly, and just before dusk Rose took over cooking the evening meal. Tom helped her get water and washed out the bowls from morning. "Tom, do you think we should bleed the goat to add nourishment to the soup?"

"No, I want to take her with us for the milk. And I'm thinking she can carry a small bundle of our bowls and blankets if I keep her on the rope."

"Then we have leeks, parsley, and barley for supper. I wish there were nettles up."

"Oh, I found eggs in the bushes near home. I was thinking we would boil them for traveling." He looked around. "I wonder where I put them." He smiled at Rose as she looked horrified, and then pointed to the ledge behind them where the eggs were lined up in a row.

She rolled her eyes and pinched his arm. "Good work. We can cook them before we make tea tonight."

The simple supper and tea was taken at dark, and after smooring the fire that night, everyone tried to sleep.

Wednesday, 7 April, The River Path

THEY WERE OFF to an early start in the morning. Tom and Ian, being the most enthusiastic to go anywhere, made the morning meal. That ended the peat supply and they walked away from the fire after Bella scooped a few embers in the tin to carry to their next hearth.

Neil and Bella helped Catherine walk down the path and at the bottom Alec and Neil carried her on the chair they made for Margaret. Rose walked with Margaret, trading off carrying Allan or their blankets.

On their way through Kildonan in the morning, they stopped at the MacDonan homesite for the last time. The soil from the garden was loose from the turning Bella had done days ago. She knelt on the ground by the rosemary bush and picked up the dark rich soil and let it sift through her fingers. The potatoes had never been planted, and it was unlikely she would have a garden like this again. She scooped up one handful of earth.

She considered carrying it the whole way and then remembered her metal herb box; maybe it had survived the fire. When she stood up to look for it, there was Alec with a collection of tools, including her herb tin. She pinched off a sprig of rosemary to carry the scent of Kildonan, and slid the soil on top.

"Are you ready to go dear?" Alec was close to tears.

"Aye, take my hand." She led the way down the path to the river.

Bella turned for one last look before the trees blocked her view. Perhaps some day she would remember the happiness she had known here. But not today.

It was slow going, but by sundown they reached the creek where Tom and Nathaniel slept just the week before. Everyone was tired, but Margaret seemed to gain strength from moving, while Catherine could hardly walk near the end. She begged to be left by the side of the road to sleep, but Neil coaxed her with the promises of rest around the next bend After dividing the boiled eggs and squeezing a bit of milk from the goat for Margaret, they rolled up in blankets next to each other, shivering at first and then finally giving up to exhaustion.

Thursday, 8 April, Helmsdale

NEXT MORNING THEY agreed that Tom should stay away from town until they were sure Sellar was not there. Catherine refused to move as it brought on coughing, so she stayed at the spot by the creek, with Neil and Tom to care for her. The rest of them walked into Helmsdale to the MacDonalds's in hopes that at least Margaret and her little one could stay indoors for a few days.

People in Helmsdale were traveling in every direction. Some led ponies laden with household supplies and others walked in an empty handed daze. Food was bought or begged as soon as it was cooked, and armed soldiers were stationed along the main street. The soldiers did not seem to be looking for anyone in particular, but were walking back and forth with their guns ready to quell a disturbance.

Bella and Rose went into the Inn with Ian, Margaret, and the bairn. Alec waited outside to watch for Walter and John.

Bess MacDonald was taking orders and directing her staff to serve food to the various people sitting inside, as well as some waiting outside at tables overlooking the harbor.

"What will you have?" She looked up and saw Ian. "Oh my stars, 'tis my dear boy Ian." She looked around at the bedraggled group standing behind him. "Ach, lad, come in our own rooms." She called to one the staff to take her place at the counter. When they all got into the private room, she shut the door.

"My, my, have you all been evicted from the Strath?"

"Yes, Auntie, even my wee bairn and wife Margaret." He helped Margaret remove her shawl and lifted the boy to show her.

"He is so tiny. When was he born?"

They looked at each other. "Today is his fifth day," Margaret said.

"Have you walked all the way here?"

They nodded and Ian spoke for them, telling of their last few days and the long trek to Helmsdale. "We want to buy some food, Auntie, enough for eight people right now. Five of us are here and three more, including Margaret's parents, are waiting for us along the river. I have the money."

"I will do the best I can for you all. We have been warned by the soldiers not to harbor anyone who has been evicted, so I will just forget you told me. You all sit in here and get warm and dry. Go in our kitchen, Ian dear, and get bread and cheese from the basket. Put the tea kettle on, and I will be back as soon as I can."

"Thank you, Auntie. We have one more person outside. If you don't mind, I will go call to him."

"Show me who it is and I will fetch him. You had all best stay out of sight for now."

When Alec was safely inside, they all relaxed a little more. Ian and Rose washed their hands in the sink, which had running water, and then cut the bread and cheese and passed around the basket for everyone to take a piece. The bread was soft and the cheese sharp, making it the best food they had eaten in days. Everyone had a second helping when Ian insisted. There was a fireplace with a chimney and a bright peat fire on one side of the room. Chairs with cushions lined the wall, one big enough for three people to sit on.

Margaret fed Allan, who had been squirming, but promptly fell asleep with a full belly. "If I get more comfortable, I will never go back outside," Margaret said.

"Ian," Bella said, "if your Aunt Bess will let you and Margaret stay here, I think you should. No one has seen either of you at Golspie or Kildonan, so if you had fresh clothes, there is no reason to think you were evicted."

"What about Ma and Da? I already feel bad that they are sitting out in the bushes," Margaret said.

"We cannot risk her coming to town," Bella said. "Sellar will never forget your mother. The rest of us will take food to them, then Alec and I will go up on the bluff to look for the Gunns and MacKays. Maybe your aunt knows what is going on up there, or where they expect people to go, if she has time to talk to us."

"Maybe if I had clean clothes, I could help cook or wash dishes,"

Rose said.

"I will ask her everything when she comes back," Ian said.

When Mrs. MacDonald returned, her husband Leland was behind her. She brought another loaf of bread, and he carried a large pot of soup. He put the soup on the stove and then gave Ian a warm welcome.

"It's good to see you, lad, for living so close to us you have been scarce the past few months."

"Aye, well, the weather's been nasty for walking. We would all be home by the fire now, if we had one."

"Rotten business, these evictions. Hundreds of people with nowhere to go, and that Sellar, riding around like he owns the place."

"Uncle, come greet my wife Margaret and meet my son, Allan Sinclair MacDonald." Ian introduced his uncle to everyone.

"You all must be starving while we stand here. Come get some soup," Bess said.

Rose was in the kitchen quickly and asked, "Could I help serve the soup?"

"Yes, dear, that would be lovely."

When everyone's situation had been explained and possible options explored, it was decided that Rose, Ian, Margaret and the bairn would stay in an extra room in the house. Ian and Rose would help in the kitchen in exchange for food, a place to sleep, and one meal a day for their families from Kildonan. They would be willing to receive messages at the Inn, but insisted everyone coming and going call themselves 'MacDonald from Beauly' if anyone asked.

"We need to get back to work now, and I want to see about some clean clothes for you young folks. If there are hungry people out in the bushes, we better find them something to eat."

She packed a sack of bread, cheese, oatcakes and baked potatoes for Alec and Bella to take with them. At the last minute, Rose wondered if she should be parted from her mother, but Bella assured her that staying there to earn food would be the most helpful thing she could do.

***

WHEN BELLA AND Alec returned to the creek with the food, Tom had been ready to set out to look for them. Alec told them all that had happened, while Bella passed food to Tom and Neil, who was sitting next to a sleeping Catherine.

"Ah, thank you, Bella. She was coughing so bad, but is now finally resting. I will save her some food." Neil took a piece of bread from the basket. "It's been a long time since we had flour to make bread."

"Aye, and wait 'til you try the cheese," Bella said looking over at Catherine, who was lying very still. "Alec and I are going across the river now and up on the bluff to look for Helen and Annie. When Catherine wakes up, be sure to tell her that Margaret is staying with the MacDonalds and your grandson is well."

"I will tell her. She will be pleased."

"I will be looking for a safe place for her to get out of the weather."

Alec and Bella took their leave and stood waiting with dozens of others at the ferry dock. It was tempting to talk with the other people to find out what they knew, but they both decided it was too risky to say they were MacDonans.

Chapter Twenty-nine

For liberty we must hope. Clan Wallace

The Moor

WHEN THEY GOT across the river and walked up the path to the bluff, a strong wind was blowing. Blankets were flapping and children stationed at the sticks were trying to keep the wind from taking their new home away. An army canvas tent was securely staked down and soldiers guarded the entrance. A line of people waited for a turn to go inside.

They took a place at the end, and then dared to ask the man in front of them what the line was about. "If your rent was paid up with the Factor, and you haven't complained about being evicted, then you will be allowed to pay rent for a spot of rock on this bluff."

Alec and Bella stood back, while the next person in line took their place.

He put his arm around Bella as they stepped away from the tent. "What shall we do?" Alec looked around for a familiar face.

"Let's walk around and look for Annie and Helen." Bella said.

The broad moor was roped off into sections. It appeared some people had already been assigned a place and had chosen a spot to start a fire and tie their canvas roof. A section near the army tent was full of women and children, the families of the men waiting in line they guessed. They were walking down the mud path when young Jamie ran for Bella, arms outstretched. "Auntie, Auntie, we are here. Come this way!"

Bella hugged him and looked back at Alec with tears in her eyes. Alec took her other hand and the three continued along until a few more children were loudly announcing their arrival. Annie and Helen met them at the "entrance" to their new home site.

Two soldiers were directing the older lads to lay rocks along the borders of the new crofts, as they called the barren ground, where the people were expected to build shelter out of nothing and grow their grain on the windblown cliff.

"We have been so worried," Annie said. "Is there news of Walter and John?"

"Aye. We were together 'til two days ago, when they started for the coast," Alec said.

"Thank God. They are free, and well?" Helen asked.

"John hurt his foot and is limping, but can walk with help. We were hoping they had found you, but they may be afraid to come this close to the soldiers."

"You found us, though, so I am sure they will," Annie said. The children ate the food as quickly as Bella could hand them a potato or oatcake. The fire was just wet scraps of tree branches that were doing little more than smoking, but it defined the center of their lives now, the hearth where people gathered.

They sat on the wet, hard ground and exchanged news of Janet's death and burial, the trek to the cave, and their present situation. The Gunns were given this spot on the bluff. Once Annie and Helen found out that the Fraser sisters were being sent to a worse spot further north, called Badbea, Annie said her name was Gunn also. For now it kept Helen and Annie together.

"Have the soldiers asked you about the MacDonans or where your husbands might be?" Alec asked.

"No. There are so many people here and all along the coast, that they only try to sign people up to work. There's the herring fishing and chopping, kelp gathering, or the army. If none of those seem lovely, you can emigrate. If you won't leave the country, then you must keep going, to wander without food or shelter," Annie said.

"What did you say you would do?" Bella couldn't imagine how they could decide, or what she would do.

"The herring, we both agreed to that," Annie said. "It's close by, on the other side of the bridge." She pointed back to Helmsdale.

Helen poked the fire with a stick. "Once they had our names and we agreed to cut up the fish, they sent us over here and said the Earl has arranged a daily serving of barley for the workers. So we may be weak, wet, and sick, but we probably won't starve to death."

Bella reached out for Helen's hand. "Is there any hope of shelter? Catherine is coughing badly."

"They say that before nightfall a cart of branches and peat will be brought and dumped at the edge there." Annie pointed to a spot of bare ground across the way, where dozens of people seem to be waiting. "I plan to run over when the cart arrives and Helen will stay with the children."

"Alec," Helen said, "would you go and bring the Sinclairs and Tommy before it gets dark? Tommy will look like every other man here, and maybe you will see Walter and John if you are across the river. You can all sleep here tonight and decide whether to give your name tomorrow. If we can get some branches, we'll put Catherine under them with a blanket roof. The children can manage another night outside."

"I will stay and help Annie," Bella said to Alec. "We will have a shelter ready when you return. Better count your steps back to the tent in case it's dark. Whistle when you get close."

"I would rather you come with me. I worry about losing you," Alec said.

"Just hurry back, I'll be here. I think Tommy will be safe, don't you?"

"Aye. I haven't seen anyone yet who was in Golspie when we were." Alec reluctantly took his leave and then counted two hundred and fifty steps before he reached the tent and the line, which was now three times as long. He saw a few people he knew, but no one from their small section of the Strath.

WHEN ALEC GOT back to the waiting place, Neil had his head buried in his arms and was weeping. "Neil!" Alec shook his shoulder. "What's wrong?"

Neil looked up through his sobs and tried to speak, but could not, he just shook his head. Alec looked around, but no one else was there, and the place where Catherine had been sleeping was empty. Alec owl-whistled for Tom and heard an answer just up the hill.

Alec started in that direction and Tom met him partway. His eyes were red too, and his hands were covered with dirt. "What happened?" Alec grabbed his shoulder to steady him.

"Uncle Neil tried to wake Catherine to give her some food, but he couldn't. He talked to her and shook her, and tried to sit her up, but Da, she was dead." Tom held onto Alec's arm. "It was awful, the saddest thing I have ever seen. Walter and John found us then. We could all see she was dead, but Uncle Neil couldn't, he wouldn't. He tried to feed her and talk to her, and put her hand on his face, but she was gone."

"Oh, Tommy. I am sorry, lad."

He began to sob in between words. "Walter finally pulled him away, and John wrapped her body in her blanket." He wiped his eyes on his sleeve. "Nathaniel was here too. The four of us dragged her up the hill and dug as much as we could with our hands, and then covered her with tree branches."

Alec held him while he cried. Walter, John, and Nathaniel joined them. "I think things cannot get any worse, and then they do," Walter said. "I am afraid to ask if you found our families."

Tom stopped crying and waited for the answer.

"They are all together, up on the bluff. Helen has been assigned a spot of ground by the Earl's plan. We think it would be safe for the three of you to go there. I warn you, there is nothing there but the women and children we love. No shelter, no food, no nice stack of dry peat. All we can do is sleep on the ground and start over again tomorrow."

"Let's go," John said. "Someone take Neil's arm or he won't leave."

Dusk, The Moor

AFTER CROSSING THE ferry with the group, Nathaniel stopped where the sea path and moor path met. The temptation to go back and see Rose was strong, but then he might never leave. "It is time for me to go home. There is no use putting it off any longer."

Alec responded first. "We would all go home with you, if we could, so cannot ask you to stay. You have done all you can for us and we appreciate it."

Walter nodded. "Aye, lad. When Jamie grows up he will remember you very well."

"I hope to convince my father to retract his accusations, but can hardly hope he will. And I plan to write an opinion to the Edinburgh news about the brutality I have seen. Maybe they will print it."

"Good luck to you, lad," John said.

Tom waved one last time.

"Please give my regards to your families." He mounted Scout and turned south toward home.

They watched him ride away, and then slowly walked up the hill. Alec and Tom took Neil's arms and Walter took John's as they struggled along. As they hoped, no one paid the slightest attention to them as they walked down the path toward the Gunns's section. Annie and Bella had been able to gather boughs and sticks, and after the reunion with the family, and the terrible news of Catherine's death, they all worked together to erect a buffer from the worst of the wind and rain.

Two people stayed awake at a time to hold the shelter together and try to keep the fire going. Before she went to sleep, Bella opened her fire tin. The ember she brought from the cave was fading. She spilled it out under a branch and blew on it until it began glow. She stared at it as she had her home fire, looking for a sign of their future until sleep overtook her.

Friday, 9 April. The Moor

THE NEXT MORNING brought dry weather for a change, and the sun shone through a haze of smoke blown this way and that. The air and ground were still damp and the early morning brought a chill that caused everyone to hold the children close for shared warmth.

The goat had survived the journey, and being tethered on some fresh grass on the edge of the moor increased her milk supply enough to give the all the children sips of warm milk to start the day.

Bella missed Mary and her steadfast quiet presence. She grieved Robbie's absence keenly, but took the smallest satisfaction in knowing the four of them were together on their way to a new life.

Neil walked around in circles, unable to talk to anyone. The spot given to the Gunns was large enough that he walked on the edges, where no one would bother him. The children started running after him, but Walter called them back and tried to explain that Uncle Neil's heart was broken, and they should give him peace.

Alec went back to the tent with a set of questions that he hoped would be answered without him being arrested. Tom and Walter went to the edge of the moor where the branches were being collected and became part of the crew to drag supplies back to those waiting. They were loaned a small saw, so were able to cut birch saplings for a roof frame.

They continued cutting until they had enough branches to frame a shelter big enough for five or six people to stretch out side by side. That way half of them could sleep at one time, or maybe everyone could sit down.

When they returned with the birch to "Castle Gunn," as they were calling their spot of dirt, Alec had come back from the tent. The MacDonans were on a list the Countess had prepared of those with special treatment. They were to have a place to build their new home overlooking the river. The Countess had arranged a delivery of stones, thatching materials, and a stack of dry peat.

"It's to pay you for raising me, isn't it?" Tom asked.

"Aye, but I am not inclined to turn it down on principle," Alec said. "We can put up a shelter quickly and get everyone out of the rain. Saving lives is more important than pride to me now."

"I still want to see her one day, to tell her how she has hurt all of us." Tom stood taller.

"I hope to be there when you get your chance," Bella said.

"Let's get busy, we have a shelter to build. Da, grab one end of this branch and we'll line them up for the roof."

"Whatever you say, Son."

Chapter Thirty

Endure bravely. Clan Lindsay

Mid-May, Helmsdale

ROSE LEFT THE kitchen at MacDonald's Inn for her daily walk to the sea. The weather was sunny and warm enough to leave her shawl behind. Life slowly improved for her family since their arrival a month ago. She saw her mother almost every day when Bella came to get the kettle of food to take back to the moor. If it was a quiet time in the kitchen, Rose would go with her and visit her extended family.

Ian and Margaret had gone to Inverness with their bairn. At first Rose cried herself to sleep each night. She knew she was crying for many losses, but it was easier to pretend she missed the wee baby.

When she had extra bread or biscuits she would take them to Annie and Helen, who were working in the herring shed a short walk along the harbor. Tom, Alec, Walter, and John went out on the herring boat every night. The Earl owned the boat, the shed, the moor, and them. Now it was required that any couple wishing to marry must go the Earl's judicial clerk for permission. Any man not working on the herring catch or the road building could not marry.

Bella had agreed to care for the small children nearby so their parents could work at one of the Earl's "improvements" as he called their new lives. Her status as the community healer and midwife allowed her to bypass the job assignments. Alec and Tom earned enough money when the herring catch was good to pay their rent and save for the winter.

The central fire was moved to the spot the MacDonans had been assigned and the beginning of a stone wall had been built with everyone taking turns. The wall was high enough to block the sea wind, so a larger, more permanent shelter was created with branches and thatch where everyone took cover on rainy days and nights.

It was lonely for Bella without Robbie and Mary nearby. The month had gone by without news and then a letter arrived at the MacDonald's Inn. Rose carried the letter, unopened, to the moor with her that afternoon. She knew her mother would want to be the first to read it.

Bella studied the envelope. It was Mary's hand, postmarked from Wick along the coast to the north. She wrote that Hugh, Les, and Robbie were laboring in the shipyard to earn passage to Canada. It turned out the passage and land in Canada was in exchange for three years' work when they arrived. They were saving their wages to bring their own food and all the supplies they would need to survive in the Red River Valley.

She finished reading the letter to Rose. "If any of you want to come with us, we would love to have more of our family and loved ones. We have decided our new town in Canada will be called Kildonan. Warmest regards, Mary MacLennan"

"It does sound exciting," Rose said. "Are you and Da thinking of it?"

"No. Only if you and Tom decide to go." They were sitting alone by the fire.

"Ma, I have never really told you, Nathaniel asked me to wait for him." She couldn't keep this secret from her mother any longer. "I love him and could not bear to leave in case he comes back."

Bella took her hand. "I have a high regard for the young man. I hope he can return, but you know it may be very difficult for him."

"I know. I want to take the chance," Rose said as she kissed her mother good-bye and headed back to work.

THE AREA ON the moor had filled in quickly with evicted people from every direction. The Countess was still in London and no one expected her to show her face in Helmsdale. A few newspapers began reporting about the cruel removals in the Highlands, but there seemed to be no way to get their land back.

A new pastor had arrived on Sunday. He traveled along the coast telling the evicted people that God had punished them for their sins. They should learn from their lesson and give up any un-Christian behavior so they had a chance for redemption. Everyone was too tired at the end of the day to even think about sin, much less do anything.

The warmer weather and longer days saved them from desperation and starvation. Children were assigned by their parents to dig in the dirt with sticks and remove as many rocks as they could from a small patch where a grain plot was started. Bella noticed a few pregnant women and began to collect wild herbs and make birthing supplies. She smiled when she saw them, and began to wonder if there were any other midwives nearby.

Hundreds of sheep were being unloaded from ships at Helmsdale and herded up the Kildonan valley. Men they had never seen before walked behind them while dogs nipped at the sheep's heels to keep them going. It was a never ending sea of bleating animals that stopped as often as allowed to eat anything growing in their path.

When the herring boat Alec worked on arrived in port early one morning, he followed the sheep along the river, curious about how far they were going. One of the shepherds yelled at him to go back and sent a dog to chase him.

"Who gives the order that I cannot walk along the river?" Alec yelled back above the barking.

"Mr. Sellar owns all this land now and no one can enter." The man whistled his dog back and continued along the river path.

Chapter Thirty-one

I love. Clan Scott

Mid-June. Helmsdale

ROSE WAS PLEASED the sea was bright blue and calm today. The shore was covered with round rocks of many colors. She had been memorizing color. The color of the sea changed every day, from gray with white swirls when a storm was coming, to the pure blue, like Nathaniel's eyes, of today.

She turned on the path when she heard someone call her name. Rose hoped it wasn't Mr. MacDonald needing her to come back to work already. No, it was a tall, red-headed fellow running toward her.

Her heart leapt in her chest. Was it really him?

His arms were open and a huge smile lit up his face.

"Nathaniel!" Her vision narrowed, the crash of the waves faded, and all she could see was his body moving toward her. Then, in a flash, she was in his arms. He held her and twirled her around and around. She held on as tight as she could and decided to never let go. Finally he stopped and when they both were done laughing and looking at each other, Rose kissed him the way she had seen Matthew kiss Irene in that other lifetime.

They kissed until she realized they probably had an audience of all the women at the fish tables. She broke away to a background chorus of hoots and cheers. Blushing, she took Nathaniel's hand and escaped in the opposite direction.

She looked around to see who had noticed them, but the women had gone back to work. She glanced at the sun and figured she had ten minutes left before Mr. MacDonald would come looking for her.

"I am very happy to see you," she said and then giggled. "I guess you knew that."

"You are as glad as I hoped you would be," Nathaniel said. "It's been two months and I thought your family might have left the area, but I would have found you somehow."

"I'm living at the Inn, and the rest are across the river on the bluff." They were walking along the shore in the sand.

"Mrs. MacDonald told me where to find you."

"So they know you are here. We should turn back soon, but tell me what's happened since you left."

"May I just say that I think about you all the time and will tell you about my travels when we are with your family. I have good news for Tommy."

"I am a patient lass." Rose stopped walking and reached her arms around his waist. "But I am so relieved you returned."

"By the time I knew enough to send a letter I was ready to come north, so decided to surprise you. I'm sorry if I worried you." He stroked her hair and kissed the top of her head and they continued their stroll. The shoreline ended abruptly at the edge of a cliff, forcing them to turn back.

When they arrived back to the kitchen, her mother was there to pick up the daily food kettle. Bella noticed how Rose was glowing and didn't think it was the fresh air.

"Ma, Nathaniel's come back." Rose let go of his hand.

"It's good to see you again," Bella said with a smile.

"I'm sorry you have not heard from me, but I have good news," he said to Bella. "Where is Tom? I want to tell him first, if you don't mind."

"He is asleep now. He goes out on the herring boats at night and sleeps during the day. Come up to our hearth with me now or," she glanced at Rose who was still smiling at Nathaniel, "after Rose is done working."

"I will wait by the sea for Rose," he said.

IN THE LATE afternoon when Tom and Alec were up and about, Nathaniel and Rose arrived arm-in-arm.

"*Failte*. Welcome, Nathaniel. It is good to see you again," Tom said, shaking his hand.

"I have missed you all," Nathaniel said.

"Ma has just made tea. Come try out one of our new chairs." Tom led him to a spot along the edge of their croft where the land sloped gently down to the river. They were well inland from the harbor so the view was more reminiscent of their old valley.

Alec arrived from a break in his project, the next section of wall for their cottage. Bella brought a new tea pot and an assortment of tin cups. They all sat on the ground as Bella poured the tea.

"It is good to see you again, lad," Alec said. "I thought you might have come to your senses and gone back to Edinburgh." Alec had doubted he would ever be back. It was hard on Tom and Rose, as they were both confident he would return, but two months had gone by with no sign of him.

"After I left here I went straight to Dunrobin and found my father was still there. He was as angry to see me as I expected. I admit it was difficult to take the insults he hurled at me, but I thought of you in the dungeon, Tom, and took it. By the time he ran out of bad things to say he softened a bit. He was staying at the Golspie Inn and insisted we have supper there together."

"Mr. Davidson would remember you," Tom said.

"Aye. I had to start telling my father where I had been. He was surprised and shocked that I left school so abruptly, but after a few ales admitted he might have done the same thing when he was young. Tom, I told him about Ross grabbing the horses reins and you, hearing the commotion, were just running up to see if it was my horse being stolen."

"Did he believe you?"

"Not at first. When I told him I was asleep just a short distance away and you could have taken Scout and left me there, he had to think about it again."

Nathaniel drank his tea and Bella refilled his cup. Rose was sitting close to her mother and grabbed her hand when she put the pot down.

"My father and I never talk to each other," Nathaniel said to Alec. "When I noticed how much you talk with your children, well, I decided to just keep talking to my father and maybe he would eventually hear me."

They all smiled, trying not to laugh at the image of Nathaniel talking for days, waiting for his father to reply.

"When I said I had fallen in love with a Highland lass named Rose MacDonan," he looked at Rose, who gave him a big smile of encouragement, "he had a lot to say to me."

"I hope that's not the 'good news' you came back to tell us," Tom said.

"Sorry, Tommy. Tom. There is so much to tell. Put simply, I made a deal with my father. We went back to Edinburgh together. I apologized to the headmaster for leaving school without permission and begged my mother's forgiveness, as she thought I must have been murdered to disappear so abruptly."

"Your poor mother," Bella said.

"She was so happy to see me alive that she forgave me, but they both made me promise to tell them when I plan to do something so foolish in the future."

"Foolish action is usually not planned," Alec said.

"Da, please. Let him get to the point," Tom said. Alec waved his agreement and refilled his cup.

"Well, the point is, my father signed a statement in front of a judge in Edinburgh swearing that he was mistaken in accusing Tommy MacDonan, Walter MacKay, and John Gunn for the assault. He admitted that only one unknown man grabbed his horse and threatened him. The judge scolded him, but he kept to the statement, and said he deeply regretted any accusations against innocent men."

Alec put his hand over his mouth to keep from commenting.

Tom said, "Will the Factor believe him?"

"I brought two copies of the judge's paper. I gave one to Commissioner Young yesterday, and I have one for you, Tom." He reached in his pocket and took out a folded scroll with an official wax seal and handed it to Tom.

"Nathaniel. My deepest thanks, but what did Young say?" Tom asked.

"He will tell the Sheriff to drop all the charges. He confided in me that Sellar has been accused of unusual cruelty during the evictions by the London newspapers and the Countess is embarrassed and displeased."

"As well she should be," Alec said.

Tom opened the scroll. "I am a free man. A burden has been lifted from my heart."

"And mine," said Bella.

Rose was more effusive. "You are our hero, again." She jumped up and hugged Nathaniel's shoulders. "Walter and John will be so pleased too. But," she paused, feeling embarrassed to ask, "what did he say about you being in love with me?"

Nathaniel turned toward Alec. "I love your daughter and your whole family. I hope for your permission to marry Rose."

Alec looked at Bella, who nodded. Alec smiled. "As long as you aren't planning to sail off to Canada with her, and of course that Rose agrees."

"Yes, Da. I want to marry Nathaniel." Now that they were pledged in front of her family they could be more physically close to each other. She squeezed in to sit between him and Tom and then turned to Nathaniel.

"What did your father say about me?"

"He was shocked at first, but my mother was very pleased and trusts my heart. Part of my agreement with my father, for him to humiliate himself before the judge, is that I would finish two more years at the University." He put his arm around Rose and she snuggled next to him. "I am done with school for the summer and would like to stay here. I can help build the cottage or go out on a boat, whatever you want me to do."

Tom had enough romance. "I am taking the judge's paper over to MacKay. Welcome to the family, Nathaniel, I need another brother."

"Our home is your home, Nathaniel," Bella said, "however simple it may be. You were part of our family the day we met." The herb tin with the soil from Kildonan was by her side. "I believe it is time for a ceremony to witness your pledge."

Bella stood up and took her daughter's hand. "Come over to this beautiful spot along the river bank." She motioned Alec and Nathaniel to follow. They all walked along the edge of the croft to the place where Bella planned to have a garden.

She put the tin on the ground and opened it.

"Rose and Nathaniel, join your hearts together this day, in this new place where we live. Reach into the bucket and each take one handful of earth." They both picked up warm loamy soil at the bottom.

"This soil and our memories is all we have left of the Kildonan Valley. It is fitting that you begin your life together by adding a bit of our beloved land to our new garden." As they spread the soil on the earth, Bella sang a blessing:

> "With tender hearts and loving care,
> We touch the Earth as she lays bare.
> We promise now with hope held high,
> To love with courage 'til we die."

Author's Note

WHEN MY DAUGHTER, LiAnna, and I drove along the northeast coast of Scotland in 2003, we passed the town of Helmsdale. I only glanced up the river as we went by, late to meet my cousin further north. The idea of writing a novel about Scotland was taking shape and back home while looking at a map, I remembered the river at Helmsdale that flowed into the North Sea and chose that glen as the setting for the story.

By chance in 2005 I read John Prebble's non-fiction *The Highland Clearances*. I was blown away to discover the valley I chose for the setting had been called the Glen of the Gunns and my distant cousins were forcibly and brutally evicted from their homes in 1813. I felt compelled to tell about the clearances and invented the MacDonan Clan with Bella, Alec, and their family at the heart of the story.

Music was a large part of my daily inspiration. Steve MacDonald's "Highland Farewell" and Dougie MacLean's "Garden Valley" tell about the plight of those forced to leave Scotland. Robert Burns's (1759-1796) poem "Parcel o Rouges" sung by Jim Malcolm kept me angry at the villains. I listened to Malcolm's album "Resonance," containing Ed Pickford's "The Worker's Song" hundreds of times. One of the verses ends "we're expected to die for the land of our birth, and we've never owned one handful of earth." That seemed to speak to the tragedy of a Clan living on the same land for 300 years and being forcibly evicted with no recourse whatsoever. And a perfect title for my novel.

To be as historically accurate as possible, I chose to have people in Kildonan speak The Gaelic. Aye, *The* Gaelic. Any attempt I have made to speak The Gaelic by looking at the words or repeating a phrase has been met with utter failure. I tried to give the flavor of the language by using a few Gaelic words followed by immediate translation. The characters speak in English with a few Scottish phrases that can be easily understood by the reader.

The birth scenes are adapted from my experiences as a home birth midwife in Oregon from 1975 to 1985. The women characters are completely fictional, but the breech birth and postpartum hemorrhage really happened and were treated successfully as described in the book.

As much as possible I tried to depict the realistic result of the clearances. There was a ship that took many young people to the Red River Valley in Canada. Some people went south to larger cities like Glasgow to work in shipyards and factories. The kinship system helped the first wave of homeless people, but within several decades most of the remaining families were forced to move also.

The windswept bluff outside Helmsdale became a village of crofters, the new word invented to describe people who could rent enough land from the Earl to grow some food, but not enough to raise grain or pasture animals. People were then forced to work in fishing and construction industries owned by the Earl of Sutherland.

Some people died sooner than expected or under circumstances directly related to their eviction. In 1816 Patrick Sellar, a real person who was the Factor/Manager for the Earl of Sutherland, was brought to trial on a charge of culpable murder in the death of Margaret Mackay, a bedridden woman whose cottage was set fire with her inside. Sellar was found not guilty by a jury of his peers. Peers in his case meant landowning gentlemen, merchants, and factors like himself. After the removals, as he called them, of the people in Strathnaver, Sellar leased the land himself by cheating on the bid and brought the Cheviot sheep to the northern valley. Eventually word of the cruelty reached London, Sellar resigned and the Countess tried to defend the clearances as being good for the people.

Other historical figures include Commissioner William Young, who was Sellar's supervisor, and Charles Reid, an Englishman who rode into Kildonan to look at pasture land for lease and claimed he was attacked by a mob.

Nathaniel Reed and his role in the novel is a product of my imagination.

Elizabeth Gordon, Countess of Sutherland, married George Granville Leveson-Gower in 1785. They had four children. The birth of Tommy MacDonan and his relationship to the Countess is fiction. A portrait of their second son that is displayed in Dunrobin Castle was the inspiration for Tommy's appearance.

Leveson-Gower became the 19th Earl of Sutherland through his marriage. He called the clearances "improvements" and either did not care how the tenants were treated or chose to let others do the deeds and take the blame. He was titled a Duke in 1833, six months before his death.

After he died a huge statue of his likeness was mounted on a hill overlooking the Dornoch Firth, just south of Golspie. When I was taking a train north in 2006, a friendly local man pointed out the monument, which is visible for many miles. He said, "Ah, Clan Gunn is gathering. Maybe you'll finally bring enough dynamite to blow the bastard off the hill." I think that summarized a sentiment that has endured for 200 years.

There is another Countess Elizabeth in Dunrobin Castle these days. She is related to the Countess and Earl from 1813, but in my opinion bears no responsibility for what happened during the Clearances.

Last, my apologies to Clan Ross for making the fictional James Ross so despicable. Needing a local villain is my only excuse.

Many Thanks

THE VILLAGE IT took to write this novel stretches back in time and across the Atlantic Ocean. The Scottish people who kept their culture and language as best they could despite attempts to suppress their unique identity have my deep respect.

I am inspired by the Scottish writer Neil Miller Gunn (1891-1973). His novel *Butcher's Broom* tells the story of the Highland Clearances in the Kildonan area during the same time period, which I did not know when I wrote *One Handful of Earth*. I traveled to Scotland in 2006 and met Neil's nephew, Dairmid Gunn. I confessed that I wrote a novel that follows the same events as *Butcher's Broom* and worried someone would think I copied his uncle. He kindly assured me that Neil would be very pleased, if he were alive, to know that someone, and especially a Gunn, cared enough about the plight of the people who were evicted to write another book about them.

My closest cousins in Scotland, Lorna Gunn, and her sister, Nancy Gibson, have been enthusiastic supporters of my writing project. I grew up with Lorna's name as my connection to the place where my grandfather was born. I would love to go back to Scotland and hand them each a copy of the book.

My Scottish grandmother, Isabel MacLennan, adored me. Her son, Les MacLennan Gunn, was my dad. They both died before I could really say thanks. My Grammy, Carrie Austing, always told me I could do anything I wanted in life. My mom, whom I still remember as Edith Gunn, created Clan within our family and supported me when I needed her.

Thanks to my brother, George Gunn, for going to Scotland first to meet Lorna and visit the Clan Gunn Heritage Center in Latheron.

The rough spots in my childhood were smoothed out when my sister, Ruth Vanderzanden, was born when I was twelve. We've shared the joy of birth and sorrow of death together and can count on each other's voices to cheer up each day.

Living in a cabin in the Oregon Coast Range with my son, John Quimby, when he was sixteen gave me the experience of walking on trails in the dark, cooking with wood, and living without running water or refrigeration. Still some of the best years of my life.

My daughter, LiAnna Davis, spent a semester of college in London in 2003 and insisted I get over my fear of flying and meet her there. We spent five days traveling in Scotland together, which gave me the courage to go for six weeks by myself the next time.

Although the characters in the Strath of Kildonan are all fictional, the circumstance of their lives reflects my own in many ways, as is often the case in first novels. I truly appreciate all the people who have trusted me with their emotions, struggles, and life-changing experiences.

As for the actual writing and continuous editing of *One Handful of Earth* over the past six years, I am especially grateful to the people who read drafts and made comments. Thanks to Carolyn Kernberger and LiAnna Davis for their line-by-line, comma-by-comma copy edits. I read the whole manuscript out loud to Martha Goodrich. Her attachment to the characters and eagerness to hear the next chapter was a spark I needed. Piper and storyteller Geoff Frasier helped me with Gaelic phrases. Any mistakes are my own.

Music was my constant companion during most of the writing. I discovered Scottish folksinger Jim Malcolm's song, "Jimmy's Gone to Flanders" and played it on repeat for a year to invoke the feeling of tragedy. Then Jim came to Oregon and I switched to his song "Lochanside," a tribute to nature and the hospitality of the Scottish people.

I joined a writer's critique group late in the process, but every suggestion they made helped me see the story with fresh eyes. Working with other people who are also writing a novel has been inspirational and a lot of fun. So many thanks, Jina Oravetz, Tom Bender, and Christine Thackeray.

Hope Hitchcock gave me enough stars when she read the manuscript to encourage me to send my efforts out into the world of readers.

Autumn Molsee donned a sweater and wool scarf to pose for the cover on a hot summer day. Donna Lee Rollins's enthusiasm for taking the photographs gave me confidence we could create a beautiful cover.

My circle of friends and family has managed to say "I can't wait to read it" enough times in the nicest ways to keep the pressure on to finish without me feeling guilty for taking so long. The friends who read a draft encouraged me to keep writing, even though I thought I was done.

And not last, or least, my husband, Mark Davis, who has had the opportunity to practice patience and kindness while I struggled, cried, laughed, and obsessed about this story. Thanks, dear.

About the Author

ELLIE GUNN HAS made her home in Oregon since 1960. She is an active peacemaker, vegetable gardener, and massage therapist. She loves everything Scottish but haggis. This is her first novel.

www. elliegunn.com